C...

"Bardsley's gift for ... r's delight. Her newes... nt charmer.... If you'r... is just what the doctor ordered." —Romantic Times

"This story more than keeps the action flowing. Off-the-wall humor, mystery, and a touch of danger add extra zing to Bardsley's latest paranormal, and fans will be delighted." —*Library Journal*

"Another grab-you-by-the-throat, laugh-out-loud addition to the Broken Heart series.... If you thought the inhabitants of Broken Heart were up against some crazy evil before, you haven't seen anything yet." —Fresh Fiction

Come Hell or High Water

"The action and humor are bountiful. Tremendous fun as always!" —*Romantic Times* (4½ stars)

"I love paranormal novels and I believe that Michele Bardsley's Broken Heart series are some of the best there are." —Fresh Fiction

"Bardsley has brought us another amazing story . . . [with] endless wit and humor. As always, I will add this to my ever-growing keeper shelf to read over and over again." —Night Owl Romance

Over My Dead Body

"I fell into this story hook, line, and sinker. I just couldn't put it down.... It has everything to bring a smile to your face: vampires, werewolves, pixies, dragons, and more." —Publishers Weekly

continued . . .

"Michele Bardsley has done it again! This is one of my favorite paranormal series for sheer entertainment value. . . . Clever, action-packed, and sensual, *Over My Dead Body* is a helluva page-turner that's not to be missed!"
—Romance Novel TV

"A great paranormal romance that I would definitely recommend to readers who enjoy a fast-paced story that will leave them guessing until the end." —Fresh Fiction

Wait Till Your Vampire Gets Home

"Has action aplenty and a free-spirited, wittily sarcastic heroine who will delight fans." —*Booklist*

"Bardsley has one of the most entertaining series on the market. The humor and wackiness keep hitting the sweet spot. Add Bardsley to your autobuy list!"
—*Romantic Times* (top pick)

"Witty. If you like your vampires with a dose of humor, I highly recommend Bardsley's Broken Heart series."
—Romance Novel TV

"An enjoyable mix of humor and romance . . . fast-paced, steamy, and all-around entertaining."
—Darque Reviews

Because Your Vampire Said So

"Lively, sexy, out of this world—as well as in it—fun! Michele Bardsley's vampire stories rock!"
—*New York Times* bestselling author Carly Phillips

"Another Broken Heart denizen is here in this newest hysterically funny first-person romp. The combination of sexy humor, sarcastic wit, and paranormal trauma is unmistakably Bardsley. Grab the popcorn and settle in for a seriously good time!" —*Romantic Times*

Must Love Lycans

A Broken Heart Novel

MICHELE BARDSLEY

A SIGNET ECLIPSE BOOK

SIGNET ECLIPSE
Published by New American Library, a division of
Penguin Group (USA) Inc., 375 Hudson Street,
New York, New York 10014, USA
Penguin Group (Canada), 90 Eglinton Avenue East, Suite 700, Toronto,
Ontario M4P 2Y3, Canada (a division of Pearson Penguin Canada Inc.)
Penguin Books Ltd., 80 Strand, London WC2R 0RL, England
Penguin Ireland, 25 St. Stephen's Green, Dublin 2,
Ireland (a division of Penguin Books Ltd.)
Penguin Group (Australia), 250 Camberwell Road, Camberwell, Victoria 3124,
Australia (a division of Pearson Australia Group Pty. Ltd.)
Penguin Books India Pvt. Ltd., 11 Community Centre, Panchsheel Park,
New Delhi - 110 017, India
Penguin Group (NZ), 67 Apollo Drive, Rosedale, Auckland 0632,
New Zealand (a division of Pearson New Zealand Ltd.)
Penguin Books (South Africa) (Pty.) Ltd., 24 Sturdee Avenue,
Rosebank, Johannesburg 2196, South Africa

Penguin Books Ltd., Registered Offices:
80 Strand, London WC2R 0RL, England

First published by Signet Eclipse, an imprint of New American Library,
a division of Penguin Group (USA) Inc.

First Printing, September 2011
10 9 8 7 6 5 4 3 2 1

Copyright © Michele Bardsley, 2011
All rights reserved

SIGNET ECLIPSE and logo are trademarks of Penguin Group (USA) Inc.

Printed in the United States of America

To Keegan James,
who changed the world, and our lives, and our hearts,
and everything

ACKNOWLEDGMENTS

I owe a great deal of gratitude (and booze) to author and friend Mark Henry (www.markhenry.us), who briefly redonned his psychotherapist's hat to answer my questions. All mistakes—and interpretations—are mine. (And yeah, I still think it's hilarious to diagnose a real werewolf with clinical lycanthropy.)

I also owe thanks to Jeff Strand (www.jeffstrand .com), creator of one of my all-time favorite characters, Andrew Mayhem. Jeff unknowingly donated his name to Kelsey's pug puppy. Yes, I often victimize—er, honor—my friends in unique ways. Ahem.

I'd like to express my appreciation to the usual suspects, who deserve gold medals for all their efforts on my behalf: Stephanie Kip Rostan—aka Agent Awesome—and her sidekick, Monika Verma, and everyone at Levine Greenberg; the goddess of editors, Laura Cifelli, and her assistant, Jesse Feldman (who secretly runs the world and who totally named this book), and the wonderful team at NAL; to my BFFs, whose support and love sustain me; and to the League of Reluctant Adults, who make me laugh every day (whether they mean to or not): www.leagueofreluctantadults .com.

And finally, I would like to thank my Minions, and all my fans everywhere, for buying my books and thereby contributing to my chocolate fund. I adore you all.

"Who are YOU?" said the Caterpillar.

This was not an encouraging opening for a conversation. Alice replied, rather shyly, "I—I hardly know, sir, just at present—at least I know who I WAS when I got up this morning, but I think I must have been changed several times since then."

—*Alice's Adventures in Wonderland*

Alice laughed. "There's no use trying," she said: "One *can't* believe impossible things."

"I daresay you haven't had much practice," said the Queen. "When I was your age, I always did it for half an hour a day. Why, sometimes I've believed as many as six impossible things before breakfast."

—*Through the Looking Glass*

"But I don't want to go among mad people," Alice remarked.

"Oh, you can't help that," said the Cat: "We're all mad here. I'm mad. You're mad."

"How do you know I'm mad?" said Alice.

"You must be," said the Cat, "or you wouldn't have come here."

—*Alice's Adventures in Wonderland*

A NOTE FROM THE AUTHOR

Three years have passed since *Cross Your Heart*, which makes it eight years since the Consortium rolled into Broken Heart. Every so often, I think the citizens of Oklahoma's paranormal community deserve a break from chaos.

But obviously that break is soooo over.

Most of the children you met in *I'm the Vampire, That's Why* are grown, and should no doubt start having adventures of their own. (Who knows, right? There are still a lot of stories to tell.) The last time you saw Adulfo, he was twelve. And now he's twenty. Those werewolves grow up so fast!

Speaking of werewolves, this story is Damian's. Well, it's Kelsey and Damian's. I know a lot of you have been waiting for the crown prince of lycanthropes to get some love. Me, too. I'm very happy that I was finally able to write not only his story, but also to delve more deeply into the world of lycanthropes.

You should probably know that I'm not a planner. Or a plotter. I don't actually know what's going to happen until it happens, and a lot of times I'm just as surprised as you are. For example: When I starting thinking about the kind of heroine that would appeal to Damian, a young psychotherapist empath was not anywhere on that list. Also, once in a while I write something in one book that really screws me up in another, so I have to find ways to explain why I'm undoing or redoing stuff. I should blame the characters in Broken Heart who keep a lot of secrets, even from me.

I've also noticed that I tend to start my Broken Heart novels with the hero naked. No one's complained, but I really didn't do it on purpose. (I will from now on, however.)

Oh, and you probably want to know that *Schätzchen* is a German endearment that means "little treasure." You'll find a couple of glossaries and some other helpful information at the back of the book, so if you wanna thumb through it now—well, okay. I won't stop you.

There's a small mention about the pool at the home of Dr. Stan Michaels and his wife, Linda. If you want to know how they got that particular addition, then you'll have to read the short story, "Tuesday, the 13th." It's included in the free e-book *The Adventures of Zombie Larry*, which can be downloaded at my Web site: www.michelebardsley.com.

Legends of the Lycans

It is said that the Moon Goddess wanted children, so she took her wolf form and mated with an alpha named Tark.

She gave birth to twins. The firstborn was a wolf of black. And the second, a wolf of gray. Her elder son had the ability to turn from human to wolf. However, her second-born could assume his wolf nature only on the night of the full moon.

The Moon Goddess's sons grew up, and soon they wanted wives and families. The Goddess offered her firstborn a beautiful female wolf, which she gave the ability to shift into a human. To her second-born, the Goddess gave a beautiful female human. Since her son assumed his wolf form only during the full moon, she gave his mate the same ability.

And so some lycanthropes are full-bloods, shifting whenever they need to, and others are the Roma, shifting only during the full moon.

This is the story told for generations from father to son, mother to daughter, of the lycanthrope heritage.

It is, however, a lie.

We must also consider the unexpected branch of the lycanthrope family tree: the *loup de sang*.

In 1807 a small group of *loup-garou* emigrated from France to the town of Vincennes, the capital city in Indian Territory. Among the newest arrivals was the widow Chantelle Marchand, who was eight months pregnant. She made the long, treacherous journey to the United States to join the pack of her father, Jacques Marchand.

Not long after Chantelle arrived, a territorial dispute erupted among the *loup-garou* and the *deamhan fola*—vampires. The pregnant widow was among the casualties of a short but brutal skirmish. Unfortunately, the vampire who killed her also tried to Turn her.

As she lay dying, her father delivered triplets: The first was a son, Gabriel, and then a girl, Anise, and another son, Ren—all with the same strange condition. They were alive, but could gain nourishment only from blood. Gabriel was given to a lycan outcast. Anise and Ren were sent to live among the Vedere psychics.

Marchand's grandchildren were the first-ever blood-drinking lycanthropes, and it was Marchand who coined the term *loup de sang*. However, in his diary, he wrote only about the birth of Gabriel. He never mentioned Gabriel's siblings.

So for reasons unknown, Marchand lied, too . . .

Then, years ago, when renowned prophet Astria Vedere was still very young, she made a prophecy:

A vampire queen shall come forth from the place of broken hearts. The seven powers of the Ancients will be hers to command. She shall bind with the outcast, and with this union, she will save the dual-natured. With her consort, she will rule vampires and lycanthropes as one.

Alas, this, too, is a lie.

Well . . . sorta.

None of these tales include a whisper about the only known royal lycans—the triplet princes of all werewolves who are neither full-bloods nor Roma nor *loup de sang*.

The story of their origin is not a lie.

It's a secret.

Chapter 1

The man was naked.

I pressed my palms against the reinforced steel door, already on my tippy toes, and peered through the small square window made of shatterproof glass. Beneath the window was a narrow slot that allowed sound to escape, which was the only way to speak to the patient inside. The setup was old-school, and a prime example of the many quirks at the Dante Clinic.

He paced endlessly, emulating an animal in a cage. It bothered me how close the analogy was to the truth. However, the safety of the staff and the other patients took precedence over his comfort. How soon he got out was entirely up to him . . . and, well, me. I was still getting used to being in charge of the clinic. I'd been given control over an entire building and the people within it after I'd already proven—in public, no less—how incapable I was of controlling *myself*.

So, yeah. Everyone here was screwed.

Mr. Dante asked only that I did my best as the clinic's administrator and full-time on-site therapist. I threw in the guarantee that I would never again square off with my famous mother on a national talk show. Uh-huh. That happened. It was fun, if my definition of fun was "humiliated and disgraced by psycho(therapist) parent in front of a live audience." Did I mention the serial killer I'd let loose on Oklahoma City? Okay, not on purpose, but still totally my fault.

What's done is done, I reminded myself. Unless someone invented a time machine and a way to give me a personality transplant, I couldn't change my past.

I refocused my attention on the new patient.

The poor guy didn't even have a pair of boxers to cover his . . . um . . . I blanked as he made another turn and revealed his front. Yep. There it was. In all its glory.

Sweet mamma jamma.

His penis was huge, and it wasn't even erect.

Heat swept through me, along with a big heap of shame. *Get a grip, Kelsey, you heartless slut.* I was behaving unprofessionally—even though it was only mentally. Just because I hadn't had sex in . . . er, ever, didn't mean I had the right to entertain the idea of sleeping with a client.

No matter how gorgeous.

Or well-endowed.

For all my faults as a psychotherapist, I'd never had sex with a patient. (See, Mother? I could *too* be ethical.) No matter how badly I had messed up last year, I still wanted to help as many people as I could. I might've chosen my profession out of duty (and maternal expectation), but I was committed to it all the same. Sometimes I dreamed about the other things I might've done with my life. I could've been a scuba diving instructor. Or a painter living in an artists' colony. Or an alligator wrangler in Florida. Ah, well. Dreams were for people with choices (and who had mothers who didn't begin every sentence with, "It's your duty to . . .").

I studied my new client. His thick black hair reached midback and swung like a dark curtain as he whipped around, his agitation growing with each long stride. He was well over six feet tall. Every part of the man was built—a beautiful body crafted by hard work, not gym time. I pegged him for a construction worker, or maybe an outdoorsman. It was wrong, so very, very wrong, to watch the bunch and flex of his muscles. *Oh, baby* . . . Okay, okay, enough. Sheesh. He deserved better from me than a hormone-fueled assessment of his physical attributes. I really needed to study him from the point of view of an open-minded, nonjudgmental, kindhearted (and mature) therapist.

He was dirty and bruised. Scars crisscrossed his torso, and there were burns on his arms, too. He'd been tortured, though he seemed unconcerned by his injuries. With my empathic abilities, I could literally know about a person's pain, whether physical or emotional. That ability was another reason I became a therapist. I thought it was God's big hint to me about my life's purpose: *Go forth, Kelsey, and help wayward souls.*

I wanted to help this man, even though he didn't particularly strike me as a wayward soul. I got the distinct impression he was strong in mind and heart—but that was more a supposition than an empathically derived certainty.

I felt the sudden, intense snap of his anger. It reached out and tried to bite at me, but I slapped it away. I was used to fending off the emotions of others, but his were somehow different.

Every so often he paused to punch at the walls. He was also cursing—in German.

The walls and floor were padded. The cell—and I cringed to call it that—had no furniture. The place was called the induction room because sometimes new clients needed time and space to calm down before being assigned a residency. Their suites were no less secure, but when an angry psychiatric patient threatened to rip off your head, he might actually try to do it.

He stopped in the middle of the room. His head rose, and he stared at the door. His eyes were like chips of jade. I saw the flare of his nostrils. He was . . . scenting?

He rushed forward so fast he was nearly a blur, and slammed his entire body against the steel. The metal actually groaned.

I squeaked and backed away, forgetting that I was the one in charge here. Could potent masculinity reach through two feet of steel to taunt me? Or was it my libido's insisting to replay the images of his gorgeousness?

His face pressed against the glass. He studied me with a cold expression. "Let me out," he said. *"Now."*

Holy crap. He was scary. But he wasn't the scariest person in the clinic. That would be my boss, Mr. Dante, and after him, the enigmatic Sven, who was in charge of security here.

"What's your name?" I asked.

His lips thinned. "What's yours?"

"Kelsey." Asking patients to use my first name was my initial salvo to make them feel comfortable, but I got the feeling he was too much an alpha personality. I straightened and put my shoulders back. "Kelsey Morningstone. I run this facility."

He gaze dropped to my breasts, which I had sorta thrust out there in an effort to create my "in-charge" body language. I couldn't back off now, so I tried to pretend that his gaze wasn't wandering over my boobs, or that I noticed his inspection.

"Let me out, Kelsey." His voice had gone low and smoky. My belly clenched as my girly parts perked up. *Stop that,* I demanded. *He's a patient.*

"Do you know where you are?" I asked.

One eyebrow quirked.

I flushed at the silent chastisement. Of course he knew he was in a padded cell. Okay. Seriously. I had to get in control of myself, the situation, and him. "You're at the Dante Clinic. You were brought in last night from another facility."

"What facility?"

I hadn't been told much, only that he'd been rescued from a private laboratory. I shuddered to think about the kind of experimentation he'd gone through, much less why he'd been chosen to be a guinea pig. I hadn't asked more questions about the patient's previous situation because one, you didn't question a billionaire, and two, the less I knew, the less I had to wrestle with my conscience about this job and all that it entailed.

"You don't remember?" I asked.

"No."

"Do you know your name?"

"Damian."

"Is that your name," I asked gently, "or is that the name your captors used?"

"Captors." He made the word sound like both a question and a statement. He pushed away from the door, his frustration bubbling through my psychic shields. I returned to the window to watch him pace. He was frowning and rubbing his temples, obviously trying to remember what he'd forgotten.

Which was his entire life.

"As soon as you're ready, we'll get you a shower, some clothes, and a hot meal. Then we can talk."

"I don't want to talk," he said. "I want to leave."

"Where would you go?"

For the first time, I saw panic enter his gaze. His anger shot out again, and wrapped deeply within it was a terrible sorrow. Staving off his emotions was difficult. They were so strong, and so . . . strange. Animalistic.

Primal.

Like him.

"When will you let me out?" He sounded like he was chewing gravel. I was sure it chafed his ego to ask even that simple question. Even without my empathic abilities, I knew he was not used to relying on the kindness of others.

"I'll make the arrangements," I promised. "Damian, you must accept that the clinic is your home now. The sooner you do, the sooner we can focus on how to help you."

He considered my words for a moment; then he looked at me solemnly. "I have nowhere else to go."

Yeah. That made two of us.

"We sure got a live one, Doc," said Marisol Brunes. "And lord-a-mercy, he's a hunk and a half. Too bad he's one taco short of a combo platter, eh?"

I looked up from my clipboard so Mari could see how unthrilled I was with her assessment. I liked Mari. She was short and chubby with silver hair and twinkling blue eyes, but tough as nails. She was sorta like a biker version of Mrs. Claus. She'd been at the clinic since opening day more than ten years ago, and she'd been kinder to me than the rest of the staff. I was younger than all of them, and certainly younger than my predecessor Dr. Danforth Laurence, who'd been a renowned mental health researcher and a well-respected psychiatrist.

Me? Not so much.

After staying silent under my chastising glare, Mari finally caved.

"I know," she said, her gaze twinkling—with mischief, not contrition. "Derogatory language is a subtle but damaging way to assert our superiority over people who deserve nothing less than our compassion and assistance."

"Glad you've been listening."

I looked back down at the paperwork, but I knew she was rolling her eyes. I'd taken over the Dante Clinic only three weeks ago—mere days after Dr. Laurence had died unexpectedly in his sleep. I'd managed to skate into the first of December without anyone dying or anything blowing up. So, you know, huzzah an' all. Poor Dr. Laurence had been in his late fifties, and had died from cardiac arrest. We should all be lucky to go that peaceably. There were worse ways to die.

My stomach took a dive as an unwanted image flashed: the knife in my hand, the gleam in Robert's eye, the blood spilling over both of us.

No. You will not go there, Kel.

I stepped off that particular dark mental path and circled back to something less soul crushing.

When Jarred Dante approached me, I was living in Tulsa and working for a nonprofit medical clinic. It didn't pay well, but I couldn't complain since I hadn't expected to work as a therapist ever again. I was one paycheck away from being destitute—I'd been sued numerous times and I lost every case. How could a conscientious jury not punish the therapist who'd failed to treat the evil Robert Mallard—especially after hearing from the grieving families of his victims? I would've nailed my ass to the wall, too. I lost everything. My practice. My new house. My Mercedes. Even my clothes.

Someone had to be blamed. Robert was dead. And I was the only visceral link left to the tragedies he'd caused. It had not mattered that I, too, had been a victim, or that I was the one to exact the final, fatal price from Robert. The cost of his actions—and of mine—had been too great. Too horrifying. (Like a Lifetime movie, only without Tori Spelling or the happy ending.) Then my mother added the whipped topping and cherries to my failure cake by taking me to task on the *Leo Talbot Talk Show*. (You're welcome for the ratings, Leo.)

After that debacle, Mother rescinded her invitation to the traditional family Christmas gathering, and had not invited me to anything else, not even her local book signings. She no longer bothered with the monthly perfunctory phone calls, either, the ones her executive assistant scheduled, so Margaret Morningstone could check "speak to youngest daughter, make her feel inadequate" off her list.

My disgrace had tainted her, and she hadn't forgiven me.

I really should've picked up the hints she'd pretty much disowned me after telling the whole world I was incompetent. *What you've done is a great disservice to our profession. You've shamed the family, Kelsey, and yourself.*

Somewhere inside me was the rejected little girl who wanted Mother's unconditional love. She'd spent my entire life pointing out numerous times that no emotion was unconditional, least of all love, and I hadn't believed her.

Until now.

After Mother's very public rebuff, my brother and sister followed suit. We'd never been particularly close anyway. I'd been a surprise child, one born eighteen years after my sister. Our father died when I was only two. My mother's psychotherapy practice was already well established as was her career as a lecturer and author. Not long after my father died, Mother hit the *New York Times* bestseller list with her book, *Lies Your Mother Told You: How to Discard Your Childhood Drama and Build a Real Life*.

Her entire career went platinum gold.

Anyway.

When Mr. Dante showed up and offered to make all my debts go away, including the pending payouts to the families, and give me a cushy job that included luxurious digs and a generous paycheck, I didn't turn it down. Granted, I didn't accept right away. I knew the folly of allowing someone else to sweep in and solve my problems. I even gave myself a stern lecture, which included phrases like "stand on your own two feet," "if it doesn't kill you, it makes you strong," and "face the music."

But . . . well, I guess I wanted the chance to redeem myself. And yeah, okay, I wanted to be free of those burdens heaped upon me by my family, the victims, the courts, and my own conscience. I could never, ever take back what happened. So I could either slit my wrists or I could take the opportunity Mr. Dante offered and try to move on.

I chose Option 2.

The Dante Clinic was a privately funded psychiatric facility that supported the care and well-being of clients handpicked by the facility's benefactor. No one knew why Mr. Dante chose the people he did—only that most of the cases were hard-core and the patients had no families. Many of them had been homeless or locked up in state facilities. Dante picked up the considerable tab for high-quality care. I had yet to understand his motivations, but maybe it was nothing more than an eccentric indulgence of the super-rich.

Okay. I didn't buy that, either.

Located just outside Broken Arrow, the facility had been created from one of Dante's refurbished mansions. It was a huge towering Gothic structure plopped into the middle of a heavily wooded ten acres. It looked like Dracula's castle and operated like a king's palace. There were never more than ten residents. With Damian added to the roster, we now had six full-time patients.

Every client had a personal maid and butler, who also served as certified nursing assistants, and when necessary, guards. They were all black belts in various martial arts forms, and they behaved in military fashion. Working in a psychiatric facility wasn't exactly safe, so I could understand why the security was intense. The suites were large and sumptuous, but impregnable. Everything could be locked down within a matter of seconds. If patients got out of line even the tiniest bit, privileges were revoked, and in the three weeks I'd been here, no client wanted to be without their Egyptian cotton sheets or nightly hot cocoa and scones. Meals were taken together in a dining room roughly the size of a football field. I supposed the more . . . er, unusual aspects of the clinic were easily balanced out by the quality of care. The facility offered the best of everything to its patients. Maybe the reason I felt unsettled was that I didn't feel like I was the best option—either as administrator or as psychotherapist. Yet I'd been given a prime opportunity, deserved or not. I would do my best to earn what I had been given.

"You look like you need a Starbucks," said Mari. "A triple shot."

Sheesh. I'd been meandering down memory lane, staring sightlessly at the clipboard in my hands. Crap. "Maybe a triple shot of vodka."

She grinned wickedly. "'Atta girl."

I signed off on the entrance paperwork for Damian NoLastName and handed her the clipboard. "I'll be in my office until my two o'clock with Mr. Danvers."

"Good luck," she said sympathetically. "Sven caught him cutting out paper feathers again."

"Oh, jeez. He's already sprained his ankle jumping

off tables." I paused. "Do you have the shock bracelets on him?"

She nodded, and I saw the distaste in her gaze. I felt the same about the bracelets, but they were effective. Until the guy stopped believing a demon wanted him to fly or we found a more palatable way to keep him grounded, he would have to wear the bracelets. The clinic employed many experimental psychiatric tools. I was not sold on the bracelets, but Mr. Dante insisted. I couldn't deny he seemed to genuinely care about the well-being of our clients. Still, he was a man who knew how to exploit the vulnerabilities of others; he was an effective manipulator.

Then again, so was I.

As I said good-bye to Mari and headed toward my first-floor office, I thought about Mr. Danvers. He blamed all his bad behavior on a demon he called Malphas, who supposedly took the form of a crow. He claimed the demon inside him wanted to return to hell, and he wanted to take Mr. Danvers with him—by flying into a portal located in a Tulsa hotel. I can Google as well as anyone, so it easy enough to figure out how my patient had come up with both the name and the ideology behind Malphas. It was on Wikipedia, for heaven's sake. A hellmouth in a hotel was a good twist, though.

What I was trying to understand was why Mr. Danvers had created the delusion. Right now, I was still building trust between myself and the patients. It would probably take a while for Mr. Danvers to reveal anything that might allow me the insight I needed to help him.

It wasn't that I didn't believe in psychic phenomenon. After all, I was an empath. I could feel other people's emotions. I knew how to tease out the hidden nuances from the main emotion. Someone who was angry almost always had strands of sorrow or hurt or abandonment woven into their fury.

Nothing was ever as it seemed.

My ability usually made it easier to connect with patients, and to help lessen their distress. Unfortunately, Mr. Danvers was a particularly difficult case. Truth and sincerity emanated off him in waves. That was the problem with dealing with delusional patients—they believed absolutely in the realities they created.

Not long after opening my practice, I'd learned by sheer accident that I could also absorb emotions. After I figured out this new facet of my ability, I started using it to just take away the pain, the anger, the confusion, even the crazy. I didn't realize I'd made myself vulnerable, or that I'd taken away the ability for my patients to work through their issues. They didn't stop engaging in the destructive behaviors that had led them to my door—they just didn't feel bad about those actions anymore. I'd given them a magic pill. And I'd taken all their poison into myself.

I was already off emotional kilter when Robert Mallard became my patient. Somehow, he'd been able to creep under my skin, get inside my head, and—*no*. I repeated my mental mantra: Let go. Move on. Find peace.

So much easier said than done.

I thought about the mysterious and very naked Damian. I picked up the phone and hit the speed dial for Sven's cell. He had an office, but he was never in it. He was a prowler, someone constantly on the move trying to anticipate problems. He was very good at his job, but not much of a talker.

"Dubowski."

"Hi, Sven," I chirped. I was well aware that my perkiness annoyed him. What can I say? I had yet to discard all my childish impulses. "It's Dr. Morningstone. Will you escort our newest patient to his suite?"

He was silent for so long, I said, "Um, Sven?"

"Too dangerous."

"Even for you?" I asked. "That's surprising. You're not afraid of him, are you?"

"Save your psych crap for the nutjobs," he said sourly.

"Aw, Sven, you say the sweetest things. You were voted Mr. Congeniality in high school, weren't you? Go on, admit it. Your sunny disposition gave you away, Pollyanna."

Sven made a snorting noise that almost sounded like a laugh, but I couldn't be sure. I'd never seen the man smile, much less chuckle. "Fine," he groused. "I'll get your werewolf settled in."

A second later, I heard the dial tone.

"You're a peach," I muttered. Then I hung up the receiver. Huh. Why had he called Damian a werewolf?

"Dr. Morningstone."

Startled by the deep male voice, I gasped and shoved back from the desk. When I saw the imposing figure of Mr. Dante standing in the doorway, I took a shuddering breath. I remembered quite clearly shutting my door; I hadn't even noticed that he'd opened it. How long had he been standing there observing me?

He was a big man—a linebacker in Armani. He had wavy black hair, stormy gray eyes, and chiseled features. I never got vibes off him. He was either completely emotionless, which was impossible, or exercised iron control over his emotional state. I believed he was very capable of encapsulating pesky feelings.

His lips flickered at the corners, and I swore he'd tried to smile.

Realizing that I'd been sitting on the edge of my chair gaping up at him, I rose to my feet. "Mr. Dante. Please, come in."

He was already inside, but he didn't call me on the

obvious flub. Instead, he strode to one of the wingbacks that faced my desk and sat down. I retook my seat and scooted closer to my desk. Mr. Danvers and Damian's files were beneath my fingertips.

"Are you settling in well, Kelsey?"

I nodded. The informality suggested an intimacy in our relationship that made me uneasy. Was he attempting to create a more congenial relationship? Or trying to throw me off-guard so he could whammy me?

Overanalyze much, Kel? Truthfully, I looked for motives in even the most mundane gestures long before I got my psychotherapy license. My mother taught me well the hubris of the well-intentioned.

"We seem to be transitioning from our perceived roles," I said pleasantly. "Shall I call you Jarred?"

"I would like that very much."

His tone was warm, friendly. I wasn't sure what to make of his change in demeanor. Oh, don't get me wrong. He'd always been polite. He'd never said or done anything indecorous. But it seemed that he was, indeed, trying to create a new level of intimacy between us.

"What are your thoughts on our new patient?" he asked.

"I might be able to offer a better assessment if I knew more about his circumstances. All I know is that you somehow rescued him from a private lab and he has amnesia. Who would experiment on him? And why?"

"I'm aware that it'll be more difficult to treat him without knowing his full story." His gaze flicked over me. "I'm disinclined to share certain details with you at this time, but I can tell you that he suffers from lycanthropy."

I took a moment to absorb what he was saying. Either he didn't trust me enough to offer complete disclosure, or the situation involved issues (legalities, perhaps) that he didn't want to confirm. After all, no one had discussed the logistics of removing Damian from his previous incarceration. I had no doubts he'd been a prisoner—his body and his manner bore the marks of a caged and tormented creature.

And then there was the diagnosis of clinical lycanthropy.

"It's a rare psychiatric condition," I said. "That kind of delusional behavior is often linked to schizophrenia or bipolar disorders."

I hadn't gotten the kind of vibes from Damian that I'd previously associated with other schizophrenics. It seemed more likely he was bipolar, but even that consideration didn't seem to fit. How could one diagnose an amnesiac?

"You told me that he lost his memory," I said. "I take it the clinical lycanthropy diagnosis is from his previous records?"

"He doesn't have records, Kelsey. But trust me when I say the information is quite accurate."

Hmm. I'd have to do some research on lycanthropy and formulate a suitable therapeutic plan. If Damian was schizophrenic, I could at least get him on meds, which would help with his delusions.

"You asked Sven to assign him a suite."

"A gesture of trust," I said, feeling rattled. I never realized how much I relied on my empathic abilities until I conversed with Mr. Dante. He spoke in a pleasant tone with a razor edge. He could be halfway into ripping me a new one before I'd even realize it.

"Do you believe his amnesia is permanent?"

"I don't know," I said. "After I meet with Dr. Ruthers to discuss Damian's physical injuries, I'll have a better idea. Of course, I'll need to speak with Damian. My gut instinct is that the amnesia is temporary."

"Oh?"

"He was cursing in German," I said.

"Born and raised in Germany, I believe," said Jarred. "But he's lived quite a long time in America."

"I thought you said he didn't have any records."

"Personal knowledge," said Jarred. "And that's all I can say."

Translation: *I know a lot more, but I'm not telling you.* His tone clearly indicated he would answer no more inquiries. Frustration zinged through me. I opened Damian's file and studied the mostly blank page. I couldn't really derive much from the intake form, but it's all I had.

"What is the importance of Germanic blasphemes?" asked Jarred.

"It may be an indicator that his memories are already returning."

"I see."

I couldn't tell if Jarred was pleased or dismayed by the idea Damian might regain his memory. An unpleasant feeling curled in my gut. Damian was different from the other patients. His case was somehow personal for Jarred. In what way, I couldn't begin to guess.

"Are you free this evening?"

I stared at him. I was free every evening. I never left the compound because there was no point. I had no friends, my family had disowned me, and going out into public venues, with all those people and their emotions, exhausted me. Besides, it had been snowing and winter driving in Oklahoma was no fun.

"Kelsey?"

"I'm sorry." I blushed, and looked down at the desk. My gaze skittered over Damian's paperwork. "Yes. I'm free."

"Excellent. Please join me in my private suite for dinner."

I blinked up at him. I usually took meals with the patients, not only because I craved the company, but it also gave me an opportunity to observe them. Dinner with the boss would be . . . nerve-racking. As far as I knew, other than Sven, no one had ever seen Jarred's living quarters.

"The purpose of this dinner is . . . what, exactly?"

"We'll talk about your plans for the clinic, and your innovative approaches to therapy," he said. His expression was bland, as usual, but there was something dangerous lurking in his eyes. Did he really want to talk about the clinic? Or did he have something more carnal in mind?

My stomach squeezed as trepidation spun coldly through me.

That almost smile fluttered on his lips again, and then he stood up. "I'll see you tonight, Kelsey." He paused, tilting his head as he studied me. "Wear something nice."

After a thoroughly unsatisfying session with Mr. Danvers, I stayed in my office to write up my notes about the session. Mr. Danvers only wanted to discuss the tensile strength of feathers, and no amount of persuasion or shift in verbal tactics had swayed him to talk about another subject. I'd been tempted to use my abilities to dig through the man's emotional detritus, but I'd forgo that route until we had a better-established relationship. I had decided not to completely stop using my gifts to help others, but I'd learned my lesson. I was very careful, and I never absorbed their emotions. Pain was a gateway—a portal to inner knowledge and true change. Humans were too stubborn to change except out of necessity.

I put down my pen and turned to stare at the blinking cursor on my computer monitor. I really should input the notes for the session with Mr. Danvers, as well as my initial thoughts about Damian's condition and possible treatments.

Instead, I filed the folders in my desk, locked the drawer, and shut down my computer. It was close to end of office hours anyway. It wouldn't hurt to peek in on the new patient and see how he was settling in. I was a tad worried that I had him released too soon, but those were more Sven's doubts than mine. Still, I couldn't help but think that perhaps my strong physical reaction to Damian was coloring my perceptions.

I headed upstairs to the west wing where the patient suites were located. The other five residents were participating in a yoga class held in the ballroom, and first-day intakes were encouraged to stay in their quarters. Adjusting to new circumstances often worked best in stages. At least according to the philosophy of Jarred Dante.

Obviously, I'd been unable to get Damian out of my thoughts. My libido wouldn't shut up about the man's body, and that was irksome. I needed perspective if I had any intention of helping Damian, especially since it appeared he suffered from a serious delusion.

I'd dealt with schizophrenic patients before, and I couldn't reconcile Damian to that diagnosis. Then again, he had amnesia, which had been confirmed by Dr. Ruthers, so who knew what manifestations would occur as his brain tried to recover memories and behaviors.

Sven had called me to let me know that Damian had been assigned Room Ten. I took a moment of pure vanity to smooth my skirt and fluff my hair. I inhaled deeply, then let out a long, slow breath.

I knocked on the door.

Mari answered.

What the—

The moment she saw me, her eyes went wide, and her gaze slid guiltily over her shoulder before she gave me a big smile. "Doc!" she trilled.

"What are you doing here?" I asked.

She blinked at my sharp tone. Then she sighed. "He's like looking at a van Gogh," she said. "I couldn't resist another peek."

I gaped at her. "You're admiring him? He's not a painting! He's a man." A virile, gorgeous, *crazy* man. I grabbed hold of my anger, and that glinting sliver of odd jealousy, and tucked them away. "I need to do my initial assessment," I said, unable to thaw my frosty tone. "Please excuse us."

Her face went red with mortification, but honestly, I expected better from Mari. I couldn't feel bad that she was embarrassed about letting her own libido get in the way of her job. At least I'd kept my inappropriate drooling to myself.

"He's all yours," she said. Then she scuttled past me, her gaze on the floor.

I couldn't reconcile her behavior with the competent, no-nonsense woman I'd come to know over the past three weeks. Still, I could, on some level, understand her obsession. Damian was unusual in many respects, and he wore machismo like some men wore cologne. His sexiness was imbued, not cultivated.

I walked in and shut the door behind me.

The apartment was much smaller, though no less luxurious than my own. The open kitchen overlooked the living room with its big leather couch facing a floor-to-ceiling entertainment system, which included all manner of high-tech gizmos attached to the flat-screen TV.

Damian stood at the large picture window—secured, of course—his hands clasped behind his back, gazing out onto the sprawling front lawn of the estate. Thanks to yesterday's snowstorm, it was a blanket of white dotted with clusters of scrabbly trees.

He wore one of the gray suits given to all the inmates—er, I mean, patients—though they seemed a tad too small, especially given how much they clung to his impressive musculature. His long hair fell like inky shadows, the strands damp but obviously combed. I stood near the couch, hesitating.

"Kelsey."

He hadn't bothered to turn around and see who had entered the room. He must've heard me talking to Mari, and I flinched. I certainly didn't need to make patients aware of any issues between the staff. Not that my annoyance with Mari's ill-advised action truly merited a real issue.

"Hello, Damian."

He turned, his pensive gaze meeting mine. "What am I doing here?"

"I'm afraid I know very little about how you came to be at the Dante clinic. I can assure you, however, that you're safe. And I will do everything within my power to help you."

One dark brow arched. "Help me what?"

The silky tone made my womb clench. I pasted on a smile, and gestured toward the couch. "Let's sit down and talk."

He studied me in a ruthless sort of way, as though trying to determine if I were friend or foe. Then he lifted his shoulder in an elegant shrug and strode across the room to sit on the couch.

I usually sought to create a professional distance between myself and my patients, but since there were no other chairs, I sat opposite him on the couch.

"What's the last thing you remember?" I asked.

"Waking up in that padded room." His gaze flicked

to mine. "And then you." His nostrils flared. "You smelled . . . good."

"You're saying you could smell me through that metal door?" I asked. It was three inches thick, for Pete's sake.

"Yes."

Okay. Chalk one up for werewolf delusion.

"What was this scent? My lotion? My perfume?"

He frowned. "Those are not the scents that attracted me."

My pulse gave a little leap. Crap. *Stop it,* I told my body crankily. *He's not for you.* "What, then?"

"It's difficult to explain."

"Perhaps you could try, Damian." I smiled at him, and whoa, big mistake.

Wicked intent blazed in those jade orbs. He slid across the couch until we were mere inches apart. He took my hand and lifted it so that my wrist faced up. "Have you ever been lost?"

"Yes," I said. Both figuratively and literally. Sometimes I still felt lost. No, more like I wasn't wearing the right skin. That my true identity was somewhere else, and I needed to find it. My heart started thudding erratically, but I didn't want to disturb his thought processes by yanking my hand away. (Also, it felt nice to have my hand held. It had been a really long time since I'd felt the touch of another, and certainly not one so tender.) I decided to let the moment unfold, no matter how unwise.

"And when you were lost, did you come across something that reminded you of home? Something that comforted you so much that you could fight off the panic, the fear?"

I could answer yes to those questions, too. Instead, I asked, "Are you afraid, Damian?"

His brows dipped down and his eyes turned icy. "No." He leaned down and sniffed my wrist. Then, much to my shock, his tongue flicked against my pulse. "That's how you smell to me, Kelsey," he said in an aching voice. "Like I have come home."

Chapter 2

Damian's gaze was so haunted that I couldn't look away. I wasn't sure why he'd incorporated me into his delusion—or maybe he hadn't. Maybe I was a reminder of someone he'd known. Sense memories could be very powerful. Perhaps I wore the same perfume as his wife (gah!) or his mother, and he was associating me with someone important to him. This strange attraction of his might only be his injured brain trying to reconcile past with present.

I pulled my wrist out of his gentle grip and folded my hands on my lap. I didn't break eye contact. "Do you remember anything—even if it seems random or strange?"

"The moon," he said. "I remember seeing the moon."

The moon would be important for someone who believed himself to be a werewolf. I couldn't be sure if this particular image was relevant to his delusion or to an actual memory. "Before you were taken?"

"I don't know."

"Okay. Let's focus on the . . . er, my scent. What image comes to mind?"

"The moon," he said again. "A forest. A castle. Home."

"You live in a castle?"

He offered a half smile. "How would I know?"

I blushed, feeling out of my element. He seemed ... I don't know. Wise and strong and experienced. He was all too aware of my discomfort. He didn't look away, or move back even an inch. Maybe it was his way of taking control. Or maybe he wasn't aware of his own actions. Being the stronger, the leader, was his nature. His gaze was heavy-lidded, his eyes shiny jade. Whoops. Never mind. He knew exactly how to wield his sexuality. He hadn't forgotten how to do that. Nope.

I took in a shuddering breath. He leaned closer. My gaze skittered along his mouth and I heard a faint sound issue from him ... something like a growl. My stomach jumped, and my pulse raced. Enough! I needed to switch tactics.

"You don't remember your captors, or what they did to you, Damian?"

He eased back just a little. A muscle ticked in his jaw. "No."

"And you don't remember being rescued, either?"

His gaze shuttered. "No."

Hoo-kay, then. He didn't like the idea of being rescued. I'd already come to the conclusion he didn't like confinement, but then again, who did?

"Do you know who the president is?"

"Why would I know that? Those are human concerns."

Bingo. "Aren't you human?"

His brows slashed down and his lips thinned. "These are strange questions." He angled closer still, and it took all my effort not to suck in an unsteady breath. "You are trying to determine if I'm crazy."

"Are you?"

"I cannot remember anything. So maybe I am."

Trepidation crept through me. Most people suffering from delusions or other psychological disorders firmly believed in their realities. They wouldn't admit that they were wrong, much less that they might be insane. It could be that even with amnesia Damian was operating within his delusional framework, but my instincts were whispering that all was not as it appeared. Still, I kept a tight wrap on my empathic powers. No way would I go delving into his emotions just yet—especially since I couldn't get myself under control. Damian's nearness was messing with every one of my senses. I knew what it was like to be attracted, and what I felt with Damian was like attraction on steroids. It took all my willpower to keep myself from inclining toward him, into accepting that challenge in his eyes.

Kiss me.

I gulped. Did I think that? Or did he say it?

"Are you American?" I asked. I hoped the question would jostle something loose. I wanted to test Jarred's information. I don't know why Jarred would lie about Damian's origins, but the man's motivations were murky at best.

"How would I know?" he countered. "I don't even know if I'm human." Amusement threaded his words.

"Of course you're human," I said. "There aren't any other options."

"Are you sure?"

I kept my expression pleasant, but it took some effort. I got the distinct impression he was screwing with me. "Okay, then. Tell me about these options."

"Mmm." He looked me over, his eyes going all smoky. How the hell did he manage that? My breath stalled in my lungs. *Way to be professional, Kel.*

"I don't know where I'm from, if my name is truly Damian, if I'm American, or who the president is . . . but

you believe I'm aware of alternatives to being human."
He slid the very last inch, trapping me against the wide
arm of the couch. "You do think I'm crazy."

"I'm trying to help you," I said, injecting calm into my
voice. "We may not know much about you, Damian, but
prior to your amnesia you believed you were a werewolf. Can you tell me about that?"

He laughed. "What a conversation that would be,
Frau." His gaze lingered too long on my lips. "Do you
like werewolves?"

The question startled me. I wanted to blurt, "I like
you," but I managed to bottle that response. "Werewolves don't exist, Damian."

"But if they did?"

"I don't know if I could like a creature that was so
dangerous."

"A very therapeutic thing to say," he said. "But not
entirely honest." His gaze darkened more, and my heart
flipped over in my chest. "You think I'm a werewolf."

"Not at all."

"I could be." His rock-hard thigh pressed against
mine. I couldn't stop the shiver that danced up my spine.
"Because I very much want to devour you."

"Th-that's inappropriate."

"Very," he agreed. "You should probably stop me,
Frau. Especially as you think werewolves are dangerous." He offered a toothy smile. "Or perhaps you find
the human me dangerous, *ja*?" He tugged the knot of
hair pinned at my nape. The strands drifted around my
shoulders like tired dandelions. He sniffed my hair
(Sheesh! He really did like my smell!), his fingers daring
to stroke my neck. Then he lowered his head and pressed
his lips against the hollow of my throat.

Hot need sparked in my belly. I put my hands on his
shoulders, intending to push him away, but I couldn't

quite work up the outrage. His lips trailed up my throat, tracing the same path as his fingers, then coasted along my jaw. I felt his teeth tug my earlobe, and I nearly jumped out of my skin.

"That's quite enough," I rasped.

"I smell your arousal. You're wet for me, Kelsey." He pulled back and cradled my face. "My memories have abandoned me, but I recognize desire."

Oh, good Lord. He was right. I was aroused. And so was he. Worse, he was going to kiss me, and then I'd be a goner for sure. I could commit the final sin—sleep with a patient. Then I would be as awful and immoral as my mother believed. (Honestly? No real down side there. But I was *trying* to have morals, damn it.) "S-stop," I managed. I cleared my throat. "Damian! You're being rude!"

He reeled back as if I'd slapped him. His hands dropped away and he scooted to the end of the couch. "Forgive me," he said stiffly.

Fierce regret rose inside me. I didn't want to hurt his feelings, but I'd already crossed the line between therapist and patient. If him being wounded by my rejection kept his hands off me, then that was good. He affected me in a way no other man had, and I wasn't sure what to do about my own reactions. My entire body was trembling, even my hands. I clasped them together tightly.

"Only if you'll forgive me," I said softly. "I shouldn't have let you touch me."

He stared at me. "You're right. Permission is needed. I'll remember that next time."

I stood up, my legs feeling like Jell-O. "There will be no next time," I chided. "I have a professional and moral obligation to help you. I cannot give in to . . . that is, I shouldn't indulge your . . . er, wooing."

"Wooing?" Once again, amusement ghosted his tone.

"Our next session will be in my office," I said coolly. Now that I was able to breathe again, I could see that he wasn't repentant about our encounter. A fire burned in his gaze; it was banked, but by no means doused. I felt another jump in my pulse. "It's not wise to be alone with you in other environments."

"Are you afraid that I will be unable to control myself?" he asked. "Or that you will?"

"Both," I admitted frankly.

He seemed surprised that I would admit my own culpability, but I'd learned well the lessons of taking responsibility for my actions.

"Help me," he said.

"I will," I promised. "I'll do everything—"

He shook his head. "Help me leave this place. I'm not crazy. I'm just . . ." He trailed off. He rubbed his temples. "I don't belong here."

"That may be true," I said. "But you don't have anywhere to go, or anyone to contact."

"And if I did?"

"Then I would call your family myself."

He peered at me as though trying to discern if I was telling the truth or just placating him. I wasn't lying. If Damian had loved ones out there, I would make every effort to find them. They would be worried sick. And having familiar faces around might well help Damian recover. I could get the medical information I needed, too.

"What's your brother's name?" I asked.

"Which one?"

I smiled. "Doesn't matter."

He opened his mouth, then paused. "I don't know." Surprise registered. "But I must have brothers, *ja*?"

"It appears so."

He nodded, and I saw relief glint in his eyes.

"If you give it some time, I'm sure your memories will return. Don't you think your sister would think so?"

"She died."

"I'm sorry," I said softly. "How did she die?"

"She was . . . taken. Killed." He frowned. "How can I know that, but not know my real name? Or where I was yesterday?"

"The brain is weird. An injured brain is even weirder. I think your memories will return, Damian. A good night's sleep may be enough to get the healing process started. Try to rest," I said. "I'll see you in the morning."

I walked around the couch and headed toward the front door.

"Stay for dinner."

I turned and gaped at Damian. "What on earth for?"

"You're the only person I know." He flashed me an unguarded smile. "I told you. You feel like home to me." He paused, and gave me a considering look. "And much more."

"Damian, whatever ill-advised attraction we may feel toward each other, I cannot let you believe that I can—or will—indulge in . . . well, anything. With you. Ever. Because that's unprofessional."

"Are you trying to convince me? Or yourself?"

The latter mostly, but I wouldn't admit that to him. "It may be wise to reassign you to one of our visiting therapists."

"No." The word was absolute. His tone held command and intent.

"Then you'll have to behave."

"I am not the only one," he said, smirking. "And if we are nothing to each other, then having a meal together has no implications."

"I already have a dinner engagement."

His glance took in my bare fingers. He may not have

remembered his life, but he sure remembered how to scope out a girl's status. "Your boyfriend?"

"With my boss, Mr. Dante. He owns the clinic. He's the one who rescued you. And it's a business dinner. That's all." *Terfreakingrific.* I was babbling. I had to go before I did something else really stupid.

"When will I see you again?"

"Tomorrow morning. I usually have breakfast in the main dining hall with everyone else. That's served between seven a.m. and nine a.m. We can meet in my office at nine thirty."

He inclined his head. "Until then."

"Good night, Damian."

"Good night, *Frau* Morningstone."

I should've been glad Damian took the hint to keep our relationship on the required level, but disappointment still whispered through me. I had to work through these inappropriate feelings if I hoped to help the man. That was motivation enough to tell my libido to take a hike. Damian needed me, and I wouldn't fail him.

"One more thing, Kelsey."

I gasped and spun around. Damian was right behind me. How he'd managed to get so close without making a sound—not to mention how fast he moved—I had no idea. He pulled me into his arms. I stared up at him, wide-eyed.

"When I get my memories back, I will no longer be your patient." His confidence bordered on arrogance. "We will be equals."

"I would be thrilled if that were the case," I said. "I want nothing more for you than for you to be happy and healthy."

"I want nothing else . . . but you." His gaze bore into mine, and I was absolutely astounded by the surety that shone there. He wanted me, he would have me, and that was that. The problem, the really big problem, was that I wanted him back. Shame washed through me. I truly sucked as a psychotherapist. I couldn't separate my libidinous emotions from my professional ethics. I hadn't ever been attracted to any of my clients like this, but that hardly earned me a gold star on the morals chart. (Yes, my mother kept a real morals chart. It would've been easier to find gold than it was to earn one of those stars.)

I slid out of his embrace. "Until tomorrow, Damian."

"Tschüss, Schätzchen."

"What does that mean?" I asked.

He grinned. "How am I supposed to know?"

I stared into the full-length mirror, examining myself from head to toe. After my shower, I'd pulled on a blue satin camisole with matching lace panties in anticipation of wearing a dress of the same color. My boobage wasn't plentiful, which is why I often wore bras that made the most of what little I had. On the up side, my B cups made it possible for me to wear camisoles instead of cleavage-enhancing instruments of torture. No way was I gonna give Mr. Dante the impression that I was interested in sexual bennies. That's why the dress I'd chosen for our evening together opened only a little at the throat and ended midcalf. I was also gonna wear decidedly unsexy black flats instead of slipping into the silver stilettos.

I studied my hair. It was dark brown, the color of mud, and since I almost always wore it in either a bun or a French braid or sometimes even a ponytail, it hardly seemed worthwhile to worry about its lack of style. It was straight and fine, and always had been. Attempts to put in waves or curls either by chemical or machine always met with disastrous results. I'd resigned myself to the fact that I could only keep it trimmed and brushed.

My eyes were blue and fringed with thick lashes, probably the most normal feature of my face. I kept my brows waxed, but as natural as possible. Once, I tried that thin, arched look, and it made me appear constantly surprised. My nose was okay, I guess, though a little too pert for my liking. I had good cheekbones, but my lips were too big. And my chin was too pointed. My face looked like a heart, especially the way my hairline curved around the top of my head.

I was six inches over five feet—not quite short, but not quite tall, either. I'd been described as "slender" by one kind high school boyfriend, though I'd heard "scarecrow" applied to my physique more than once. I was a shade too pale (me and the sun broke up a long time ago), but my skin was smooth and once-upon-a-time unblemished. I couldn't erase the scars on my ribs, stomach, and back—courtesy of Robert's blade. Even so, my skin was the only physical attribute for which I had any vanity, and so I often indulged in long bubble baths, spa treatments, and expensive creams to keep it pearlescent and supple.

After I finished inventorying (read: criticizing) the rest of my body, (Pointy hips! Knobby knees! Bulgy ankles!), I looked down at my unpainted toenails. I regularly indulged in mani-pedis, especially since there was an on-site spa in the clinic, but I never wore polish. It made me feel whorish, and I'm sure that has to do with the fact that when my eleven-year-old self returned from a slumber party with red nails Mother told me that sprinkling gold on a pile of manure didn't make it smell any better. Yes. My mom basically called me a pile of shiny poop. And yes, I understood why I had issues.

I glanced at the digital clock on my nightstand and sighed. It was just past six o'clock and I was less than an hour away from my private dinner with Mr. Dante—

with *Jarred*. Nerves made my stomach squeeze, so I fell face-first onto my bed and tried to smother myself in the pillows. Unfortunately, my survival instincts were too strong and I ended up rolling onto my back and staring at the ceiling.

What did he want from me? We could discuss my plans for the clinic anytime. Actually, I had no plans for the clinic. It practically ran itself. I knew Jarred had chosen me for my desperation rather than my skills (obviously). He needed someone in the profession to run his clinic, but more than that, he needed to control that someone.

Despite that whole serial-killer debacle, I wasn't a bad therapist. Not that my session with Mr. Danvers was any proof. I sighed. I wanted so much to help him, and the others. It wasn't entirely an altruistic goal. I wanted to feel like I was doing something right, something good for people. I wanted to wash clean my sins by paying penance here. Unease fluttered through me. Why couldn't I ignore the feeling that all was not as it seemed at the clinic? I couldn't point at anything or anyone and exclaim, "Aha!" I had no proof of nefarious dealings. I just . . . freaking didn't like it here. My mind circled back around to Mr. Danvers. Should I have at least poked at his emotions, see what was twisting him up? No. Not yet. If I hadn't tried to use my gift to manipulate Robert, to fix him, things might've ended differently. You can't fix empty. You can't give a soul to a man who has none. As much as I'd wanted to wiggle into the cracks of Mr. Danvers's emotional barriers and help him see the truth about the nonexistent Malphas . . . I would wait.

I yawned. I hadn't realized how tired I was until now. Lolling on the bed was a bad idea. But maybe . . . a teeny-tiny nap would help delay the threatening headache. No doubt that was a physical response to the stress

of having dinner with Jarred, who so did not want to talk
about the clinic.

I yawned again and let my thoughts drift. Then I
curled up around a pillow and fell asleep.

In the dream, I wore a frilly blue dress. Its crinoline skirt
brushed my knees. My feet were bare, my toes digging
into the soft grass beneath my feet. It was dusk. I stood
next to a large tree that was an amazing shade of purple.

"Late," said a growling voice. "Late. Always late."

I looked around, trying to see who was speaking. The
forest around me looked as though it had been created
by a five-year-old on a sugar buzz. I saw no one else—
nothing else.

A huge black wolf jumped over a mossy log and
stopped short. He looked me over, tilting his head. I saw
the jade green eyes, and gasped. "Damian?"

"Late," he said with a bark. Then he turned and took
off.

I followed.

"Wait!" I cried.

The wolf was fast and nimble. He sailed over fallen
limbs and scrubby bushes, and darted past trees in Eas-
ter egg colors. I tried to keep up, but he was too quick.
Then I stumbled into a small clearing. We were at the
massive purple tree again, only this time, I could see a
gaping, dark hole in its thick, gnarled base.

The wolf looked into the hole, and then at me.

"What?" I asked. I crept closer, staying clear of the
hole. "You want me to go in there?"

He nodded.

"I can't," I said. I smiled weakly. "I'm not Alice."

"Mate," he said. "Mate."

"Don't you mean late?" I asked.

"Save me," he said. Then he leapt into the hole.

I screamed, and lurched for him, my arms wide, and then I fell, tumbling, tumbling into the dark.

I awoke gasping for breath. I shot off the bed, the pillow still clutched in my arms. I tried to get myself together, but I was shaking. *Way to be helpful, subconscious.* I sucked in some steadying breaths, not even remotely ready to dissect the meaning of that dream.

I glanced at the clock on the nightstand and cursed. If I didn't get my ass in gear, I would be late for my dinner with Jarred. Like it or not, he was my boss, and I wanted to keep my job.

Damian. I paused. I really did want to save him. Despite my stern self-lectures, my unrepentant pulse gave a little leap. How could I ever hope to treat Damian if I couldn't stop drooling over the man?

Argh!

I plopped back onto the bed, thinking about Jarred, which wasn't exactly a safer area. Maybe my discomfort with this place had to do with the niggling suspicion that Jarred had picked me for *me*—a far more terrifying consideration than the idea my patheticness had driven him to an act of unimaginable kindness. Despite my lapses in judgment over the years, I had never told a soul about my empathic abilities. I can't exactly remember what it was like for me as a child, but I'm sure any weirdness I displayed was shrugged off as my imagination gone wild. I was nine years old when I figured out two things: First, being able to "feel" the emotions of others was not something everyone could do. Second, people didn't appreciate it when you dug around their emotional landscape and talked about their unsightly weeds.

So, yeah, very early on, I learned to keep myself to myself.

A low, mournful howl lurched into my thoughts.

I blinked and sat up. For a crazy second, I had a

dream-within-a-dream moment, like maybe I hadn't actually woken up from the weird forest and the talking
wolf, but instead had fallen into this space that looked
like my bedroom, but wasn't.

The howl echoed again.

What the hell?

I stood up and looked around trying to get my bear-
ings. I wasn't in Wonderland. I was awake. Probably. I
pinched my arm and yelped. Oh, yeah. Definitely awake.

My apartment was at the end of the facility's east
wing. In fact, my living quarters were the only thing at
this end of the second floor. The place was huge and
luxurious, filled with marble counters, hardwood floors,
silk fabrics, oversized furniture, and an impossible array
of polished knickknacks. I mostly stayed tucked into my
bedroom, which had its own fireplace, big-screen television, and mini-fridge. The rest of the place felt too much
like a museum (or like my mother's own haughty abode)
for me to feel comfortable within it.

Another howl reverberated, much louder this time.
Whatever creature was making that racket was in this
part of the facility. Did Oklahoma have wolves? I didn't
think so, but getting the skinny on the state's known
wildlife had never been a goal of mine. Of course, I dismissed the idea of a patient causing the ruckus because
none had ever displayed animalistic tendencies.

Except . . . well, Damian.

I hurried into the living room, bumping into the various tables and chairs positioned just so around the or-
nate fireplace. Above it was an abstract painting of red
slashes and purple spatters, which lifted to reveal the
flat-screen TV hidden behind. I had only flipped on a
couple of the numerous lights available in the cavernous
space, so I was maneuvering (ineptly, of course) through
the shadowy recesses.

Despite bruised shins and one stubbed toe, I made it to the door. I grasped the knob and hesitated. I was not gonna be the too-stupid-to-live girl (er . . . again), so I pressed my ear against the thick wood and strained to listen.

I heard rhythmic thumping, a series of noises that sounded like . . . okay, like light sabers clashing, and then . . . *hooooooooowl!*

"Shit! He's going for the doc," yelled a woman's voice. "How the fuck did he find her?"

"Goddamned werewolves." Sven! He sounded pissed off. I mean, more so than usual. And werewolves? Really? I'd never be able to help Damian if people catered to his delusions. "Dante will strip our hides if this asshole gets close enough to touch her."

I had a terrible moment where I almost yanked the door open and demanded an explanation. I managed not to turn the knob, though my fingers were trembling with the urge to follow through.

I heard shouts, pain-filled cries, bangs, and thuds.

And then there was nothing but an awful silence.

Something large smacked into my locked front door. I bounced off and stumbled back, heart thudding as I heard ominous splintering sounds. I stared at the cracking, buckling door in horrified awe. I had automatically put up my mental shields, so I had no empathic sense of who was trying to get in . . . but I knew anyway.

I wouldn't open myself up to him—keeping myself as closed as the door. I knew too well the mistake I'd made last time and what it had cost so many.

I wished I could say that I did something sensible, like run away, or lock myself in the foyer closet, or grab something with which to defend myself. But since it was me, and not someone with common sense, I stood there like my feet had been glued to the floor.

The door snapped in the middle and the man on the other side grabbed the pieces and yanked them out, tossing them into the hallway beyond.

Damian crouched down, naked and bruised and furious. His nostrils flared, his eyes narrowed, and even through my psychic shields, I felt the sudden, brutal shift of his anger into fierce, ugly need.

"Mine," he growled.

Then he leapt through the door, howling in triumph.

My fight-or-flight impulse finally kicked in. With my heart trying to claw its way outta my throat, I spun around and darted back through the living room.

Damian followed. Sorta. I heard the whumps of his feet hitting the couch cushions and the crash of items he knocked off tables as he cut across the area I'd avoided. Just as I got to my open bedroom door, he landed in front of me, crouched on all fours, his head cocked as he studied me.

Why the hell was he naked again? And what could've possibly triggered his need to go into werewolf mode? I noted a small circular burn on his shoulder. What weapon in Sven's arsenal made that sort of wound?

Oh, God. What had Damian done to Sven and the security team? Had he killed them? Nausea roiled and I pressed a trembling hand to my stomach. What on earth had made me believe that I could help this man? That I could help anyone? I'd demanded Damian be assigned a room because I wanted to believe he wouldn't hurt anyone. I'd made a terrible mistake. *Again.*

I had no idea what to do now. I wasn't anywhere near a panic button, and there were several located within the apartment. Just how many homicidal maniacs did a girl have to face in one lifetime? Granted, this situation was different from the one with Robert, except that I still didn't have a clue how to handle myself. I had no weapons, no clever ideas—just a terrible, numb sensation that felt too much like surrender.

Damian's nostrils were flaring, and his eyes were strange. The pupils were large and round. They looked so different. I couldn't quite wrap my brain around this observation. Could a person so lost in their delusion physically create characteristics that confirmed their beliefs? Damian believed he was a wolf, and so he was trying to become one. And rather succeeding.

His nostrils continued to flare as he stared at me. Then he growled low in his throat, baring his teeth at me. The growl sounded very much like it had issued from a wolf rather than a man pretending to be one. Fear chilled me.

I stepped back, and the growl got louder, meaner.

Catering to the delusion was not the correct therapeutic approach, but right now, I was more worried about survival. It seemed to me that responding to him as though he were, indeed, a wolf, might serve me best. Unfortunately, I knew zipola about wolf behavior. Why oh why didn't I watch more National Geographic? All that knowledge gleaned from the Style Network certainly wasn't helping me now.

Screw it.

"Damian," I said in a sharp, firm voice. "You're being rude."

He stopped growling, and once again cocked his head, his gaze on mine. He looked startled. He sat back on his haunches, blinking. Panicked as I was, I couldn't help but note that he had a fully erect penis, which did not reassure me about his intentions.

"Rude." His eyes somehow changed again, reverting to a more human gaze. "I do not wish to be rude." Slowly, he rose to his feet. My fear receded just a little. While I no longer saw evidence of the injuries I'd noted when observing him in the induction room (which was weird because those kinds of wounds shouldn't heal in mere hours), I saw fresh bruises and cuts—no doubt from Sven's attempt to recapture him.

And he still had that impressive erection, too.

Damian crossed to me in two long strides and grasped my arms. He had a firm grip on me, though not a painful one. His gaze was intense as he studied my face.

"What are you?" he asked.

"I'm not sure what you mean," I said carefully.

"You smell so good. But not human. You're wolf. You smell like wolf." He inhaled, his eyes closing, his lips pulling back in a feral grin. Then his eyes popped open. He lowered his face to mine. "I want you."

Dry-mouthed, I licked my lips, which drew his attention in a way that made my heart skip a beat. I couldn't allow him to kiss me, even though a tiny dark part of me hoped he'd take what he wanted. Then I could have that kiss guilt-free. (Being a therapist made me an ace at creating justifiable behavior.) He was so close that his hard-on brushed my stomach, which was bare, thanks to the way the camisole's filmy cloth parted in the middle.

"Permit me," he said.

"I . . . uh, what?"

"I cannot take what belongs to you."

What an odd way to express . . . um, whatever he was trying to express. Oh. He said the next time he'd remember to ask permission. And I'd assured him there would be no next time. Silly me. I quaked as emotions tumbled through me. My shields were feeling too thin, and no doubt I was honing in on Damian's passion, which was mixing in with my own fear and consternation. Still, I had an opportunity to regain control, and I took it.

"Let me go, Damian," I said softly.

"No," he croaked. My shields dissolved under the

weight of his desperation. His emotions flowed over me in tangled waves. He was afraid that if he let me go, he would be lost again. I ascertained he had not regained his memories, but obviously, his delusion of being a wolf was wholly intact. His emotions rioted through me— anger, terror, confusion, and, most of all, a passionate, urgent need to claim the female in his arms. His lust was more frightening than even the fury that had driven him to my door.

"Permit me," he begged.

I swallowed the knot in my throat. If I thought for a moment that letting him kiss me would secure my release, I might've considered it. But I knew it was merely the gateway to a larger problem. Damian was obviously infatuated with me and even the smallest concession would lead to other expectations that I could never, ever fulfill.

No matter how much I wanted to.

He stiffened, his gaze sliding toward the living room. The front door wasn't visible from where we stood, and I hadn't heard anything to indicate someone had arrived. But given Damian's reaction, I knew someone had either awakened from the hallway scuffle (which meant they weren't dead . . . yay!) or a secondary team had arrived. Relief tumbled through me for a nanosecond.

Damian yanked me fully into his embrace. He was all taut flesh and hard muscle (and did I mention his enormous penis, which was now pressed between the vee of my thighs?). My body and my brain argued over the appropriate response. My knees wobbled, and I felt all liquidy and faint. Then Damian leaned down and sank his sharp teeth deeply into the flesh between my neck and shoulder.

"Ow!" I cried. I smacked Damian on top of the head as if he were a pesky schoolboy taking liberties rather than a delusional schizophrenic. He straightened. And he was grinning with blood-flecked lips.

"I didn't give you permission to do that!"

"I can mark you if I so choose," he said imperiously. "I am the royal alpha."

I gaped at him. The spot where he'd bitten me stung like crazy. I should've been asking him questions that helped me understand his delusion, but I was too pissed off. "You need permission to kiss me, but you can *bite* me?"

"No!" The angry shout came from Jarred. "Damn it! Sven!"

"Got him," came Sven's icy voice.

I heard a low, soft whine; then a circular silver object thudded into Damian's shoulder. Oh. That explained the other wound. But why had they tried to tranq him earlier? What had triggered his delusion?

"You are protected now," he said. His hands slipped off my arms as his eyes rolled back into his head. He crumpled to the floor.

"Christ Almighty," muttered Jarred as he grasped my wrist and pulled me away from Damian's prone form. I watched in a daze as Sven and his female partner shouldered past us and crouched down to check the unconscious man.

"It's nice that you're not dead," I said to Sven.

He glanced up at me, his gaze widening as he noted what I was wearing. Then one corner of his mouth tugged up. "Back 'atcha."

Sven didn't completely hate me. Well, that was progress in one abysmal corner of my messed-up life. While Sven and his team dealt with Damian, Jarred led me into the kitchen. The whole area was open plan. The kitchen overlooked the living room and to the right was the formal dining room—complete with chandelier. Just ten feet away, I heard Sven on his walkie-talkie making arrangements to put Damian back into the induction room.

I wheeled around and leaned over the marble counter that separated the kitchen from the living room. "No! Don't cage him!"

Sven's gaze traveled past me, and I followed it to Jarred, who stood less than a foot behind me. He was as emotionally shuttered as usual, his expression stony. "He's too dangerous to be allowed a suite."

I had to agree with him, even though I didn't want Damian tossed into the padded cell again. "Isn't there a more secure location that's not so . . . well, prisonlike?"

"No." He nodded toward Sven. The big man picked up Damian and tossed him over his shoulder like an unwieldy sack of potatoes.

I turned away, unable to stomach the sight of yet another of my failures being carted away. At least Damian was alive. Robert had been dead, and deservedly so.

Jarred stepped closer, chopping in half the small distance between us. He looked as an ancient and stoic as an oak tree. His tense demeanor set me on edge. I couldn't sense his emotions, but I got the impression something significant had changed—something that very much displeased him. His gaze slid over me, lingering on the gap created by the way the camisole's fabric split. He had a decent view of my navel and the lacy edge of my panties. He might be able to block my empathic abilities, but I knew desire when I saw it—even in the tiny flicker Jarred allowed into those cold gray eyes.

"I'll go put on a robe."

"I would prefer that you didn't," he said.

I heard the command in his tone, and I didn't like it. I had the childish urge to yell, "You're not the boss of me!" Except that, you know, he actually was.

"I'm not particularly comfortable conversing with my employer while in my underwear."

"You may as well know," he said in thoughtful tone, "that I had fully expected to bed you by evening's end."

I swallowed the knot in my throat. I hadn't been incorrect about his intentions at all. "I don't care how desperate I am, Mr. Dante. I will not sleep with you to keep my job."

He blinked down at me, the slight widening of his eyes the only indication of his surprise. "Our sexual relationship has nothing to do with your employment." He frowned. "I find it disturbing that you believe I need to blackmail anyone into my bed."

"I find it disturbing you think we're going to have a sexual relationship."

His lips thinned. "I hadn't counted on the competition."

Competition? I looked at him blankly, and he sighed. He put his hands in his pockets and rocked back on his heels, ever the casual man (only so not . . . everything about Jarred Dante was calculated).

His gaze meandered over me again, which I tolerated with some annoyance. Being wealthy and good-looking and autocratic had made Jarred somewhat a spoiled bully. I crossed my arms and glared at him, but he didn't relent in his inventory of my assets. His mouth tightened almost imperceptibly.

"I'm surprised you championed Damian at all," said Jarred. "He could've killed you."

"If he wanted to kill me then I would be dead."

The blame for Damian's escape was mine. I hadn't judged the situation appropriately. Worse, I allowed my attraction to him to cloud my judgment. I was entirely out of my league. I could no longer pretend that I was capable of running the facility when it was so obvious I couldn't even run my own life. It appeared that I would never regain my confidence (or was that my own arrogance?). I would always second-guess myself—forget about regaining full trust in my own decision-making skills. *Why are you even a therapist, Kelsey?* The question was a blend of my mother's voice and my own conscience. Pure stubbornness had propelled me forward. Despite losing civil lawsuits, and being convicted in the court of public opinion, I had received no reprimands from the state nor had the federal government sought charges against me. And I'd spent quite a few days in the company of FBI agents. So, with license (and the proverbial hat) in hand, I'd sought a therapy job. And I'd eventually gotten one—a very crappy, unrewarding one. Then Jarred found me and offered me redemption through his largesse.

But still I was plagued by the idea that I hadn't found my place in the world. I always felt like I was going in the wrong direction.

I reached up and felt the wound on my neck. Even the light pressure sent a jolt of pain down my shoulder. *Ouch.* "The question is why Damian tried to find me at all. And how did he manage it?"

"He caught your scent."

"That's ridiculous." Unless my theory that his delusion was so powerful, his body was actually accommodating it. "I can't believe how embedded he is in the fiction he's created. It's amazing that it survived the amnesia, but not any of his other memories. He told me that he could mark me because he was the royal alpha."

"Did he?" Jarred's gaze flicked to my neck. "Let me see."

He lifted my hair. He was such a large man that I couldn't help but feel intimidated by his nearness. He was dressed in a gray suit with a striped tie, no doubt for our dinner date, and I had to admit, his spicy cologne was rather nice. He uttered, "Goddamnit." Then he stepped back. "I'll call Dr. Ruthers."

I shook my head. "I'll put on some antibiotic ointment and bandage it. I'll be fine."

Jarred quirked a brow. He removed his cell phone and pressed one button. "Dr. Ruthers, please come to Kelsey Morningstone's suite. She's been bitten by a werewolf." He ended the call and stuck the phone back into his jacket pocket.

"Yeah. Funny," I said. "It's nice that you take Damian's case so seriously."

"Believe me, Kelsey, I take Damian's case *very* seriously." He reached into an upper cabinet and pulled down an elaborate bottle with a gold spiral around it. In another cabinet, he pulled down two snifters.

I looked at him, surprised. "I had no idea those were in there."

"I stocked the kitchen for you. It doesn't look like you use it much."

"I don't cook."

"I'll get you a chef," he said as he handed me the glass. "Then you won't have to."

I didn't particularly want alcohol to soothe my jangled nerves. I thought the whole gesture was rather cliché, but with Jarred staring at me expectantly, I took a small sip.

I grimaced. "Ew. That's yucky!"

His eyes went wide, and he nearly choked on the drink he'd just taken.

I put the glass on the counter. "I don't think I'm a brandy kind of girl."

"If you can't enjoy a one-hundred-twenty-year-old brandy with a seven-thousand-dollar price tag," he managed hoarsely, "then no, you are not a brandy kind of girl."

I studied the bottle, wondering why on earth he would spend so much money on such a silly thing. "Maybe you can get your money back."

He shook his head. "On my soul, I will never tell the Frapin family that you called their Cuveé 1888 'yucky.'"

I shrugged. "It's your liver."

He put his glass next to the one I'd abandoned. Once again, he moved very close to me, leaning a hip against the counter. He reached out and curled a strand of my hair around his forefinger. "You are not impressed by the trappings of wealth."

"I used to measure my success by the amount and quality of possessions I acquired."

"And now?"

"Now I'm beholden to a man trapped in his wealth."

He actually chuckled. His eyes crinkled in a way that made me think he had once been a man who laughed easily. I wondered what had happened to him to make him so closed off. He let my hair drop. Then he crossed his arms, his enigmatic gaze on mine. "I won't allow you to quit."

My mouth dropped open. He'd discerned my intent before the idea had fully formed. Hadn't that really been what my mind had been circling around? My heart just hadn't caught up. Once he said the words, however, I knew quitting this job, hell, quitting as a psychotherapist altogether, was exactly what I needed to do. I had never felt in charge of my own life. Part of it was because my mother was controlling—always pushing me toward the goals she thought I should accomplish. Still. I was twenty-eight years old. I could hardly keep blaming my mommy issues. Okay, I could, but I wouldn't. The other part, of course, was my fear. What would I do if I wasn't a therapist?

I couldn't think of a thing.

It was scary to look at a road stretching out in front of me, endless and spiraling with no familiar landmarks.

After all I'd been through, I was still a coward.

"It's not your choice," I finally said. "You would think after I let a serial killer loose, I would've gotten the universal hint that I shouldn't be a therapist."

"What Robert Mallard did was not your fault."

"It was, actually."

He considered me for a long moment. I was feeling too tired to defend my position on anything else, and the pain of my injury had been worsening every second. It ached so badly now, I just wanted to pop some Advil and go to bed. I resisted the urge to touch the wounded flesh again. I had no idea what would soothe a bite, but suddenly I was glad Jarred had called Dr. Ruthers. Surely the physician had some magical ointment that would fix me.

"You will continue to work for me," said Jarred. "Or you'll have to deal with the legalities of walking away from your obligations."

I felt the blood drain out of my face. I'd agreed to three years as administrator and head therapist in exchange for Jarred paying off my debts, a generous salary, and this luxury apartment. "You would sue me for breach of contract," I said flatly.

"As a start."

I tamped down my anger. Jarred was probably expecting me to get upset, so I tossed aside my impulse to tell him to take a flying leap, and tried to appeal to his sense of reason. "We both know I'm not cut out for this job. The staff doesn't respect me. The patients don't trust me. Sven thinks I'm an idiot. And you have the gall to believe that I'll fall into bed with you because you're rich and smart and handsome."

"What's wrong with those qualities?" he asked, ignoring everything else I'd said.

"When you can buy anything, or anyone, then nothing truly has worth. How can you cherish what you hold, Jarred, when you did nothing more than pay for it?"

He didn't look away from me, but he didn't respond right away, apparently mulling over my words. Then he shrugged. "It's the way my world works. Everyone, and everything, has a price. One I can always pay."

"I suppose that's true. There's no doubt you bought me," I said. "But you don't own me. Every female within a hundred miles would warm your bed tonight, but in the morning, what would you have left?"

"Some very good memories."

"I don't want to be someone's very good memory," I said softly. "Is that all you aspire to, Jarred?"

He didn't answer, and though I still wasn't getting any real vibes off him, I believed I glimpsed into his soul—maybe just a teeny-tiny bit. What Jarred was seeking, either through his work, this clinic, me, or that fancy brandy of his, he would not find. He wanted what we all wanted, what we all sought from each other on a daily basis. Connection. If we were lucky, we found our equal, the partner who balanced our weaknesses with their strengths, who offered us companionship and faith and security.

Jarred Dante wanted love.

"You look pale," he said. I detected the barest whisper of concern in his words.

It was as if his words sparked the reaction. Cold rushed through me, followed by a wave of prickling heat. My knees buckled, and he caught me. I stared at him, wide-eyed. "I don't feel well."

The room started to spin, and I clutched Jarred's arms, trying to right myself. Instead, I tumbled into the awful vortex. I spun and spun . . . away from the light, the room, the man holding me . . . and into the thick, cloying darkness.

Down, down, down into the rabbit hole once again.

Chapter 3

"You were quite unexpected."

The woman's lilting voice drew me out of the spinning dark. When I opened my eyes, I stood within a circle of trees so tall that their myriad thick branches nearly blotted out the moon overhead. Lights glimmered among the branches, and I had no doubt the flickering dots were fireflies—and there were certainly a lot of them. I wore a blue dress of the sort I associated with Greek goddesses, my hair loose and flowing over my shoulders. I clutched the soft fabric in my hands, wondering at the significance of being dressed in such a manner.

Before me, sitting on a throne carved out of beautiful polished wood was a woman so gorgeous, she couldn't be real. She had long black hair that coiled in tight ringlets down to her waist. Her skin was as pale as cream, her features refined and delicate. Her dress was a dark blue satin, it seemed finely cut and expensive, yet her feet were as bare as mine. On her head rested a crown that seemed to be woven from both polished wood and gold; in its center was a bloodred ruby the size of a kiwi.

"I am the Moon Goddess and this is my mate, Tark."

My gaze was drawn to where the woman's hand rested on the scruff of a very large black wolf. His collar was made of the same materials as the lady's crown, with the same size and shape ruby. His jade green gaze assessed me in such a haughty manner that I immediately felt unworthy of his scrutiny.

He reminded me of Damian—not only that familiar green gaze, but the proud stance, the arrogant tilt to his head. He didn't look too thrilled with me, and I took a step back.

"You're frightening her, darling. Be nice."

Tark snorted and raised his snout. Hoo-kay. Was that wolf gesture for "I won't eat you now, but watch it"?

"Where am I?" I asked.

"I redirected your consciousness. I couldn't resist the opportunity to visit Damian's intended. You are an unusual choice for a lycan bride," she said, her brown eyes assessing me. "But I approve."

The wolf barked, turning his visage to the lady, his head cocked in a silent query.

"What else can we do?" she asked him. "Damian has been lost to us for so long. He must reclaim his rightful place as the crown prince. He must heal the wounds of his past and look to the future."

"I know I'm dreaming," I said. "And I know I have this very inappropriate . . . er, thing for Damian. But maybe you could explain. You know, everything."

"There's no time to explain it all," she said. "I'll try to cover the basics. Damian and his brothers are royal lycanthropes—the only ones. You see, they can trace their bloodlines directly to me. They are different from the other lycans, just as the full-bloods are different from the Roma."

I blinked. I latched on to the last of her words because the rest made no sense. "What's a Roma?"

The lady sighed. "I'm going about this completely wrong. We have so little time and there is much you must know."

The wolf yipped, putting a paw onto her thigh. She leaned down and planted a kiss on the wolf's snout. "Yes, darling. Of course." She looked at me. "Damian abandoned everything he once held dear because he believes that he failed his people. He also believes that I abandoned him. Neither he nor his brothers will talk to me. Not anymore. I used to hear their prayers every night. After Danielle died, they stopped."

The wolf at her side whined and she tugged on his ear.

"Who's Danielle?"

"His adopted sister. She was orphaned when she was only an infant and she was raised as royalty with the triplets. She was killed, and her death broke Damian's heart. He couldn't forgive himself for not saving her."

Damian had said his sister died. Was this . . . No. I was creating this fiction. I was dreaming, and wow, my mind was working overtime to fill in the blanks of Damian's life.

"The full-bloods are dying, their numbers dwindling. They have no faith," she said sadly. "They are lonely for the old ways, the times when they had a real community. Damian believes that his time is past, that another rules that which belongs to him. This is, of course, incorrect."

Tark barked in a way that seemed to convey annoyance.

"They are still werewolves," she admonished. "And you know they have a different destiny from our dear ones." She drew in a breath and offered me a dazzling smile. "Damian has chosen you."

"Chosen me for what?" I felt a vague panic swishing around inside me.

"To be his mate." Her tone had gone quiet, serious.

This was the craziest dream I'd ever had. I wasn't the mate of anyone, much less the schizophrenic who'd attacked me. "Damian thinks he's a werewolf. You're saying he bit me so he could . . . uh, marry me?"

"I really wish we could skip the 'convince you it's the truth' part of this process," said the lady. "Perhaps you could simply believe all that I'm telling you."

Yeah. Right. If I believed even a tenth of the crap she'd just spewed, I'd be getting my own patient suite at the Dante Clinic.

Tark pawed her thigh, his nails rustling in the folds of her dress.

"Yes," she said. "I know." She glanced at me. "Our natures include robust passions that prove wearisome for lesser creatures. It is rare that a lycan will choose a human for anything other than a temporary lover. You see, our children have been unable to breed with humans." She stroked the wolf's head. "Tark is worried about your ability to procreate—even with your unique attributes."

"You mean my sunny disposition and gazellelike legs?"

Her laughter was like the ringing of wind chimes. "You don't yet know the secret locked within you." Sadness flickered in her gaze, but she still managed to keep her hopeful smile. "Sometimes that which begins in sorrow ends in joy."

I couldn't think of a response, so I said nothing and tried to keep my stare polite. All I had to do was wake up. When I did, this dream would fade like any other. I would probably even laugh at the way my subconscious had played around with my attraction to Damian.

"You must help him to find his way again, Kelsey."

The wolf turned toward me and dipped his snout in recognition of the lady's words. I wanted to help Damian, but I knew the reality of his situation. His delusion held him in thrall, and apparently me as well. We both needed to shake free of this madness.

As I watched, the wolf rose to stand on his hind legs. His fur receded with feathered hushes as his bones snicked under his flesh. Within moments I beheld a naked man as strong and handsome as Damian with jade eyes, an aquiline nose, and thin-as-blades cheeks. His curtain of black hair brushed his buttocks. The collar around his neck remained. He was tall, well muscled, and regarded me with something between curiosity and suspicion.

"You know how stubborn these humans are," he said in a low, raspy voice. "They require proof." He looked at me reproachfully. "Faith is too often discarded by your kind."

"Sometimes it's taken from us," I said softly.

"Yes," he agreed. "How pathetic that you give it up so easily." He sighed. "If but one would stand and hold firm, others would follow."

"Doubt is its own monster, with teeth and claws and poison," said the Goddess, "which is why two faithful souls are stronger still." She pointed at me. "I bestow this symbol so that both you and Damian will embrace the truths we have given you."

Blue light sizzled from her fingertip. The bolt smacked into my flesh inches above my left breast and seemed to burn a hole right through me. Pain exploded. I cried out, grabbing on to my shoulder, only to let go when the spikes of agony worsened. The ground beneath my feet gave away, and once again I was spinning into the clasping darkness.

When I awoke, I was in my own bed. My eyes felt puffy and heavy, my limbs ached. Fever flushed my skin, the heat of illness buried into muscle and bone. A single lamp on the nightstand offered a small glow of light that did nothing to dispel the shadows of my bedroom. I was tucked in tightly, the covers thick and suffocating.

I wanted to push them off, but neither my arms nor my legs obeyed the commands to move. I turned my head, my mouth dry and my lips cracked.

Just outside the circle of light sat a man in a chair that had once graced the left side of my bedroom hearth. He was leaning forward, his elbows balancing on his knees as he cradled his head.

"Water," I managed. "Please."

His head came up instantly, his eyes wide. "Kelsey."

"Mr. Dante." Even through the haze of pain and unbearable heat, I saw how crumpled his suit looked, how his hair looked as though he'd furrowed his fingers through it numerous times, and how worry weighted a gaze I once thought so cold.

He rose from his chair and moved into the darkness where I could no longer discern his figure. I heard the clink of ice and the sweet sound of pouring liquid. He returned to the bed, sitting gingerly on its edge. Carefully, he slipped his hand behind my head and held me gently as he lifted the glass to my mouth. "Sip only," he said.

I did as he asked, even though I wanted to gulp it all down. My stomach roiled at even the small tastes I allowed myself, so I reluctantly stopped imbibing.

"What's wrong with me?" I asked.

His expression was wintry. "Nothing that you asked for, I assure you."

His response confused me, but I couldn't croak out any more questions. Exhaustion battered me, competing viciously with the streams of agony that flowed from temples to toes.

He put the glass on the nightstand, and then readjusted the mountainous bedding that covered me. "We are dealing with too many unknowns. Despite the legends and myths surrounding werewolves, the truth is that until now, lycans were born, not made."

Something about his tone, not to mention the actual, crazy words, caused alarm to leap through me. "Lycans?"

Not this again! It seemed as though my contact with Damian had infected me with his delusion, for why else would I keep having conversations with people who believed werewolves to be real?

"This is not how I wanted to introduce you to my world," he continued, his words clipped. "But the choice was taken from me. I did us no favors by rescuing Damian from his captors." His smile was thin and sharp. "Had I known he would take what I sought for myself, I would've left him to rot in his prison."

His tone was strangely formal, and the words still on this side of infreakingsane. I was trying to take it all in, but my aching head felt stuffed with cotton. Surely I was dreaming again, having dropped out of a forest where a goddess and her wolf-mate told me outrageous lies and into this nightmare of Jarred spouting nonsense.

"Lycanthropes are real," he insisted. He brushed limp strands of hair away from my face. Bitterness turned his gray eyes as flat and hard as river stones. "Like it or not, you've been claimed by the prince of werewolves."

Jarred's preposterous announcement propelled me back into the exhaustion of illness and nightmares. Every so often, I would surface from the fevered terrors, feeling as though I had somehow ripped away my own skin to reveal my true self: a dark, craven creature that pawed and growled and bared its teeth. This was the very creature Robert Mallard had said that I bore inside me, the one he wanted to set free. He'd wanted to kill the "outer me," so that the "inner me" could join him in his life's work. He'd even brought along a present for the occasion: a seventeen-year-old girl with long blond hair and terrified blue eyes.

No! I pushed away the images. I couldn't relive those moments again. I'd gone through that agony numerous times already—talking to police detectives and FBI agents and psychiatrists. I knew the firmament of my own mind. I was not broken. Robert had taken so much from me, and from the world, I would not give him anything else.

"Sshh." I felt a tender hand upon my brow; then a cold, wet cloth was pressed against my burning face. "Rest, Kelsey. It's all you can do now."

I closed my eyes again and slipped once again into nightmare-ridden slumber.

"How long will it stop the change?"

Jarred's voice filtered through the twilight of my consciousness. I struggled through the thickness of sleep that didn't feel natural.

Had I been drugged?

The thought panicked me. I couldn't get my limbs to move, or my eyes to open. My ears were working fine, however, and I strained to hear the low conversation. I teetered on the edge of sliding back into oblivion, which made it difficult to concentrate.

"You know we haven't had enough trials," said another man's voice. Dr. Ruthers? "My preparations were for Damian. Giving it to the girl is risky."

"How long?"

"If we're lucky, she'll get a month's reprieve."

"Damn it!" Jarred's voice seethed with frustration and anger. "Damian has ruined everything. All that planning, all that research—all for nothing!"

"Not necessarily," said Dr. Ruthers. "It may well be she completes the transition, which means your supposition about the theria genotype is correct."

"So is its rarity," said Jarred. "You know how long it took for me track down Sylvia. And it was only by chance we discovered she'd had a child. There must be a way to strip out Damian's DNA."

"You know how the theria genotype works. Once the shifter's blood was introduced into her system, it activated the process."

My heart started to thud so loud, I was sure the two men would be able to hear it. I wanted very much to believe that I was caught in yet another dream, but I couldn't deny this seemed all too real. Somehow Damian's bite had affected me in ways I didn't understand. I had little faith that Jarred wanted to help me because of any altruistic motivations. Given the heavy languidness I felt, it was likely he had indeed drugged me.

"We should be glad ETAC has not discovered this anomaly," mused Dr. Ruthers. "It's bad enough lycans have been disappearing or turning up dead in recent months."

"They've figured out the blood of a royal has different properties than commoners. That's why they kidnapped Damian. Bastards aren't satisfied with their mutant vampires. Now they want to fuck with the lycans, too. If only we'd gotten to him sooner, damn it!"

"They'll want him back, no doubt."

"Don't worry about that," said Jarred tersely. "Give her the serum."

I heard the doctor sigh. "As you wish."

I heard someone approach and the snick of a case opening. Fear bled through the stratum of my addled weariness, but I still couldn't get my eyes to open much less get my body to move away.

"I'm sorry, my dear," whispered Dr. Ruthers.

I felt my arm being gently extracted from underneath the stifling covers. I was still wearing the stupid camisole, so I didn't even have the protection of a sleeve to prevent the feel of something round and cold against my shoulder. *Hiss. Pop.* Sudden, sharp pain radiated from my shoulder.

A terrible chill stole across my chest. I felt the aching tendrils worm into my heart and within moments, the sting of its cold poison invaded my veins.

Pain flared, and I cried out.

I felt hands on me, nonsensical comforts whispered as my body quaked and raged at this systemic invasion.

Then, blessedly, I slipped once again into the inky waters of unconsciousness.

I woke up with a clear mind and firm intentions.

I lay in bed, slitting my eyes so that I could assess my surroundings without revealing I was awake. I listened carefully for any activity, but it appeared I was alone. Certainly my bedroom was empty, and the door was mercifully closed.

Slowly, I sat up, afraid I might alert someone.

Once I had reassured myself I was alone and would remain so, I allowed myself to think about all that had transpired.

Werewolves. I couldn't dismiss the idea of their reality as easily as I wanted. No, I wanted to crawl into my disbelief and rout out the ridiculousness of believing shape-shifters roamed among the human population. For heaven's sake! Wouldn't someone notice such creatures? How would anyone be able to keep that kind of secret?

I couldn't believe I was actually considering the idea that werewolves existed. Between my dreams and my drugged state, along with my inappropriate empathy (and attraction) to the delusional Damian, I could surely justify the need to think werewolves were real.

Jarred had told me as much, hadn't he? And if he was trying to mess with my mind, what was the point? A test of some kind? To what end?

It was all so damned confusing.

There was one thing, however, of which I was certain.

Jarred Dante had used me as his personal guinea pig. And he'd rescued Damian from his previous incarceration to experiment on him as well. Even if I still had a sterling reputation, I would be hard-pressed to convince anyone that the billionaire was using his money and influence to conduct medical trials on helpless people with no families and no options.

The callousness of Jarred's actions burned me to my soul.

I had no proof, and honestly, I hadn't gotten any emotional vibes that indicated subterfuge from anyone here. The patients seemed happy and content. Those emotions might well be drug-induced, but if they were, I'd know it. Emotion rendered by a pill was distinctly different from a raw feeling pulsing in the figurative heart.

The fact remained that Jarred Dante and Dr. Ruthers had injected me with something. And while I remembered their fiercely whispered conversation, not much of it made sense, especially if I was to consider that they believed werewolves were real. And if I factored in my own strange dream of the Moon Goddess and the wolf named Tark ...

Oh, please! Was I really going down into this ugly, little rabbit hole?

I was no Alice, and this was no Wonderland.

I clenched the bedspread and let the full force of my own anger soak me from skin to bone. I felt utterly betrayed, but I could blame no one but myself for my current situation. I'd bargained with the devil and now I was paying the price.

My bed was framed by two large picture windows. Sunlight darted through the gaps in the curtains, dappling the wood floors. I was reminded sharply of the dream in which the fireflies flickered like diamond speckles tucked into the velvet night.

You must help him to find his way again, Kelsey.

The Moon Goddess's words were no doubt echoes of my own conscience. Dreams could be very important messages from the subconscious, from those hidden, dark parts of ourselves we tried to ignore. I couldn't leave Damian to his fate here. All I had to do was rescue him and then figure out a way for us to escape one of the most secure facilities in the state, if not the nation. And avoid Sven. Oh, crap.

What if Jarred had stationed guards outside my door?

Well, I'd just have to pretend like everything was fine and that I didn't know about Jarred's nefarious endeavors. For the first time I considered that perhaps the man really didn't have emotions. Quite possibly he was a robot. Humph. I nibbled my lower lip as my thoughts whirled. I had never really been very good at comportment (not that my mother hadn't tried to turn me into an obedient milksop). I had learned to hide my empath abilities rather well, and that ability to smile while feeling another's pain had taught me guile in nearly all things. I was, I'm almost sorry to admit, an excellent liar. No doubt all those theater classes in college had helped with this flaw of my character. I sighed. If I had mastered my gift, instead of just the hiding of it, Robert's poison would've never seeped into my soul. Since that moment, I had tried to live honestly. Forthrightly. But even before my vow to be . . . well, good, I had the annoying habit of speaking my mind, which made Mother cringe. (That, and my impulsiveness. I was definitely a let's-push-the-red-button kind of girl.) Granted, I had learned the value of shutting up every now and then. When I got really upset or angry, the words tumbled out of my mouth before my brain had processed the consequences. During one of my mother's lectures on my lack of sophistication and my wayward nature, my stepfather, Ames, had interrupted to say that he thought I was a "delightful smartass."

Thus far, that was the nicest compliment I'd ever received.

My thoughts circled back to my escape plan. I wish I knew some karate or at the very least that I'd paid closer attention to those Steven Seagal movies that Ames so loved.

Trepidation spun through me, but I wasn't going to stay in bed and wish the world was different. I had to act, and fast, if I was to save myself and Damian. I wasn't sure what I could do about the other patients. If only I had some proof about Jarred's illegal activities! Then maybe the authorities would believe me and I could shut down the clinic and see justice done.

A knot clogged my throat.

Jarred was too rich and too clever. The moment he realized I'd disappeared and taken Damian with me, he'd no doubt use his considerable resources to track us down. Maybe even silence us. I felt dizzy, and as I swung my feet over the bed and let my soles rest on the floor, I had a terrifying vision of Sven and his team aiming monstrous guns at us and firing. I sucked in a steadying breath and stood up. I had to take the chance. Besides, I knew I could live with the fear already blossoming inside of me.

Terror and I were old friends.

*   *   *

I discovered the scar while toweling off from my hasty shower. It was just above my left breast, its shape distinctive enough to be mistaken for a tattoo. It sorta looked like a hook bent in two directions with the ends straightened. A small, upright slash bisected the slanted middle. It seemed almost pagan. I remember distinctly feeling Dr. Ruther's injecting me with something in the *shoulder*.

I stared into the mirror and traced the odd marking, frowning.

Whoa. In the dream, the Goddess had zapped me in order to bestow her symbol. I didn't know what to make of it all. How could I gain a scar from *that*? If this . . . this branding was real, then I had to believe that the so-called visitation of the Moon Goddess and Tark were also real.

Okay. Whew. *Okay.*

I sucked in a couple of deep breaths. Well, I had to keep an open mind about everything at this point, didn't I? I could hardly judge the worth of psychic phenom beyond my experience. Still. This was not an issue I could deal with presently, so I tucked it away for later.

I couldn't arouse suspicions, so I took care with my appearance, as though I were merely returning to work after a bout of the flu. Yes, that lie fit nicely with what had happened. I realized I had no idea how much time had passed, or if Jarred had made other excuses about my absence. Hell, I didn't know if I was going to be able to walk out of my apartment, much less if I'd be able to make it to wherever they'd stashed Damian.

I put on light makeup and, unable to get my trembling fingers to create the French braid, I decided to just blow-dry it and leave it down. After dressing in a blue lace bra and matching panties, I slipped into a pair of black pants and a blue silk blouse, along with a pair of simple, comfortable flats. Normally I'd wear my ankle boots with the ensemble, but if I had to run, I wanted shoes I could shuck off. Unfortunately, walking around with my Nikes on might prompt suspicion. And so would wearing a coat. Sven noticed details like that. I grabbed a sweater, which wouldn't offer too much extra warmth, but it was better than nothing.

I wasn't much of a jewelry person, especially after having to sell all my previous baubles to pay bills and creditors. The only adornment I allowed was a pair of silver hoop earrings. Carrying my purse would seem out of place since there was no real reason to have it on me. The clinic was its own little town where currency wasn't used, much less needed. However, another of my mother's "life lessons" had led to the personal habit of keeping some sort of cash on me at all times. Since my salary was so generous, I had five hundred dollars stashed in my wallet. I took it, and my driver's license, and tucked it all into the right cup of my bra. No way would I leave it in a pocket to bulge or to be discovered if Sven didn't buy my ruse and decided to search me. I had no doubts Sven wouldn't spare my cleavage if he thought I was hiding anything.

Yet another chance I would have to take.

I went to my nightstand and scooped up the key card as well as my cell phone. I hesitated, staring at the Black-Berry. I had seen far too many movies where the intrepid heroes were tracked by their cells. Had my paranoia reached the level where I believed my Black-Berry could lead Jarred right to me?

Yes. Yes, I had.

And if he could (or did) the BlackBerry might prove useful as a red herring. No. I didn't want to risk it. I stuck the key card in my pocket and returned the phone to the nightstand. My heart started to thud, and I suddenly felt so reluctant to follow my plan (and therefore my principles) that my knees threatened to buckle. *What am I doing?* I plopped down onto the unmade bed and dug my fingers into the covers.

Surely, said a tart voice that sounded suspiciously like my mother, *I have the good sense and moral fortitude to confront Jarred with my concerns.* Did he not deserve to hear my accusations so that he could allay my fears? Or at least lie to me convincingly enough that I would no longer feel it necessary to leave with a mental patient in tow?

I had ignored my instincts with Robert. No matter how much dread balled in my stomach, I continued to treat the man. I told myself over and over again it was not my place to judge, but to heal. I had purpose, strength, hope—all things I could give to him. And I did. I used my power to push them all into his heart, where they took root and flourished. Oh, yes. I gave him all that he needed to take his first victim, and the five after that, too.

My internal alarms were clanging, rusty to be sure, but certain all the same that my too-good-to-be-true situation was closing in on me. For a fraction of a second I considered bailing without Damian, but I dismissed the idea. I couldn't leave him—and no matter what the motivation for that decision, I had to follow through.

I took a deep breath, strode through my apartment, and with a confidence I didn't feel, I whipped open my front door. I plastered a smile on my face and stepped through. Relief shuddered through me as I realized no one awaited me in the hall.

I was too tightly strung to wait for the elevator, which would deliver me only one floor down anyway. I took the stairs, trying to steady my nerves with inner pep talks. When I reached the hallway where my office was located, I felt slightly more in control.

As I strode toward my office trying to look as though it was just another day at work, the realization sunk in that the clinic had cameras all over the place. That's why no one needed to be in the hall or anywhere else—no doubt someone in the control room had been observing me from the moment I stepped out of my apartment.

And yet no one approached me.

Maybe they were expecting me to act as if nothing had happened. As I reached the locked door of my office, it occurred to me that perhaps I wasn't supposed to remember anything at all. Maybe they had hoped that whatever Dr. Ruthers injected into me wiped out my memories.

Or warped them.

Huh. Everything I believed to be true could be part of my illness's crazy dreamscape. Had I actually awakened from a rough bout of the flu believing hallucinations created by a fevered brain?

Dear Lord. Was *I* crazy?

A quick gut check told me to stay the course. I used my key card to open the door and went inside. Everything was as tidy as I'd left it, which calmed my tattered nerves a little. I flipped on my computer, which hummed to life instantly. If the date was correct, then I'd been out of it for four days. It was also late afternoon and that meant my chances of getting Damian out of the facility were lessening by the minute. I needed the activity of the place to hide our escape.

I heard a gasp and I looked up to see Mari standing in the doorway her hand flattened against her chest. She looked ashen. Her reaction certainly did not reassure me.

"Hello, Mari," I said. "Are you all right?"

"I . . . um, yeah. We were told you were really sick. Mr. Dante mentioned he might have to seek a specialist."

"For the flu?" I asked.

"The flu!" She warbled an unsteady laugh. "The way he was carrying on, we all thought you were dying of some horrible disease."

"Mr. Dante was carrying on about me?" Genuine surprise threaded my tone.

She shrugged. "Well, maybe I'm exaggerating a bit. He was worried, is all. And here you are looking right as rain."

"I feel very well," I said. "Although I thought I might head to the cafeteria for a bite. Would you like to go with me?"

I had invited Mari to take breaks with me before so the request wasn't out of the ordinary. Still, I couldn't help but think suspicion lingered in her blue eyes. I opened my shields, just a little, to get a read on her emotions. Her concern was real enough, but it didn't seem to be attached to me. Beyond the warmth of that feeling, I felt the chill of her wariness.

I rose from my desk, noting the key card in her hand. She had intended to come into my office and had been shocked to find me in it. I couldn't imagine Mari doing anything wrong—at least not before I caught her in Damian's suite. Before today, she'd always emanated sincerity. Her change of behavior made me wonder if I had managed to misjudge everyone in the clinic. She watched me carefully, and I had to resist the silly urge to jump up and scream, "Boo!"

"Could you hand me that book?" I asked. "The one on schizophrenic disorders. You see it?"

Reluctantly, she turned toward the bookshelf behind her and studied the embossed titles on the bindings. I slipped my key card off the desk and into my pocket.

"None of these seem to be about schizophrenia," she said.

"Really?" I edged disappointment into my tone, and stood up. "Where on earth did I put it?" I joined her at the bookshelf and studied the tomes. "I know it was there. I remember looking for it when I started creating Damian's treatment plan."

I was close enough to her that I felt her stiffen, and then seemed to force herself to relax. Her gaze slanted toward me. "You think he's schizo?"

"Mari," I chided.

"Right," she said on a sigh, "slang is inappropriate when talking about the conditions of the patients."

"You know, I think you're the only one who paid any attention in that meeting." I smiled down at her. "I really need to check on Damian before we eat. I'm starving, too. Do they have chicken salad today?" I turned as if to go toward the door and made sure our shoulders connected. I rammed into her so hard that she staggered backward. The key card in her hand, which she'd obviously forgotten about, went flying. I hadn't wanted the poor woman to fall down. I clutched at her arm, while she stared at me with wide eyes. Did I imagine the fear that flickered in those blue orbs? Well, that was a first. Startled by the idea of anyone being afraid of *me*, I let her go abruptly. "I'm such a klutz. Forgive me."

"No problem. Really."

I didn't think she was aware that she'd taken a step back from me, apparently trying to create distance between us. Even though I was fascinated by her fearful actions, I pretended not to notice. "What happened to your key card?" I asked. "Oh! There it is."

I heard her mutter, "Shit." But before she could compete with me in trying to get it, I scooped hers up with one hand and retrieved mine from my pocket. When I returned, I handed her mine. "I'm terribly sorry. I feel like such a dolt."

She snatched the card and shoved it into her front pocket. The cards were assigned to individuals by codes embedded in the magnetic strip that only Jarred and Sven understood. There was no other identifying information on them. Jarred explained to me that he didn't want anyone careless enough to lose their card to have it returned to them by merit of a picture or a memorized number. Basically, it was his way to make sure everyone was very, very careful about what he gave to them. Anyone who lost their card was immediately fired. And here I was tricking Mari into giving me hers. At some point when Sven saw me via video feed slinking around the wrong places, he would revoke my access, so I needed someone else's. I felt a smidgen of guilt, but I ruthlessly tamped it down. Mari had worked here since the day the clinic opened. If Jarred could forgive anyone a single transgression, it would be her.

"I'll have to skip the chicken salad today," she said. She was striving for jovial, but missed the mark entirely.

"Oh," I said. "All right, then. Tomorrow?"

Her smile was too bright. "Sure. Absolutely. Look forward to it, hon." She hurried out the door and didn't look back.

I didn't take the time to ponder her odd behavior. I couldn't risk that she was trotting off to tell on me—for what, I wasn't sure since she couldn't know anything, but I wasn't gonna risk it. Still, I had to act normal, so I straightened my desk, flipped off the computer, and locked the door, which was my habit when leaving my office.

It was time to rescue Damian.

And myself.

Chapter 4

Once again, I skipped the elevator in favor of the stairs. The induction cells were in the basement below the massive house. Even though the place was sparkling clean and the walls painted soothing shades of blue, it couldn't quite the hide the dungeon feel of the place.

I wanted to pause by the stairs and look around for patrolling guards, but that would be too obvious. The guy monitoring the cameras might think it strange enough to report. So I strode down the secured hallway to the induction rooms as if I were doing nothing out of the ordinary. Mari's access code would get me in now and out later, but only if I hurried. I couldn't count on my game of switcheroo to protect me for too long. If we got trapped inside the clinic during a full shutdown, no one would get out.

I started walking faster, hoping that Damian was still in the same induction room as before. My pace faltered as I realized I hadn't even bothered to check where he was located. He could've been placed in a suite by now, especially if he had regained his memory.

Damn it.

If he wasn't down here, then I would have to return to my office and log in to the clinic's server to see where they'd put him. I felt like such an idiot! I was in full-on self-chastisement when I rounded the final corner to the section where the hard-case inductees were kept.

I smacked into something solid and reeled backward.

"What the hell!" The words were uttered in a low, harsh tone. I gained my feet and looked up into the stony expression of a young man dressed in the black uniform worn by Sven's security personnel. His eyes were as blue and icy as a glacier's. He was tall and thickly muscled, but young—too young to be one of Sven's usual recruits. However, he gripped a big, nasty gun and looked as though he might aim it at me.

Behind him, I saw Damian. He was dressed in a gray jumper and on his wrists were a pair of shock bracelets. He grimly assessed me, looking as though he'd hoped to never see me again. I have to admit, that hurt just a little.

"Patient transfer," growled the man in front of me. "Please excuse us."

"Um. Yeah. To me. I can take him from here," I said, smiling. "And you can take off those bracelets. I'm sure Damian will behave." I looked at my new charge. "Won't you?"

Damian's eyebrows nearly hit his hairline. He looked nonplussed, but he said nothing. I wondered if Jarred and Dr. Ruthers had tampered with him, too.

"You remember me, don't you?" I asked.

His gaze went to the guard and he grimaced.

"I'm Kelsey Morningstone," I said softly, the irrational seed of hurt lodged in my chest bloomed into dismay. He'd almost seduced me; then he'd broken into my apartment to claim me, biting me so deeply my neck would surely scar, and he didn't know me. "Damian, I'm your therapist."

The guard made a strange sound, and I glanced at him. His face was red, his eyes wide. He started to cough violently. So much so that he bent over to try to regain his breath. I felt solicitous for all of a second. Then I realized I was wasting a golden opportunity. I yanked the gun out of his hands and whacked him on the head with it. He fell against the wall and then slid to the floor, unconscious.

"Oh, my God." I stared at the man and then swung my gaze to Damian. "That was easy."

"What the hell are you doing?" he said, his tone furious. His eyes were as cold and shiny as emeralds.

"I'm rescuing an ungrateful idiot," I responded hotly.

He gaped at me. Then I realized I'd lost my temper with a mentally ill man. With a *patient.* "Oh, dear. I do apologize. That was unconscionable."

He snorted. Then he yanked the gun out of my hands. That's when I noticed the shock bracelets were not actually linked together, much less activated. "I'm not insane," he said. "And you are not the only one trying to rescue me, *Schätzchen.*" He leaned down and tapped the guard's face. "Adulfo!"

"What's going on?" I demanded. "How did he get in here? Why do you know his name?"

Damian didn't respond. I wasn't completely idiotic. I mean, *duh.* I'd obviously interrupted a much better planned effort to get my patient out of the facility. I was flabbergasted by this idea, especially if . . . *oh.*

"You got your memory back, didn't you?"

"Ja," he said tersely.

As I dealt with this new information, I glanced at the man he was trying to shake into consciousness. How in the world had Damian managed to contact anyone? And how had this guy gotten inside?

"Are you sure you can trust him?" I asked.

"It is you who causes me worry," he responded. "I trust my son."

"Your *son*?" My stomach sank as I considered what I had done. Wow. I really knew how crash a party. Then I realized he'd expressed doubt about my motives. Well, I couldn't blame him. I didn't trust me, either. I peered at the man I'd knocked down, and frowned. "You don't look old enough to be his father, unless you were ten years old when he was born."

Damian glanced at me, amusement thawing the coldness of his gaze. "Perhaps we could discuss my virility at another time."

The one he'd called Adulfo groaned, and his eyes rolled around in his head for a couple of seconds until he regained his mind. His watery gaze met mine. He bared his teeth and growled.

I reared back, startled by his response.

"Nein." Damian tugged the man to his feet and handed him the gun. "A little human female knocked you on your ass. You'll have to live with the shame."

"At least she's not my therapist."

"Mention that ever again," said Damian in a dark tone, "and I'll shoot you myself."

"Way to parent there, Skippy," I blurted. Both men flicked surprised gazes at me. I put my hands up in a gesture of mock surrender. "Sorry. Please continue insulting each other. I'll just wait for the alarms to go off."

"We've taken care of that," said Adulfo brusquely.

Damian's expression blanked, his eyes returning to the same chilly green as before. I stifled a groan. What was wrong with me? It was like I'd forgotten everything about being a therapist. Maybe it had to do with my jangled nerves. Fighting the urge to run was making my feet tingle.

"All we have to do is get to the lobby," continued Adulfo. "Should we lock her in one of the cells?"

Just like that, the tables had turned. Here was the point where I could be rescued or kidnapped or stuffed into an induction cell to await Jarred's wrath. Still, I couldn't form the words to plead my case, even with Damian's indifferent gaze studying me. After begging for my life, and the life of one who died anyway, I'd lost the taste for it. Mercy was either in a man's soul, or it wasn't. No words of mine could sway a conscience that did not exist.

His gaze dropped to my neck, which was covered by the high neck of my blouse. The evidence of his bite was still there, and always would be. That's what he'd meant to do—mark me.

And he remembered doing it.

I kept my shields wrapped around me like a blanket. I didn't want to seek out his emotions, but I could see the ghost of guilt that fluttered briefly in his eyes.

"She comes with us," said Damian.

"What!" Adulfo eyed his father. "We didn't plan for her. How the hell is she supposed to get out?"

"Patrick will have to make two trips."

Adulfo's blond brows slammed down and he sent me a look of such intense loathing, I took another step back. Damian sent his son a warning glance, and Adulfo looked away from me, a muscle ticking in his jaw.

Damian took his place behind Adulfo, holding his wrists down to hide the fact that the bracelets weren't linked together. "I am awaiting your rescue, *Frau* Morningstone," he said in a mocking tone.

Adulfo rolled his eyes, but stood at the ready.

I harbored no illusions that I was still in charge. I had no idea how they planned to extract themselves from the lobby, but since I'd started off with only half a plan to begin with, I either rolled with theirs, or struck out on my own.

I led them to the elevators and we crowded into the car together.

"Be ready," warned Adulfo, but I didn't know if he was talking to me or to his father. In the next instant, the doors slid open, but before I could step out, someone stepped in and leaned against the elevator doors to keep them from shutting.

My heart dropped to my toes as I met the icy gray gaze of Jarred Dante.

"Get in, please," said Mari's voice from behind him. "I really don't want to zap you."

I moved aside so Jarred could join us. Mari followed him, her finger digging into his back. I couldn't believe the kind of gall she had! Threatening a man three times her size with a fake gun was ballsy. Then I realized she was in on the whole rescue-Damian operation. I glanced at her, and she winked at me.

"Hello there, Kelsey," she said cheerfully. "I'm glad you're on board with us. I was worried."

I gaped at her.

"Top floor," she said. "We have to do a roof exit." Her grin widened. "You believe in werewolves now, dearie?"

"I . . . uh . . ." I gulped. "Do you think you're a were-wolf, Mari?"

She laughed. "Don't be silly. I'm a *sidhe*."

"She," I repeated. "I kinda knew you were a girl."

"Sidhe," she said more forcefully. "Otherwise known as a fairy or the fae."

"Oh."

"Why the roof?" grumbled Adulfo as he pushed the button labeled R. He shot me a dirty look as though it were my fault their original escape route had been thwarted.

"He caught me resetting the security cameras," said Mari.

"Was zum Teufel!" exclaimed Adulfo. "He's coming with us, too?"

"No," said Damian. "He is not." The inoperable cuffs clanked to the floor and he moved around his son so that he could plant himself between me and my ex-boss.

"I'll come for her," said Jarred. "You know you can't hide her. Not from me."

I opened my mouth so I make sure he knew I'd chosen this path and I didn't want to be found by him, *thank you very much*, but Damian's arm snaked around my waist and squeezed. I took the hint to keep quiet, though I had no idea why he wanted Jarred to believe I wasn't leaving of my own accord. Damian didn't let go of me, instead bringing me fully into his embrace.

Jarred noted Damian's genteel capture and his eyes narrowed. "I didn't think kidnapping was your style."

"And I didn't think the great Dante would ever break his word," said Damian tightly.

"I assure you that my honor remains intact. Is yours?"

Damian's fingers dug into my hip, but it wasn't so much a warning to me as him trying to get control of his emotions.

Ding. The cheery little sound pierced the tense silence of the car, and then the doors slid smoothly open to reveal the rooftop. It was dusk, the purple sky slivered with clouds. I looked over the flat square space that must have once been meant for entertainment. A few decrepit chairs hinted that my supposition was correct. The snow had been cleared away, probably so Sven's sentries could do their jobs.

Damian slid his arm off my waist and grasped my hand. He was the first to step out, and tugged me out with him. The chill of the air crawled over me, burrowing deeply. I shivered. Mari followed. Adulfo took over guarding Jarred since he had an actual gun as opposed to Mari's tiny blunt finger.

"You're throwing your lot in with them?" he asked her bitterly.

"You would, too, if you weren't so stubborn. We're all of the same cloth, my boy."

"Are we?" he bit out. "I think not. You betrayed me."

"I am still your loyal friend, Jarred, but grief has hardened your heart. What did you plan on doing with Damian?"

"He stole her."

"She chose him." Mari shook her head, her pity evident. I couldn't imagine why anyone would feel sorry for Jarred. "I'm doing this for you." She patted his shoulder, which made him flinch. Then she scurried ahead of us, her eyes lifting to the darkening sky above.

Jarred sent me a bleak look. "I will find you, Kelsey."

"Don't bother," I said.

For a fraction of a second, he looked shocked. Then his features smoothed out, and he was the same implacable, robot-faced Jarred. I realized I didn't know the first thing about what was unfolding right now. Obviously, Damian and Jarred shared a history—and I felt the cut of betrayal deepen. Whatever Jarred's purposes for me or for Damian, I couldn't believe them benign.

"If you knew the truth of it all, you wouldn't be so charmed by him," said Jarred.

"But she would be charmed by *you*?" Damian turned and pulled me to his side. Then he pulled down the blouse's collar. He brushed aside my hair, and let his fingers trace the bite mark. "It doesn't matter what either of us wants now, does it?"

"Bastard. You don't even want her!" choked out Jarred. "Will she pay the same price for your selfishness that Anna did?"

Damian went white. His whole body tensed and I realized he was seconds away from socking Jarred in the jaw. I held firmly to his arm. "That's enough," I said quietly. "I don't know what's going on, but I feel like a steak being fought over by two starving dogs."

"My apologies," said Jarred swiftly.

I ignored him. "He's trying to anger you," I said to Damian. Fury made his eyes glint like shards of green glass. "He's distracting you from leaving, delaying us until Sven arrives."

"Come on!" yelled Mari.

"Adulfo," said Damian, "I believe Dante needs a nap." His grip on my hand tightened, and then he spun on his heel and started to walk away, me in tow.

"Damn it," yelled Jarred. "Wait."

Damian stopped so abruptly, I stumbled. We both turned.

"Dr. Ruthers gave her the serum."

"And you accuse me of trying to harm her?" Murder gleamed in Damian's eyes, and this time, I didn't think I'd be able to stop him from breaking Jarred's neck. Then again, did I want to? Jarred had admitted to giving me some kind of drug. More surprising, however, was that Damian knew about whatever this serum was—though he seemed genuinely outraged I had been given it.

"You *bit* her," said Jarred, sounding like a little boy denied the cookie jar.

"To mark her," snapped Damian. "To keep her from *you*. No shifter will dare touch her now."

For the first time ever, I could feel a whisper of emotion from Jarred: desperation. "You arrogant asshole! Your bite infected her with werewolf DNA. If we hadn't given her the serum, she'd be dying from trying to shift."

I stared at Jarred, completely flummoxed. He believed

he was telling the truth, and no one else seemed to think he was crazy. Except me. And even I couldn't deny that on some deep inner level, I believed him. I swallowed the knot in my throat, and clung tightly to Damian's arm. The world as I had known it was falling away. Dear God. I really had jumped into the rabbit hole.

"You're lying," said Damian. "There is no such power in a lycan bite. Not even in mine. You know that I cannot turn humans."

"She's not just any human. Tell Dr. Michaels to test her blood," said Jarred dully. His shoulders sagged. "If she's lucky, she has thirty days."

"And then what?" I asked, my voice trembling.

Jarred's gaze flicked to mine. "Your body will try to complete the transition by forcing you into a shift. If you live, then you'll be fully lycan."

"And if she took the serum again?" asked Damian. His impatience crackled right through my shields. I wasn't exactly doing a bang-up job of keeping myself protected. After all, it wasn't every day a girl was told she was turning into a werewolf.

"You know why we made it," said Jarred. "What it was meant for."

"Damian!" yelled Mari. "Get your ass in gear!"

Adulfo brought the weapon up and rammed the butt into the back of Jarred's skull. His eyes went wide and then rolled back into his head. He was felled like a tree; I swear the roof shook when he landed.

Damian guided me toward the edge of the roof. Even through the haze of my disbelief, I realized he was being gentle. His strength flowed to me and I grabbed on to it, feeling almost like I would drown if I let go.

Three men stood near the edge of the roof line. They looked like a boy band—all in their twenties with the same good looks, shaggy dark hair, and gazes as silver as my earrings. They wore T-shirts and jeans and the one on left wore Converse sneakers.

"Ruadan," said Damian. "I didn't expect you."

"Me boys asked me t' come along," he said with a roguish Irish accent. He was the one wearing the Converse. He executed a courtly bow. I could tell now that though the other two had the same hair and eyes and even chin, he was different from them. Older, maybe, but that was more a feeling of inner age than outer evidence. "I'll take the lovely girl."

"The hell," said Damian. "She can go with one of the married twins." He turned toward Mari. "We'll meet you in Broken Heart. Make sure there's an access key ready for Kelsey. She'll have only a minute before the Invisishield activates." He sighed. "You might as well tell the queen we're in deep shit, too."

"Delighted," said Mari with a grin.

Then to my utter shock, she disappeared in a shower of pink sparkles. It was like Mari had burst into glitter. I looked at Damian, but he didn't seem all that surprised. I wasn't sure I was all that surprised, either. I fully expected a unicorn to show up next. Yeah. A unicorn ridden by a leprechaun holding a kettle of gold. Or a box of Lucky Charms.

"Go with Patrick," Damian said to me. "When we get to Broken Heart, we'll debrief you."

"What?" I asked dazedly. Who the hell was Patrick? I started to sway, but Damian's grip tightened on me. It was freezing out here, but I felt cold on the inside, too. "You take me," I said, clutching his arm. It felt like my whole world had shifted, and I couldn't get my balance. I did not want to let go of Damian. "I can't . . . you have to . . . *please*." I sucked in a breath and realized I was staring at my former patient through a sheen of tears. "I'm not exactly being brave, am I?"

"You are very brave," he whispered. I saw tenderness in his gaze; then he stiffened. He let go of me abruptly, and I staggered. I stared at him, wounded, but he pushed me toward the trio of silver-eyed dudes. "Go, Kelsey."

"Come now, darlin'," said the one in the middle. He put his arms around me, which forced me very close to his rather nicely built chest. "You might wanna close your eyes."

A long, low growl startled us apart. I looked over my shoulder at Damian, then up at the shocked face of my benevolent captor. "What the bloody hell?" He stared at his friend with raised brows. "You all right, Damian?"

"I don't like your hands on her."

Now *everyone* was staring at him and then all eyes turned to me. I found it laughable that I could be held accountable for Damian's demeanor, which was obviously—given the various expressions of amazement—out of character for him. Then again, I'd been accused of causing much worse behavior. Also, I was hurt that he'd let me go so easily. It was stupid and irrational, but feelings often were.

Damian looked as though he wanted to rip me from the man's arms. I almost pushed out of the Irishman's embrace, but I didn't. We had to get outta of here. All of us. And I wouldn't delay this crazy rescue because I felt better when I was with Damian.

"I'll take him first." Ruadan grabbed hold of Damian and they both almost instantly turned into a shower of gold sparkles.

Adulfo dumped his gun; then he strode toward me. "You are my father's," he said, "so you are my family, too. Welcome, *Frau*."

"Um . . . thanks."

He nodded stiffly and then stepped near the other man. "Let's go, Lorcan."

I watched as Lorcan put his hands on Adulfo's shoulders and then they were gone with a gold-sparked *pop*!

"It's been a very strange day," I said to my rescuer. I was trying to absorb everything happening, and I felt close to fainting.

"'Tis about to get stranger," he said with a smile. "Hold on t' me, and close your eyes tight."

I did as he asked, wondering if maybe I was still in my sick bed having another dream. Maybe no one had escaped at all. I was trapped in this Wonderland, spinning from one weird adventure to the next, doomed to never find my way back to the reality I had known.

"Kelsey! Hold!" yelled a strident voice.

I looked over my shoulder and saw Sven and two guards running toward us. One stopped to check on the prone form of Jarred, but Sven and the remaining man continued on full throttle.

"Hang on," murmured Patrick.

I felt a burning sensation in the pit of my stomach. It suddenly burst into a thousand pinpricks, which felt uncomfortable, but not painful.

I heard a popping sound. Something solid and hot slammed into my shoulder. Agony ripped through me— sudden, intense, unrelenting. I heard Sven yell, "Don't shoot *her*, you fucking idiot!"

Then my entire being exploded.

"Patrick!" The female's concerned cry was the first thing I heard when the world swirled back into solid form.

"Sshh, Jess. She's the one injured."

My eyelids fluttered open. I was still in Patrick's arms. My shoulder throbbed in excruciating pain. Something warm and sticky dribbled down my stomach and soaked my clothing. I sagged backward and saw the crimson stain on Patrick's shirt.

"I'm terribly sorry," I said. "I'm sure some soda water will take that right out."

Patrick stared at me, and so did the pretty brunette clutching his shoulder.

"Give her to me, damn it." Damian's strong arms slid underneath me and he yanked me out of Patrick's embrace.

"Turn your neck." The gentle command came from the brunette. I did what she asked and I felt something wet and cold slapped against my skin. There was a blaze of heat—and I swear I heard a *snick*. Then it was over.

Damian whisked me away, and I got a vague impression of white walls and long hallways.

"I don't think my rescue is going very well," I told him. "Then again, it is my first time."

He looked at me, one dark brow arched. "You are trouble."

"And you like trouble?"

"Not particularly."

I sighed. "Then you should probably drop me off at the nearest bus stop. Because I'm not very good at being good."

"No bus stops." He entered a small white room that smelled like antiseptic, and then he laid me on a soft, narrow bed. He sat down next to me. "We will discuss your inability to be good later."

"Spankings don't work," I said morosely. "Just so you know."

He gaped at me for a microsecond, then something like speculation entered his eyes. "Perhaps we'll test this interesting theory of yours later."

"What theory?" I asked, perplexed.

He flashed me a grin, and then pressed the back of his hand against my cheek. "Lie down," he directed in a soft voice.

I hadn't realized that I was leaning up on my elbows. I collapsed onto the bed, and pain shot through me. "Ouch!" I touched my neck where the brunette had slapped on whatever-it-was. "What did she put on me?"

"It's a temporary tattoo," he said. "It allows you to stay within the protection of the town's borders."

"What town? Where are we?"

"Broken Heart, Oklahoma."

Memory flickered. "Wait a minute. Wasn't that the town that got blown up after a gas leak? The whole place got turned into a crater."

"That's what we wanted the humans to believe. The Invisi-shield gives the impression that nothing is here, but there was no gas leak, no explosion. We are hidden from the human world."

"Oh." I touched the tattoo on my neck again. I was getting all kinds of lovely additions to skin. "Better than shock bracelets, I guess."

"You are not a prisoner," he said. "You are a guest."

"Well, it's not like I have anywhere else to go. I won't return to the clinic so they can finish me off."

"Dante has no intention of killing you," he said. Then he offered gruffly, "Do not worry. The doctor has been summoned." Damian grabbed the edges of my blouse and ripped it open. The fabric fluttered onto the bed. I looked down and studied the quarter-sized hole in my upper shoulder; blood gurgled from it. The flesh around the wound was blackened, as though it had been burned. Despite how bad it looked, the agony was receding.

"That's not normal, is it?" I asked.

"It's not a bullet wound. More like a . . . laser."

"Oh. I've never been shot before so I'm not sure what to expect."

Damian's gaze flickered with what I pinpointed as

guilt. "It seems you're experiencing many firsts today, *Schätzchen*."

"Why do you keep calling me that?" I narrowed my eyes. "Does it mean stupidhead in German, or something?"

"Or something."

"Your cheerful manner certainly helps allay the pain," I chirped. "Why, I bet you're the best candy striper in this hospital!"

He glared at me. And I smiled widely at him. Sometimes the best way to disarm someone intent on being grumpy and ill mannered was to be terrifyingly sweet. I'd learned this particular technique in dealing with my mother's constant criticisms. She hated when I responded to her sour comments with sugary responses. It was very difficult to harangue someone who agreed that she was every bad thing you'd said and more—especially when expressing such sentiments in a relentlessly cheerful tone.

He lasted a full twenty-eight seconds (which was eighteen seconds more than my mother's record) against the inanity of my smile. His eyes dropped to the wound, which had, to my relief, stopped bleeding. Then he studied my blue lace bra rather intently. He went completely still. His gaze was riveted to the scar visible above my left breast. The blood drained from his face. "How did you get that?"

Since he looked as though *he'd* been shot and I couldn't very well admit a dream goddess zapped me, I said, "College indiscretion."

"Explain this . . . indiscretion."

"Drunken lark with my girlfriends," I lied. "Never mix tequila with a tattoo parlor." I gazed at him solemnly. "It can lead to regrets."

His expression offered skepticism. He opened his

mouth, no doubt to begin another round of interrogation, when the door opened. I looked up and saw another Damian—and then *another*—stride through the door. Damian placed his hand over the scar, his palm centimeters away from my breast.

The other Damians stood at the end of the bed, arms crossed as they stared at me. Their gazes skimmed my blue bra, and both men noted the way my (sorta) Damian was touching me. Obviously he didn't want his clones to know about the mark.

"What?" I asked to draw their attention away. I frowned down at the bra. "If I'd known I'd be showing off the girls, I would've gone with the black lace." I looked up. "What do you think?"

They had matching grins.

"I like her," said the one on the right.

"Can we keep her, *mein bruder*?" asked the one on the left.

Tweedle Dee and Tweedle Dum, I thought. Who would show up next? The March hare?

Damian ignored his brothers, no doubt from habit. "Where is Dr. Clark?"

"Delayed." The man on the right executed a formal bow. "I am Drake."

"And I am Darrius." He dipped his head.

"Triplets," I said.

"Yes," said Damian.

"And you were firstborn," I murmured.

He looked at me askance, but I sent him a blinding smile. He actually flinched before he looked away.

"Would you guys mind if I covered up?" I asked pleasantly. Damian couldn't conceal the mark forever, and honestly, the warmth of his hand (not to mention its location so near my breast) was making me shiver. "Not that being injured and exposed to strangers isn't fun and all."

"Turn around," he told his brothers.

Their grins widened before they pivoted. As soon as their backs were turned, Damian helped me tuck under the single white sheet that covered the bed. He pulled it up to my chin, probably hoping to cover up evidence of the mark. Then he drew my hair forward so that it shielded my neck—and his bite—as well.

I felt like evidence at a crime scene.

Drake and Darrius turned around and both were eyeing me with interest. The door opened again, and a tall man with short blond hair and kind blue eyes strode inside. He had that doctor air about him, probably due to the white lab coat he was wearing. "Good evening, Damian," he said. He smiled at me. "I'm Dr. Clark. Let me have a look."

I could tell, even without dipping into my empath abilities, that Damian was reluctant to give the doctor access. I wasn't sure what the rules were for werewolves, but I had a sneaking suspicion that him claiming me had flipped some kind of possessiveness switch. Staking territory—like when dogs peed on trees. Oh, great. He was the dog. And I was a urine-soaked tree.

"Move," I told him rather grumpily. "Or would you prefer I bleed to death? That would solve your problems, wouldn't it?"

He blanched. "You are not a problem."

"Then move!" I yelled.

Damian shoved himself off the bed and went to sulk in the corner. His brothers watched our interaction with a combination of surprise and humor. The doctor's gaze widened, but he said nothing. He sat on the bed and peeled the sheet down. I clutched the right side so that it covered the scar. He examined my wound, but didn't touch it. He frowned.

Crap. It was never good when a doctor frowned.

"Don't you have anywhere else to be?" asked Damian. His question was directed toward his brothers.

Drake pretended to think, one finger on his chin. Then he shrugged. "No."

"Me neither," said Darrius with a doleful shake of his head.

Damian glowered at them, but they countered with innocent expressions and beatific smiles. I decided that I liked the pair of them. Anyone unafraid to give Damian shit was okay in my book.

"I need to clean the wound," said Dr. Clark. "I'll get some supplies and return shortly." He glanced at me. "Do you need anything for the pain?"

"It doesn't hurt that much anymore," I said.

"Hmm." He leaned down to take a closer look. Then I saw his gaze shift. "What's this?"

He moved my hair aside to view the bite mark.

Damian growled.

Dr. Clark looked over his shoulder. "Is there a problem?"

"He has issues with other men touching me," I said. I glanced at Drake and Darrius to see what teasing gestures they'd make now. However, I found them staring at their brother, concern and shock mirrored on their faces.

"You *marked* her?" asked Darrius.

"You were trying to hide it," accused Drake.

Thick ropes of anger spiraled out from all three brothers. There was no shielding myself from that kind of triple fury.

"You've claimed a human," said Darrius in a shaking voice. "What have you done, *mein bruder*?"

Chapter 5

"I don't need to explain myself to you," said Damian viciously. His gaze was on the doctor's fingers, which were resting lightly on my collarbone. "Could you *stop* touching her?"

"I can't help her if I can't touch her," Dr. Clark said reasonably. He drew the sheet up to my chin, winked at me, and then got up. "I'll be right back."

He glanced at me, then rounded on the brothers. "Behave." Then he strode out the door—leaving me at the behest of three angry werewolves. *Nice bedside manner, Doc.*

I didn't understand the reason for everyone's distress, but I totally got that Damian had done something important—and unusual. And they didn't even know yet about the serum or Jarred's belief that Damian's bite had morphed me into a werewolf.

"She doesn't understand, does she?" asked Darrius. His solemn gaze met mine. "My brother's bite is an ancient and powerful protection. It means he's claimed you as his child—or his *mate*."

I tried to ignore the way my stomach lurched. "Oh.

Um—" Sooooo not gonna address the mate issue. "He bit Adulfo?"

"Yes," answered Damian. He was glaring so hard at his brothers, it's a wonder they hadn't melted from the molten anger directed at them. "He's my adopted son—and my heir."

"And how many people have you bitten other than Adulfo . . . and me?"

His jaw tightened. "None."

"None?"

My voice had gone up a decibel higher. I sat up, clutching the sheet. "Why does everyone want me to marry you?" I gasped. "Oh, my God. We're hitched already, aren't we? We've done the Vegas version of a werewolf wedding. Tell me the truth!"

Three sets of jade eyes zeroed in on me.

"What do you mean—*everyone*?" asked Damian in a low, hard voice.

I blinked at the fury in his tone. "Did I say everyone?" I asked weakly.

"Kelsey."

"I had a dream. After you bit me," I admitted hastily. "I was in this glen at night. And th-there was a l-lady and a wolf there. Um, Tark. Anyway, she s-said you'd chosen me. She said it was time for you to t-take your rightful place." My teeth were starting to chatter. "Did someone t-turn up the air c-conditioning?"

"The Moon Goddess has blessed your choice," said Drake. I could feel his relief. My shields were all but gone by now anyway. "That is something."

"She has no right to interfere," said Damian.

Darrius studied me. "All these years gone from us," he said, "and she shows herself to a mere human."

"Hey!" I said, instantly offended. I wrapped the sheet

around me tighter. It was really, really cold. But no one else seemed to notice. "Does anyone have b-blanket?"

Damian walked to the bed. Then he leaned down, tucked the sheet around me securely, and scooped me up. He sat on the bed, scooting until his back was against the wall. Then he wrapped his arms around me. I huddled into his warmth and nearly purred when he started rubbing my back. Well, I guess I couldn't purr since I was half doggie now. Maybe I should ask for a belly scratch.

"We will not discuss the Goddess. She made her choice, and we made ours." Anger pulsed within Damian. It was old, familiar. He had nursed this rage for a very long time.

Obviously they were no fans of the Moon Goddess. Maybe that's why she contacted me—because they had rejected her. But my concern was the tension between the brothers. They obviously did not keep things from one another, and Damian's attempt to hide the bite mark had offended his siblings.

"Tell them the rest," I whispered against his throat.

His arms tightened briefly. Then he said, "Dante thinks my bite has started an irreversible process. He believes Kelsey is turning into a lycan."

"That's not possible." I wasn't sure which brother spoke. I was very much enjoying my current location. Damian smelled really good. I had a sudden insane urge to flick my tongue against base of his throat.

"Apparently, I'm not just any human," I offered, mostly so I would be too busy talking to plant kisses on Damian's neck. I knew I was attracted to him, but these urges were almost beyond my control.

"She will be able to shift?"

I pressed against Damian's solid, warm (oh-so-muscled) chest, but I heard the incredulity in the voice of whichever brother asked the question.

"We won't know for a while. He gave her the serum." He paused. "He thinks she will be unable to . . . to transition."

Following this announcement, there was a double round of swearing—a mixture of German and English.

"We'll have to tell Patsy," said Damian.

"Everything?"

I felt the tension gather in Damian's body as he said, "Yes. Everything."

I glanced at Drake and Darrius. Even though I could feel the swirl of emotions from all three, I still liked to gather information from facial expressions and body language. Mostly to see if it all jived together. Damian's brothers were worried, not about the confrontation with Patsy, but about something else. Something . . . important. The feelings associated with secrets felt like being draped in spiderwebs—soft and sticky and disconcerting. I resisted the urge to scrub at my hair.

"She won't be happy," muttered Darrius.

"She doesn't know about the new prophecies," said Drake.

"Not really new," argued Darrius. "Left out is more like it. Those Vederes pick and choose what they give to us. Had we but known—"

"What?" croaked Damian. "Would we have returned to Germany? Tried to rebuild the pack?"

"It would be better than letting our people drift," said Darrius. "They need a leader."

"They have Patsy!" Damian gripped me so hard, I let out a squeak. He immediately relaxed—a smidgeon. "She's been blessed by the Goddess, remember?"

"Accepted by the temple priestesses," said Darrius in

a bitter tone. "And that's not the same as a blessing from the Moon Goddess."

"It doesn't matter," said Damian.

"You've chosen a mate," said Drake quietly. "Like it or not, the prophecy is coming true."

The chills pervading my body worsened. It was almost as if my body was repelling Damian's warmth. I shivered uncontrollably, and my teeth started to chatter.

"What it is wrong?" murmured Damian.

I couldn't answer him. Instead, I burrowed closer trying to suck the heat of his body into my own. I pressed my face against his chest again, clutching his shirt with quaking fingers. Gawd. He smelled so good. Like freshly baked chocolate chip cookies. Or the first day of spring. Or a Yankee Candle store. Really, like everything in the world that had ever made me happy. And there was color in it, too. Ribbons and ribbons of color fluttering and swirling.

"Here we go." Dr. Clark had obviously returned. I heard him tell the other two men to leave. I could feel their reluctance, but neither argued.

"You'll have to put her down so I can—"

"No." Damian clutched me tighter as if afraid the doctor would try to rip me out of his arms. He was good at shutting off his emotions, even from me, but I felt the echoes of my own reactions within him. What was happening to the two of us?

"Lay her on the bed, Damian," said Dr. Clark gently. "Stay next to her if you must, but let me help her."

Carefully, Damian put me on the bed and then stretched out next to me. There was barely any room for one person, much less me and a big guy like Damian. He cradled me close, his legs intertwined with mine. He propped himself up with one arm and the other arm he draped over my stomach. I felt safe so long as he was nearby, and I feared the world outside of our bubble. I didn't feel like myself . . . although, I couldn't actually be sure I'd ever felt like myself. How was one to know?

"She's freezing," he said. "Why?"

"Shock most likely," said Dr. Clark. "She's been through the wringer, Damian."

"I-is it b-because of the w-werewolf thing?" I managed.

Dr. Clark tugged down the sheet and started rubbing my shoulder with some kind of smelly, wet cloth. It was like a combo of antiseptic and rosemary and sandalwood. Weird.

"What werewolf thing?" he asked as he cleaned the wound.

"It's possible she is becoming lycan," said Damian. He sounded like he was chewing glass. "But she was given an experimental serum that prevents the change for thirty days."

"Well, those two points of information are certainly of interest," said Dr. Clark. "But nothing I can treat. That's more Dr. Michaels's area of expertise. However, it might be . . ." He was staring at the wound, which FYI, didn't hurt at all anymore.

Both Damian and I looked down.

The injury was gone. Once Dr. Clark cleaned off the blood, dirt, and singe marks, my flesh was unblemished.

"Oh, my God." I stared at the space where the bloody hole had been. "It's like I was never shot." I glanced at the doctor. "That's . . . er, different."

"Not in Broken Heart," he said.

"You're sure it's not Wonderland?" I asked.

"Feeling like Alice, are you?" Dr. Clark laughed. "You're not far off. It'll take a bit of getting used to, but it's really a nice place." He glanced at my wound again. "You certainly have the ability to heal like a werewolf."

"And the strength, too," said Damian. "She knocked Adulfo out."

Dr. Clark laughed. "If she managed to do that, Damian, she might well be able to shift."

I stared at Damian. I was processing all the information, all the experiences, and I finally had to accept that all that had unfolded wasn't some dream. I could still be crazy, though. "This is not a dream."

"No," agreed Damian. "It is real."

"Hoo-kay," I said. *Holy freaking crap,* I thought.

Dr. Clark stood up and picked up the tray of supplies. "Let's get her some blankets. Try to keep her warm, make her feel safe. I'd offer Valium, but if she is werewolf, drugs won't affect her system."

"I will take her to my house," said Damian, "and care for her there."

I don't remember much about the trip to Damian's house. He wrapped me up like a human burrito in two fluffy blankets. There was a car involved, which was better than the atom-explosion mode of transport that had gotten me to Broken Heart. Why would anyone call a place Broken Heart? It hardly created a sense of welcome and security.

I must've drifted off at some point because I woke up in a dark room with my heart knocking in my chest and a scream lodged in my throat.

I see you, says Robert. Nobody else does, but I do. I know what you are, Kelsey. We are the same soul. You must shed your old skin. You must walk in the darkness with me. And she will help us.

I tried to block out the images. The sounds. The feelings. But he was there, always there, the other voice in my mind, the one louder than my mother's, than my own. *I know your secret. I know your secret. I know your secret.*

I struggled out of the mountain of blankets piled on me, panic tearing at me with teeth and claws. It was so goddamned dark. I was in a huge bed and I couldn't find the edge of the mattress. It felt like Robert was in the room with me, standing in the shadows, laughing, taunting.

I fell off the bed. I landed on my side, and an ache vibrated up my arm. I righted myself, rubbing my elbow, and tried to figure out where a light might be, or better yet, the door.

This is important, says Robert. It must be done a certain way, you see. Otherwise, you miss out on the essence. It'll be your turn soon. Watch, Kelsey. Watch me and learn.

No, no, no. My heart pounded—faster, faster, faster. Cripes. I was going into a full-blown panic attack. I hadn't had one for months. The nightmares had stopped, too. Well, mostly. It had been a year, but I still felt poisoned. Tainted. Dirty.

I started crawling, too afraid to stand up. *What if he's there? What if he's not dead? What if he found me again? What if . . . what if . . . what if . . . ?*

I saw a sliver of light smudging the carpet, and realized I was close to a door. I launched myself at the knob and wrenched it open, stumbling into a very well lit hallway. On the left, just a couple feet away, was the bathroom. Across, there were two closed doors and to the right . . . to the right was more beautiful, wonderful light.

See the light in her eyes? That's the spark we must imbibe. That's why we cut her like this, so that we preserve the essence for as long as possible. Don't cry, Kelsey, Robert says. Tonight, we will be reborn. You will be who you were always meant to be. I understand my purpose. I understand your purpose.

I skittered into a small living room that had a big brown couch and matching ottoman, and floor-to-ceiling bookshelves crammed with books. Ah, there was the front door. And to the left was the doorway to a cozy kitchen.

The rooms were empty.

I was alone in someone else's house. Where was Damian? Was this his place? Or had he dumped me off at a safe house or whatever?

I couldn't calm down. I couldn't get Robert's voice out of my mind. I couldn't run away from my own psychosis. I wanted to scream for help, but there was no one to hear.

I skittered into the kitchen. There was a breakfast nook that had bench seating and a small whitewashed table. There was a back door next to it, and I nearly jumped a foot when it swung open and Damian strode inside. Cool air swirled in behind him, but I was already shivering.

He looked startled; then he frowned. "Kelsey, are you—"

"Damian," I whispered. All I wanted was to feel okay. To feel safe. I ran toward him and leapt into his arms. He caught me easily. I wrapped myself around him.

"What is wrong, *Schätzchen*?"

I burst into tears and clung to him tightly, afraid he would reject me, afraid he would find me too needy, too cowardly. I was still in Robert's clutches, and I hated it. I realized that even though I'd done my time in therapy, and I'd answered a bajillion questions asked by law enforcement, and I'd sat through the recriminations of my mother and the hand-patting of my stepfather . . . no one, not ever, had hugged me and told me it was going to be all right.

That I would be all right.

Oh, God. I just wanted to be all right.

"Don't let me go," I begged. "I . . . n-need . . . please. I just . . . oh, Damian. Don't let me go. *Please.*"

His arms tightened around me. "I'm here," he said. "You're safe."

I believed him.

He walked back to the bedroom, and with me clinging to him like a barnacle, he managed to turn on a lamp on the nightstand. Then he sat down on the bed.

Damian kept his arms wrapped around me, and he whispered to me in German, and we stayed that way for a really, really long time.

It took forever for me to feel like I could loosen my grip. My breathing and heart rate had steadied, even though my mind still felt bruised from the dream, the memories.

Also, my bladder was starting to complain.

"I have to go to the bathroom," I said.

"Okay." He stood up, still holding me, and started for the door.

"Damian!"

He chuckled as he stepped into the hallway. "What?"

"You can't go with me."

"But I think we are fused together."

"Well, *un*fuse us!" I demanded.

He released me, and I unfolded my legs. My feet touched the carpet, but I stayed in his embrace, waiting until I felt steady enough to walk on my own. I estimated it would be some time next decade.

"Thank you." I met his gaze. "I'm really not a wimp. Not much, anyway."

He cupped the side of my face, his thumb sweeping over my cheek. "You are amazing. And strong. And beautiful."

My shields had dissolved long ago, so I could feel the truth imbued in every word. And underlying those compliments was the heat of his lust. He desired me, but his need to protect me, to comfort me had taken priority.

But the slow burn was there, and it wouldn't take much to get the flames roaring.

"You won't leave again?" I asked.

"No," he said. "I only left to take out the trash. I'd been checking on you every half hour."

"Oh." I leaned in, because I couldn't help myself, and pressed my cheek against his chest. His heartbeat was so strong, so steady. "Thank you."

His arms went around me again, and for the first time, I realized that I was giving something to Damian, too. His emotions felt a little . . . I guess "musty" would be the best word. Yes. A little unused, as if he'd locked them away for a long time. Well, at least the ones I was beginning to associate with me. He liked holding me. And doing so allowed him to feel affection. Knowing that he was receiving comfort, too, made me feel less selfish.

"I'll fix you a snack," he said. "Meet me in the kitchen."

He pulled back, but I clung, not quite able to let go. Shame filled me. I was so freaking pathetic. All this non-judgmental warm-fuzzy-type notice from Damian had turned me into a piping hot bowl of Cream of Wheat.

"I can wait for you," he offered.

"You can't listen to me pee," I said, horrified.

He laughed. An all-out burst of genuine hilarity, too. His response made it easier for me to move away, especially since his chest was jiggling so much. I pried my fingers off his arms and took a wobbling step back. "Obviously, I can cling to you like a beauty queen clings to her tiara," I said crossly, "but I hardly think we're to the point of being comfortable with bathroom . . . um, noises."

He laughed harder.

"Damian!" I whopped his arm. "I'm serious!"

"I know," he said, "that's why it's so funny."

"Whatever, Mr. Sensitive." I pushed past him, and looked over my shoulder. As soon as he had left the hallway (laughing all the way to the kitchen, thank you), I went inside and took care of business.

A few minutes later, I entered the kitchen. Damian was seated at the table. A built-in bench seat accented the window, which jutted out from the kitchen like a pointy chin. He sat in the middle with a tall black can of something in front of him, and to the left, a triple-decker sandwich filled with meat and slathered with spicy mustard. I could smell it—even from the doorway where I stood surveying the counter where jars, bread bags, and meat containers were strewn across it. I was starving, and that sandwich looked delicious squared.

"Oh, baby. Come to mama!" I scooted onto the bench seat until I was thigh to thigh with Damian. There was a can of Sprite, too. Meat *and* sweet, empty calories. If there had been a cupcake, it would've been the perfect snack. Still, I was a happy, happy girl.

Damian had apparently spent his time making sandwiches and neatly boxing away any residual kindness or humor. It didn't take a psychotherapy license (or maybe it did) to figure out he didn't like the way I invoked his emotions (not on purpose, mind you). He liked me, and he wasn't thrilled by his attraction to me.

He was giving me that stone-faced, mean-eyed look again. I didn't understand his need to create distance, but I wasn't having it. I liked him. We were in this big ol' muckety-muck—together. For all I knew we were really were werewolf married. I wasn't sure how to feel about that (Just because I was an empath didn't mean I had my emotional shit together—haven't you figured that out already?), but I did know that I didn't feel bad.

"Don't start that again, Skippy."

"Start what?" he asked coldly. "And don't call me Skippy."

"Yeah. That'll happen. *Skippy.*" I waved my hand in the air. "You know, where you go back to being all stoic and serious. You wanna act that way with other people, then okay. I think it's stupid, but you know . . . *okay*. But not with me."

"And how should I act with you?"

"Like you like me." I took a huge bite of sandwich. The bread was homemade—sourdough, OMG—and there was ham, salami, and roast beef layered with spicy mustard and dabs of mayonnaise. "Mmmmphhggggrrrr."

"What?"

I swallowed the bite. "Mighty phenomenal sandwich."

One eyebrow arched. "All that noise sounded like dialogue from a bad erotica novel."

"You read a lot of those?" I asked.

"Every chance I get."

"You should try some of the good ones," I said.

His eyebrows hit his hairline. The chilly look in his gaze melted. You know, he had really nice eyes. And his face was *GQ* model material, all sculpted cheeks, square jaw, and aquiline nose. I wondered how he would taste. Better than my sandwich, I bet . . . and that was a mighty fine sandwich.

"What?" I said primly. "I'm allowed to read dirty books."

"Hmm." He sipped on his can of—

"What is that barf you're drinking?"

He choked. It took him a full thirty seconds to get his breath back. "It's not barf!"

"Smells like it."

"It's the werewolf version of an energy drink. It's good."

"If by *good* you mean *barf*."

"Stop saying 'barf'!"

I smiled at him sweetly. Then I ate my sandwich.

Damian apparently lost his taste for the werewolf go-juice. He pushed the can away and stole my Sprite. I was only a few bites away from finishing my snack, but I was full—and now soda-less, so I pushed away the plate. "That was awesome. Thank you."

"You're welcome."

"I can't help but notice that I'm in a big T-shirt." It covered my ass, and I was still wearing my bra and panties, but I really wanted a shower and more appropriate clothing. "Where are my clothes?"

"The shirt was destroyed and the pants are in the bedroom." He frowned. "I will get you new clothes."

"When?"

"Ah. When you run out of my T-shirts." Then he looked at me, I mean *really* looked at me, and this wave of red and heat and lust roared over me.

My nipples went hard, and my breath left in a rush, and my panties got soaked.

"You're flushed. Are you okay?"

I swallowed the knot in my throat. His desire beat through me like ancient drums, so primal and raw that I was held hostage by the intensity. I sucked in oxygen, but my body was on fire, as if he were touching me, and kissing me, and . . . oh. *Sweet mamma jamma.*

The more he looked at me, the worse it got. Well, the better it got, I should say, because pleasure tingled through me, gathering hot and tight between my legs. I bit my lip and dug my fingernails into my legs.

This had never happened before.

I stared at him with wide eyes.

"What's going on?" he asked softly. He was studying me, his own body tense, his gaze burning. "I can smell your arousal."

"It's your fault," I managed through clenched teeth.

"I haven't touched you."

"Well, duh."

He wanted to touch me. Badly. There was so much color in his emotions. Like those emotionally colored ribbons I'd discerned earlier. This, however, was mostly red, mostly passion, and I could hear whispers of words like "beautiful" and "need" and "take."

What the hell? Emotions had never come in colors and I wasn't telepathic, so I didn't understand why I could hear words. It all pulsed together, a living, breathing thing, amazing and powerful.

"I'm an empath." It was the first time I'd ever told anyone about my gift. "And I seem to be absorbing your lust."

He grinned.

"Seriously?" I was flabbergasted. "Me being an empath doesn't freak you out?"

"Why would it?" His grin widened. "I'm more interested in my ability to make you come."

"What?"

"I'm not touching you," he pointed out again, "and you're nearly vibrating." His nostrils flared. "You're close, aren't you?"

I gulped.

He captured my gaze; another wave crashed over me.

I pushed my thighs together and sucked in air. "I can do it back," I threatened.

His lips hitched. "Go ahead."

Knock, knock, knock.

"I may have to murder whoever that is," said Damian.

His passion receded, but not by much. I tried to get myself together, but I couldn't enact my shields. Something about Damian—about whatever *this* was between us—forbade me from closing the connection.

It was really a day of firsts for me.

Knock, knock, knock.

"Stay here," he said. "I'll be right back."

The kitchen doorway opened directly onto the foyer, so I could easily see Damian answer the front door, and the two people who came through it. They both stamped snow off their feet. The woman was blonde, and had a classic beauty. She was well dressed—though I thought it odd she wore no coat. She definitely had that air of wealth about her that I knew from my mother and her circle of friends. The gentleman with her was a tad more . . . well, blue collar. He wore a light jacket, jeans, and Nikes. His raven hair was shaggy, his eyes a gold-green, and his casual stance could not hide the raw power that swirled around him. He was dangerous, in the same way Damian was dangerous.

"Oh! You must be Kelsey." The woman hurried past Damian, who flashed me a look of worried surprise. She settled on the end of the bench, and smiled. "You are quite lovely." She extended her hand. "I'm Elizabeth Jones," she said. "And this is my husband, Tez."

"Hey," said her husband. I noticed then he was holding a Louis Vuitton suitcase—one that cost six grand by my estimation. He put it down, then leaned over the table to shake my hand. "You're the shrink."

"Psychotherapist," I corrected. "We do the same thing as shrinks, but we use smaller words and keep our egos in check."

He laughed.

Neither he nor Damian chose to sit. Since I was connected to Damian, I could feel his need to protect, to stay alert even among friends. He was not the trustful sort. I couldn't help but wonder about the events that occurred that caused his current emotional responses.

And here I thought I was gonna give up psychotherapy.

"We understand that you had to leave in rather a hurry. I hope you don't mind, Kelsey, but I brought you some clothes." She waved at the suitcase. "They may be a tad big," she said, frowning. "But I think they'll do until you can get a new wardrobe."

I glanced at Damian, but he'd gone all stoic. He'd shuttered his emotions again, or at least tried to, but I could still feel wisps. He couldn't hide from me—and I couldn't hide from him, either. I felt a rush of warmth for the way he'd been caring for me. It felt nice to the recipient of someone's concern. "You're very kind," I said. "Thank you."

Elizabeth smiled. "It's our pleasure."

Scents were tickling my nose. Elizabeth's perfume, yes, but underneath a sorta crispness, like dried leaves. And coming from Tez was a musk I associated with maleness, but something else, too—the closest example would be the dark, rich scent of wet earth. He was like Damian, but not. The scents I had associated with Damian did not match Tez's.

Wait. I'd been associating scents with Damian?

Oh, my God. I really was turning into a werewolf. And it appeared that there was a whole world of beings that populated secret corners of the world. It was amazing and terrifying all at once.

"Forgive my rudeness," I said. "But what are you?"

"I'm a vampire," said Elizabeth. "And Tez is a were-jaguar."

Dazed, I looked up at Tez, who grinned widely. The Cheshire cat, I thought, feeling a bubble of hysteria rise within me. Then I turned my gaze to Elizabeth. She'd brought me clothes, so I couldn't help but think of her as the Hatter. "You drink blood."

"Yes. But only Tez's. It's a lot to take in, isn't it?" She reached over and patted my hands, which I had clasped on the table. "It will be dawn soon and you look tired. Get some rest. Things will look better this evening."

"It feels as though the world has gone upside down," I said.

"It has," said Tez. "But it's a much better viewpoint. C'mon, Ellie Bee. Damian's girl looks as though she's gonna fall over." He stretched out his hand, and Elizabeth took it. Their connection blazed as bright as a golden rainbow—linked together in a way I'd never seen or felt, unbreakable and shining.

"Good night, Kelsey." She laid a hand on Damian's arm. "Good night, Damian."

He gave them a short nod. "Elizabeth. Tez."

Tez smacked Damian's shoulder, his grin still wide, and a little knowing, and then he escorted his wife out of the house.

For a moment, Damian and I stared at each other, saying nothing, but feeling everything. Then he had to go and ruin the moment by saying something stupid. *Men.*

"I shouldn't have bitten you. I had no right, but I cannot take it back."

I slid out from the bench, watched as his gaze dipped to my bare legs, and then how his jaw tightened. He was having a difficult time boxing away those emotions of his. "Can the effects be reversed?" I asked.

"Doubtful."

"Can you nullify the mark? Remove its protections, or change its implications?"

He shook his head.

"So I will either be werewolf, or I will be dead."

He looked at me, his gaze haunted. "Yes."

"And I cannot change either of those outcomes."

"No," he admitted. "And neither can I." He meant to move away from me, but I wrapped my arms around his waist. He stilled immediately. "Don't do that, Kelsey."

"Why?"

"It makes me want what I cannot have."

"I killed someone a year ago." My confession threw him off—in fact, he was so stunned by my admission, he forgot to feel guilty and tormented. I could sense him trying to regain his control, and not quite succeeding. "Let's go in the living room," I said kindly. "I like all the books."

"All right." He sounded guarded, and I felt the weight of his caution. And his ever-present ardor. He couldn't hide that he wanted to have hot, feral, sweaty sex with me.

I had no doubts that we would have each other.

It was inevitable. Like sunrises. And taxes.

I took his hand and for a second, I thought he might try to shake free of my grip. Instead, he brought my hand up and turned it to show my wrist. He planted a kiss on my fluttering pulse.

I almost melted into a puddle right there.

He led the way into the living room and settled onto the couch. I considered my seating options, and chose his lap.

"I'm not sure I will be able to conduct a rational conversation this way," he said.

"You'll manage." There was a green throw draped over the back of the couch. I snagged it and put it around us. "Better?"

He rolled his eyes.

"I'll tell you about what I did," I said. "But you have to answer one question first. You have to be honest—no omissions. And you have to buy me cupcakes."

"What do cupcakes have to do with this question?"

"Nothing. I just really want some. Okay. Here it is: Are we married werewolves?"

He blinked down at me. "I am a werewolf, you might be a werewolf, and we are not married."

"Oh." I felt disappointed. I don't know why. I'd never had the urge to be married before, mostly because I had never been able to find a guy who was emotionally honest. It was why, too, I'd never had sex. There were a few almost scenarios, but men couldn't hold back their true feelings when lust ran rampant—and I couldn't focus on keeping my mental shields strong during an act of so-called love. All too often (okay, every time), I would find out how a guy really felt about me, and it ruined the moment. Doused the fires. Killed me a little inside. I hadn't found a single man who'd wanted *me*. Sex, yes. To impress my mother, yes. (Not the sex part, the dating-me part.) Show me love and tenderness, no. Sad, wasn't it?

"The nightmare you had earlier . . . it has something to do with you killing this person?"

"Yes." No regular nightmare would propel a reasonable woman into the arms of a werewolf. The longer we were together, or maybe it was proximity thing, the harder it was to build psychic walls. I wondered if this new aspect (aka empath fail) was because of my werewolf issues, or because of Damian's bite, or because of the connection I felt with him. Maybe it was all three, tangled in knots as emotions often were.

I wanted to tell him the whole story. Maybe because I wanted to see how he'd react. Or maybe I just needed to share with someone who didn't know anything about what had happened—and maybe wouldn't judge me as harshly as everyone else. And he knew more about me, about my secrets, than anyone else.

"Tell me what happened, Kelsey."

"Okay." I took in a breath, and began again. "The whole empath thing is why I became a psychotherapist. That, and my mother really wanted me to be one. Anyway. I had this patient named Robert Mallard. He was a sociopath. Well, a psychopath, but he was trying, at least

I thought he was trying, to get well. Not that you can fix a sociopath—or psychopath. You can't. So I . . . I gave him what I thought were good emotions. I tried to give him what he didn't have, but I didn't consider that he wouldn't know what to do with emotions. Sociopaths don't really have a moral core.

"He started killing girls. Blonde, blue-eyed teens. He wanted to drink their essence. He had this whole ritual, you see. He brought the last one to me . . . to my house. He'd figured out I was an empath—and that was my secret, Damian. No one knew. But Robert said he saw me for who I really was, and he wanted to free me. He wanted us to be together, so he brought me an essence to share."

I told this story many times before—except for mentioning I was an empath. That little nugget of information was mine alone. Until now, of course. But the other stuff had become rote. I knew which facts were more important than others, what the police and then the FBI wanted from me. They had case files, some had written books, Robert became a footnote in a couple of psychological profiles, and closure. Everyone had closure— except me. Robert had killed his first girl in Texas—while on vacation with some of his friends. The next three . . . and the final fifth (if you didn't count me, and no one did, since I'd lived) he had killed in Oklahoma. Crossing the state lines had made it federal—that and when they'd established he was a serial killer.

I looked up at Damian. I was blocking his emotions because . . . well, I didn't want to know how he'd feel after all. I'd opened myself up to his judgment, but it wasn't like I could hide from my past. The whole world— well, the human world—knew about me and my mistakes. "I've known for a long time that I was an empath, but it was only a few years ago that I figured out I could do more than sense what someone was feeling. I can absorb other people's feelings . . . and I can give them feelings, too."

Damian's expression went flat. "*Give* them feelings?" He stared at me, his whole body stiff with sudden, righteous anger. "Is that what you did to me?"

Chapter 6

My psychic shields slammed down, hard and cold and fast. Me and my romantic notions of being connected to Damian . . . *Hah!* I easily severed our emotional link—and he felt it, too, because he flinched as if I'd slapped him.

"Really?" I asked with only a slight quiver in my voice. "You're so nettled by your attraction to me, you're gonna blame me for how you feel? And should I return the favor by blaming you for turning me into a werewolf? Oh, but wait. I'm sure that's my fault as well. After all, if I hadn't forced you to like me then you wouldn't have bitten me."

I clamored off his lap; then I looked down at him, deeply hurt by his accusation. "If you want to believe that I used my abilities to manipulate your emotions, then you're a coward. You feel what you feel—you can own it, or you can discard it, but don't you dare try to escape responsibility for what *you've* allowed into your heart."

I felt numb and exhausted. I had nursed a sliver of hope that I'd found something different, something just for me, no matter how little time I had to enjoy it. I was scared, no, terrified, of what the future held. What would it be like to be a werewolf? What would it be like to die? Would it hurt? Would it be quick? Would I be missed?

It was a morbid turn of thought, but unsurprising, really. This was a familiar place. When Robert attacked me, I didn't think anything. It was instinct and fury and motion and terror. But before that moment, I had plenty of time to ponder my mortality—while he cut the girl, while he waxed poetic about essences, while he wooed me with blood and death.

Damian stayed on the couch, slipping into his Statue Man mode. Inside the maelstrom of my own mind, I heard my mother's voice say, "Whatever is begun in anger ends in shame." She did love a good Benjamin Franklin quote. I often responded by quoting back Dr. Phil—complete with Texas twang. Margaret Morningstone did not like hearing the advice of her competition flung at her (which is, of course, why I did it).

"I would like to rest, if you don't mind."

"I'll take the couch."

"Thank you." I walked to the bedroom. The lamp was still on, the huge bed with its oversized pillows and thick covers. I wanted to cry, and I knew the value of a good keening, believe me. But mostly I was exhausted and sad and really not in the mood to indulge my tear ducts. Something hot and heavy and dark sat in my chest, like an ancient stone, moldy and crumbling.

I plopped on the bed, pulled my knees up to my chin, and sighed.

"Kelsey."

Startled, I looked up to see Damian standing in the doorway.

"Do you need a pillow and blanket?" I asked. It was inane, but the only reason I could think of why he would unbend himself, and his pride, to approach me. It felt kinda weird offering the man comforts from his own bed—then again, it was the least strange thing to happen today.

He entered the room, just a few steps, his solemn gaze on mine. "Forgive me."

"Tomorrow," I said softly. "Promise."

"I'm sorry." His voice sounded like a rusted hinge.

"Don't apologize much, do you?"

He shook his head.

"I appreciate how hard it was for you, Damian, but I was kinda hoping to drown in my own self-pity while lamenting about the sad lack of cupcakes in my life. It's something a girl has to do alone."

"You've been alone too much."

"True," I said. "But that's always been the way of it."

"Please. You needed me and I failed you. I never want to do that again, Kelsey. Tell me the rest."

"I'll share my secret, if you'll tell me one of yours."

"All right."

I shrugged. "He killed the girl. I begged for her life. Pleaded for mercy. I tried to give him some, even, but he'd built this psychic wall. He was furious that I rejected his gift. He decided I wasn't worthy of being his soul mate. He had the knife. And he knew exactly where to puncture her heart. I felt her die." This part . . . *this* part I hadn't told anyone. "She wasn't scared—not at first. She'd resigned herself to dying. She felt sad, and then when he stabbed her, there was this sudden fierce blaze of terror." I looked up at Damian through my lashes. "That shouldn't be anyone's last emotion. How can you have peace after this life if you've left it in abject fear?" I shook my head. I didn't really want a response. Besides, I wasn't finished. "I fought with him over the knife. I got a few cuts, a couple of punctures, but somehow I turned it on him. It pierced his heart, the same as it had hers. There was blood everywhere. I don't remember calling the police, but when they found me, the phone was in my hand, and the nine-one-one operator was still talking to me. I couldn't speak. I don't know where I went"—I tapped my temple—"I just sorta realized I was in the hospital. Two days gone. I can't remember a single minute." I huddled into myself, drawing the throw around me tightly. "That's why I was scared. I woke up and it was like he was there all over again . . . It was a dream, I guess. Or being in the dark. I don't know."

"I'm sorry he hurt you, and that he took the girl's life," said Damian. "But I'm glad you killed him."

"I've never been sorry that I killed him," I said. "But I'll always regret not being able to save her."

"I know well that feeling." He said nothing for a while, his eyes shifting away, his stare turning distant—not coldly, more in a remembering kind of way. "I was married once."

It had never occurred to me that Damian had been married. Other than the fact he was the loneliest soul I'd ever met, and he tried very hard to stand apart from others, I had started thinking of him as mine. The idea he had belonged to someone else grated on me. It was irrational, but I think we've established my lack of logical approach to most things.

"Our marriage was an arrangement. We liked each other. I would even say that we were happy. I am a royal lycan." His lips turned up in a sarcastic smile. "The crown prince. She was a noble from the Roma, not by blood like I am. The Roma have their own ideas about nobility." He paused. "Her name was Anna."

Her name was a soft rush of sound, as if he'd been afraid that by saying her name, he was giving it power. I understood the hold that the dead had over the living. I saw a young girl's tear-streaked face, her blue eyes wide, her life draining away. I had no doubt that Anna was dead. I couldn't imagine any female walking away from Damian. He had his own orbit. If you got too close, like I had, then you were pulled in.

"What are Roma?" I asked. The Moon Goddess had mentioned them, too. I supposed I should learn the lycanthrope hierarchy, especially if I was gonna switch species an' all.

"They are considered cousins of the lycans because they can only shift during the full moon. They are mostly human."

"And are arranged marriages common between Roma and royals?"

"No. Ours was the only one. Roma are Roma and full-bloods are full-bloods."

"And royals are royals?"

"Yes. We shared a lycanthrope heritage, but are worlds in apart in every other way. Our populations were dwindling. Infertility was high among our females, and our children were dying very young. I believed that interbreeding with the Roma might save the full-bloods. I was wrong."

My shields were snapped firmly in place, but I detected the horror in his tone. He felt guilty and responsible, which seemed his driving motivation for all his decisions. His sense of duty was hard-core.

"You were the experiment. If it had worked . . ." I trailed off, and he nodded.

"The full-bloods and Roma would truly be one people." I knew that this was difficult for him. Damian was not a sharing kind of guy. I was pleased he was trying to connect with me again, that he recognized how he'd hurt me, and was trying to make up for it by talking about his own secrets and his own regrets.

"It was my idea to start the village. Full-bloods and Roma living and working together. The Roma tended to wander in small groups. They've always had restless hearts. And feet." He flashed a smile. "But I was alpha of all lycans, so I created a council with full-bloods and Roma. I even had a vampire adviser—Ruadan. We had, earlier in our history, before mending the rift with the Roma, been protectors of the vampires.

"We built the village, learned to intermingle. Then I married Anna and she became pregnant. For a while, everything was good. Very good."

"And then?"

"We were attacked. Our buildings burned. Our people slaughtered. My wife and our unborn children killed. I saw our babies. They were mutated. They would not have survived even had they gone to term."

"I'm so sorry, Damian."

"It was a long time ago," he said.

"It couldn't have been that long ago. You're what? Maybe thirty-five?"

"Lycans age very slowly," he said. "What I've told you took place more than sixty years ago."

I stared at him. "How old are you?"

"It's a discussion for another time." His tone was stern. Then he paused, and offered, "Okay?"

"Okay." I chewed on my bottom lip. "It's the werewolf thing. It gives you immortality."

"Werewolves are not immortal. Most live into their eight hundreds."

"That's almost like being immortal."

He laughed, but it held no humor. "Eight hundred years isn't close to being immortal." He joined me on the bed, sitting close, and took my hand into his. "I did not bite Anna. Do you understand what that means? I married her, and took her to my bed, and put my seed into her womb, but I never gave her the protection of my bite. I never claimed her."

"Why?"

"Duty takes a man only so far, Kelsey. I know my own heart—though there are some who claim I do not have one. It is very simple. I could not offer to Anna what was meant for another."

"You loved someone else and married her anyway?"

"No." He pressed my wrist against his lips; then he clasped my hand once more. "My mother used to say, 'The heart wants what the heart wants.' There is, I believe, within everyone a core that houses our truths. It is who we are, and who we were meant to be. Sometimes, we act out of accord with this place, and it will correct our course, however hard or dangerous, to achieve realignment. Or it will act for us, even before we consciously understand what we're doing."

"Our instincts."

"That, yes, and more. Even when I didn't know who I was, I recognized you. The truth of who you were was already locked inside me, waiting. I didn't know my own mind, Kelsey, but I knew you."

"You said I was like coming home."

"*Ja,*" he said roughly. "I could not stop thinking about your dinner date with Dante. I could not accept that you willingly went to another man when you were meant for me. Eventually I got so agitated that I shifted. Then I didn't understand at all who I was, but I knew what I wanted. And I had your scent. The first time Dubowski shot me, whatever was in the disc reverted me to human form, but it held no sway over my intentions."

"That's why you showed up naked."

He nodded. "I claimed you because I knew, as I know now, that you are mine. I regret that you had no choice, that I could not control myself."

"If you hadn't taken me, Dante would have."

Damian growled.

"Not by force," I defended, though I didn't know why. I was angry with Dante, with his machinations. "But eventually he would've gotten what he wanted. It's who he is."

"You should have had a choice."

"I do," I said. "I still do." I cupped his face. "Your mother was right. The heart wants what the heart wants. It doesn't matter how we got here . . . we're here. And we can worry all day about the realness of it all, or we can let go and see where it takes us. I'm willing. Are you?"

"Yes," he said. He let the gates open then, and his emotions shattered my shields in an instant. There was pain and sorrow and hope and desire and . . . so much more, all with color and words I didn't quite understand. It was such a jumble, and I knew he was trying to show me how willing he was, and it was both wonderful and terrible.

I blinked at him. "I expected more blustering and glowering."

"I do not bluster or glower," he said, his lips quirking. In his gaze, I saw passion tempered by tenderness.

Then something changed between us, in that moment, just as quick and bright as lightning strike.

"Permit me," he whispered.

I couldn't speak, so I nodded.

And Damian kissed me.

You know in romance novels when the cute hero kisses the sassy heroine? There's this single quiet moment before his lips descend—it's a nanosecond freeze frame of longing and accepting the inevitability of their passion and then finally, oh *finally*, his mouth gently claims hers and her belly quivers and his heart pounds and everything feels perfect?

Yeah. Damian's kiss wasn't like that.

He didn't woo my lips into compliance.

He conquered.

It was hot and messy and . . . and thrilling.

My belly didn't quiver. My whole body did. His passion poured into me, and all I felt was *his need, his need, his need* for me.

He wanted *me*. Not just a woman. Not just sex. Me. Only me. It was a raw feeling, jagged with desperation, with a yearning that was soul-deep.

I had never been wanted.

Not by anyone.

His tongue swept boldly into my mouth, and I met his fervent demands for submission. I offered him everything, and he took it. It was his due. His right. *I am the royal alpha*. And I knew that I would be his. I was always his. This was where I belonged. With him.

His fingers ran through my hair; his nails scraped my scalp. He pulled on my hair until I was forced to expose my neck. Then he nipped my bottom lip, and continued those erotic love bites down my throat—a fervid line of need drawn with teeth and tongue.

Once again, Damian's feelings were color and sound. So different, so much *more*, than any I'd experienced before. Red clung to me like a silk cloak, and the words beat like primitive drums: *Mine, mine, mine.*

"Yes," I said. "Yes."

"All of you," he murmured. He pressed lips against the hollow at the base of my throat. "I want all of you."

"S-sex?" I yelped.

He pulled back and looked at me, and I saw how scarily close he was to losing it. He had iron control, I knew that, but it was thin. Even if my empathic abilities weren't on alert already, the look in his eyes was proof enough of the danger.

"I will not take from you, Kelsey. Not ever. You must give yourself freely. But you must decide now. Decide, or I will have to break my promise to leave you so I can . . . regain control."

"I'm a virgin," I blurted.

Damian's mouth dropped open.

"I don't have a hymen, of course. I mean, I've been to the gynecologist and all, and I'm big fan of masturb—oh, I see that you . . . um, don't want to know that part. Long story, short. I'm a virgin in the sense of never having sex."

"Never," he repeated in a stunned voice.

"I've gotten close-ish. It's complicated." I made a face. "I want to have sex. With you. Of course, with *you*. Only you. But I figured you should know what you're getting into. Oh, God." The heat of embarrassment swept over my cheeks. "I didn't mean literally."

"You did, actually."

"Oh. Yeah. I guess so." Misery crawled inside me and squatted like an unwelcome guest. "Me being a virgin changes things, doesn't it?"

"Yes."

He hadn't let go of me, but I could feel his withdrawal. His passion burned as hot as ever, but his logical mind had taken over. He was already harnessing his emotions, tucking them away into those little boxes he kept in his figurative heart.

"Don't reject me." I slapped a hand over my mouth. What was wrong with me? Could I sound any more pathetic? Well, truth was truth. I wanted him like I wanted no other man. No, no other *life*. I didn't want to be turned away.

"I have claimed you," he said, brushing aside my hair to touch the bite mark.

I swallowed convulsively. "No," I said. "You haven't."

It was both the wrong and the right thing to say. It

was jumping off the cliff and knowing the inexplicable joy of free fall mere seconds before the slamming into the earth.

One moment I was sitting on the edge of the bed, Damian's hand curled around my shoulder, and the next moment, I was flat on my back with my T-shirt shredded and a very aroused shape-shifter straddling me.

"This is the only opportunity you will have to change your mind." His voice almost a growl.

"I'm yours," I said.

He left the bed only to rid himself of his own clothes, and I watched him hungrily. I'd seen him naked before, but this time I would get to touch him, feel him, take him.

I started to tremble.

He returned to me, kneeling between my thighs, his hair flowing over his shoulders like black silk.

He ripped off my panties.

Then he destroyed my bra.

My heart thumped wildly. He was glorious—a god who'd deigned to lay with a mortal woman. He feasted only with his eyes, his gaze burning, and his passion . . . barely contained. I couldn't deny that I had unleashed a creature I didn't understand.

I feared him.

But I would not deny him.

He lifted my legs. As he leaned down, he placed them over his shoulders, that beautiful hair sliding along my flesh, and then he was kissing me . . . you know, *there*.

Then he started to lick.

And I died.

Well, I stopped breathing long enough to die, but then I got distracted by the pleasure sparkling through me like stardust.

My thighs shook, and I grabbed on to his skull because I felt like I was gonna float off the bed any second.

Damian's very talented, persistent tongue would've been enough, really, but Damian hadn't forgotten about our little session in the kitchen. If Elizabeth and Tez hadn't arrived, I might've well lost my virginity on the kitchen table (which wouldn't have been a bad thing ... note to self: Check sturdiness of kitchen table). He sent his passion into me. On purpose. I could feel it like an ocean wave, rolling toward me, inevitable, and the heat of his need, and the deep, dark red of it, and the words, oh the words ... *beautiful ... mine ... perfect ... she's perfect.*

And his mouth was on me, his tongue rasping over my clit, and my own lust crashed with his ... and then I was crying out, my fingers digging into his hair, my hips arching, and ... *ohmyfreakinggod.*

Yeah. It was like that.

Only times infinity.

And I was shaking, and crying, and he was gently lowering my legs onto the bed, like they were ceramic, and then he was kissing my hips and letting his hands trail down my thighs. He was murmuring, in German, and he moved over me like a dark lord, a conqueror, and he was ... he really was.

He covered me, his cock pressing hotly against the vee of my thighs. I was still slick, still throbbing and swollen. His thick length offered the sweetest kind of torture.

I moaned.

"There's more," he promised.

"You're trying to kill me."

"Just a little," he admitted with a raspy chuckle.

My hands coasted over his shoulders, over the corded muscles of his back. His skin wasn't smooth. It was marked with little dips and lines; I understood the lines, I had a few of those, too, thanks to Robert's dagger.

Damian nipped my neck, his sharp teeth scraping my flesh. My heart fluttered like a wounded bird; and my lungs were no help at all. I was gasping and panting, but so was he—although his harsh breathing was punctuated by the occasional growl.

And every time he did, my womb clenched. There was something powerful about making a werewolf growl (at least during sex).

He claimed my mouth, his tongue mimicking no doubt what his cock would soon do, and I felt another slow building of bliss. He wasn't moving his hips, but the weight of his shaft was enough to make my clit very, very happy.

He released my mouth, and leaned down to suckle my aching nipples.

Electricity zapped me.

I squeezed his buttocks, which was apparently code for "move slowly and torment Kelsey until her eyes cross and her lungs collapse."

I clung to him, my body straining toward another peak.

He cupped my bottom, rubbing against me in earnest now, his lips clamped around one nipple.

I soared into sparkling pleasure once more, my nails digging into his ass.

I think I screamed, too.

After about a year, I managed to get some air into my lungs. Then I said, "My turn."

He gave a rough bark of laughter. "Greedy, aren't you?"

"I meant my turn to torment you," I managed.

"Too late for that, *Schätzchen*."

I pushed on his massive shoulders until he rolled onto his back. I straddled his hips, and he groaned, his eyes rolling back in his head. "Now you are killing me."

"Just a little." The hard length of his penis pressed against me and I shuddered at the erotic contact. His hands drifted to my hips; the warmth and strength of his stroking fingers were distracting me. Now that I had Damian where I wanted (er . . . I think), I wasn't sure what to do.

"What now?" he asked.

"Hmm." I tilted my head and studied him, tapping my chin as if in deep thought. "How about this?"

I leaned down and kissed his naked chest. His skin was taut, all muscled curves and ridges, with dips and lines similar to those on his back—battle scars, I was sure. He was a warrior—fierce and dangerous and mine. I feasted on his pectorals, peppering kisses on every inch of delicious flesh. I laved his tiny brown nipples into hardness, then flicked my tongue across each nub until a soft growl issued from Damian. Glancing up at his face, I saw his gaze on mine, and his expression was one of tortured pleasure.

I licked the space between his pecs, tasting the faint musk of his skin. Moving upward to his neck, I used my tongue to trace patterns from collarbone to ear. He allowed me to explore, to play, to kiss, and to touch. And boiling like lava under a thin layer of rock, was his passion. For me. It was a heady stuff—like good wine or gourmet chocolate—to know he wanted me. His only motivation was to give me pleasure, and through that, he would take his.

Emotions could not lie.

His hands were restless on my back, my shoulders, my buttocks. He threaded his fingers into my hair.

Then he looped his hands under my arms and pulled me forward so his mouth could ravage my breasts. I forgot that I was supposed to be in charge, that it was my turn to torment him with pleasure. I think I was reaching that particular goal, although certainly not because I was being proactive. Damian tugged one peak, then the other, between his teeth and flicked his tongue rapidly against the turgid points. The need built—an ache that bloomed between my thighs, a heat that engulfed my whole body.

"Damian," I cried.

He used his chin to gently abrade the space between my breasts. He looked at me lazily, as if I didn't realize his cock was rubbing against my clit again. He wanted to be inside me, but he was being far too kind about my virginity.

I wiggled back onto his thighs, which popped my breasts out of his reach. He looked at me reproachfully, an expression that changed quickly as I wrapped my hand around his hard-on. Well, as much as I could. He was big. I squeezed it, loving the silky hard feel of his cock. I stroked it—just experimentally.

His moan zapped the pit of my stomach.

I crawled between his legs, my hands coasting up his rock-hard thighs. I had promised torture, so I spent several minutes fondling his balls and caressing his cock. His hands fisted in the bedcovers and his hips thrust, a silent begging for relief.

I had never given a blow job. I'd read about them, seen them in certain movies (shut up), and generally understood the idea. Prior to this moment, I had thought that putting my mouth on a penis would be an interesting experience. You know, something to try, but not necessarily an act that would bring me any pleasure.

I had not considered how turned on the idea of sucking on Damian would make me feel.

He said something low and harsh, German, I guess, and that's when I realized I had sorta zapped him with my own eagerness. He was tense, his gaze glittering, as he watched me.

I squirmed between his legs and then I put my lips against his flesh. I inhaled a musky scent, which was not unpleasant. He tasted salty, which I liked. I wished I had some whipped cream or chocolate or . . . well, the possibilities were endless. And this wasn't the only time, I reminded myself. This was only the first. The beginning of more, a lot more. There would be plenty of opportunities to explore edible options.

I just went with instinct—and tried to remember some of those videos I'd watched in college. Mostly, I savored him. Worshiped him. I kissed his cock from base to head; then I took sucked on the tip.

"Just. Kill. Me."

"Working on it," I murmured. Then I proceeded to torment him with endless tongue swirls and long licks.

I laved his shaft, sorta getting the hang of it—at least I thought so. Damian's fingers were digging into the mattress, his body so tense, I thought he might break in half.

"I want to fuck you," he said.

The raw words burrowed like arrows. My breath went out in a rush, over his engorged cock. His hissed.

Then I sucked the top part of his shaft and I gripped the base, giving short hard strokes that matched the rhythm of my mouth.

His hands dove into my hair and held me captive. No longer content (well, if he ever was) with my gentle movements, he started moving. I held on to his thighs and took his strokes, trying to keep my throat relaxed. My tongue teased the cock pumping between my lips.

With a persecuted groan, Damian released me, shuddering as he sucked in deep breaths. I did the same. Then I saw a bead of white on his penis, and impulsively, I gripped his shaft and sucked it away.

"Don't." Damian's demand was delivered between

clenched teeth. He looked at me. "I want to come inside you."

"Oh," I said. "That would be nice."

"Nice," he said, murder in his tone.

His gaze dropped to my mouth. His nostrils flared as though he were scenting me, which, of course, he was. Then his eyes filled with an intensity that made me want to leap off the bed.

Or into his arms.

He took the choice from me.

He looped his hand around my wrist and yanked me on top of him. Then he rolled me onto my back, and I was smushed against the solid flesh of his chest.

His breathing was harsh, erratic.

Like mine.

I felt his heart thudding, and its wild beat matched the savageness of my own.

He breathed in my scent, his tongue flickering up my neck. This . . . this intensity of need vibrated from him and sank into me, until I felt the growing heat of his lust, the thickening of desire in my womb, the shredding of control. Mine. His.

This was different now. There was no more tempting or cajoling or bantering.

His control was slipping—I could feel it uncoiling, loosening, and soon it would be falling, and there would be no escape for me.

I would soon be left with the wolf.

I scored his tiny brown nipples with my nails.

He reciprocated by sucking on my nipples, making noises in his throat—whimpers and growls. One of his hands slid between us to stroke my aching clit.

"Damian," I said. "Please."

He rose above me, and I could feel his cock at my entrance. He refused to let me look away—not that I wanted to. I wasn't sure what to expect. No amount of intellectual research could prepare me for the utter intensity, the giving and taking, and the mess of sex. It was barbaric and powerful and splendid.

Slowly, he buried himself within me. God, he was big. He sucked in breaths as he struggled with his control. I was grateful. It felt strange to be pierced in such a manner. It didn't hurt, not really, but it was uncomfortable.

I think, maybe, Damian understood that I was sorta losing the mojo. Not on purpose. I was just unnerved by this part, and I really wanted it to work and be wonderful. But I wasn't sold on the idea that it would be. (I know, I know. We virgins can be so melodramatic.)

He kissed me. "Relax," he murmured.

Then the red-*beauty*-passion rolled over me. His. A sparkling gift that made me gasp, and arch, and moan. "Again," I said.

He sent me his feelings again, and again, until I was squirming beneath him, begging for motion, for completion.

"Wrap your legs around me."

I did.

He started slow, but I was past that. I dug my fingernails into his back and bit his earlobe. "Please," I begged him. "Please."

He let go then, and within the beat of a heart, I was being mastered.

His teeth sank into my shoulder as he pounded into me. Sweat dripped from us both. Pleasure crashed through me. I couldn't stop the wave, the explosion. I gulped in breaths as I orgasmed, and still, Damian didn't stop.

I was holding on, a complete sopping mess, and then he stiffened, his seed jetting into me as he bit down harder on my shoulder. Pain pulsed dully, joining the ache of my thighs and the throb of my well-abused clit.

But Damian's passion was not easily satisfied.

He slipped out of me, and then began to pleasure me again with stroking fingers and a devouring mouth. He tortured my nipples, and rubbed my clit. My body responded to his touches, to his demands. Tingling heat spread through me. He slid two fingers inside me and worked me until I was soaked all over again, or maybe it was just more, and I was panting, my heart racing, and overwhelmed.

Was it always like this?

I couldn't imagine anyone ever sleeping or eating (food) or going to work or being able to think if sex was always like this.

He rolled me onto my stomach.

"What are you—"

"Not. Now." He knelt over me, planting his knees on either side of my hips. His big palms slid down my back, massaging. My sensitized nipples rubbed against the soft sheets. I bit my lip as he built the need within me once more.

I moaned as he worked the knots loose from my shoulders. How I could have stress knots in my muscles when I wasn't sure my bones hadn't liquefied, I don't know. He stopped rubbing my back, and shifted so that he was between my legs. He lifted me by the hips, and then he worked his cock into me and started all over again.

My hands fisted in the pillow.

I had unleashed the werewolf fully. I understood now why the Goddess had cautioned me about werewolf sex. Damian was relentless and insatiable.

And somewhere inside me was the growing awareness of the same ravenous creature. The one who could meet Damian's passions with her own, the one who could stand as his equal, the one who soon make her own demands—and he would meet them all.

Yes, he possessed me.

But I possessed him as well.

Damian groaned, shoving deeply, and came.

I was panting, trying to recover, when he flipped me onto my back. He knelt between my thighs and leaned down to suckle my clit.

Sweet mamma jamma. I came so hard I nearly levitated.

Then he sat up, looking as regal and arrogant as the prince he was, and said, "I have claimed you, Kelsey. You are mine."

Chapter 7

"I've claimed you, too," I said.

"You certainly have," he said. "I am a lucky man."

"The luckiest," I agreed.

I would've never pegged Damian as the cuddle type. But after we collapsed to the bed, he pulled me close. I rested my head on his chest, my arm draped over his abdomen.

"Are we mated?" I asked.

"Do you want to be?"

"I don't know. Do you?"

He said nothing, and I knew he was trying to answer the question. You'd think it would be a simple yes or no, but complicated seemed to be our shtick. His emotions were a mixture of contentment and worry and, if you can freaking believe it, the ever-present rumbling of his lust. No doubt he was considering the idea that I might not make the full transition. I couldn't blame him for not wanting to marry someone who might not be alive in a month. I felt a little hitch in my heart. Dying would so suck.

"I want to mate with you," he finally said. "But it

would be unwise to do so until we know that you will survive the shift."

"Will it hurt?"

"Yes," he said. "But you can handle it." He stroked my back, and the light touches felt good. Affection was so very nice. "I will not allow anyone else to touch you. It's . . . primal. I cannot stop it. I have this ache for you. Always."

"I feel the same way," I said. I glanced up at him. "I could survive the shift. What then?"

"One day at a time, *Schätzchen*."

I was disappointed that he hadn't proclaimed his undying love for me, but I guess he was too much of a pragmatist. He had claimed me, after all, which was definitely an emotional move. I supposed I would have to be satisfied with that until the situation played out.

"Werewolves are born in their human forms," he said. "They usually attempt their first shifts after a year. It's a natural process for our kind, but difficult. They still have to be taught so much. You are unique. You are . . . made. Not born."

"Teach me, too."

"I will," he said.

Silently, I promised the same to him. Damian had a lot to learn about his own heart. I think I'd finally figured out my purpose—one that would certainly sustain me over the next month as I waited to see if I would be werewolf (or dead). I'd do my best to help Damian find himself again. And when he did, he would uncover his destiny and he would find freedom and hope and laughter.

That was my vow. And I would do everything in my power to honor it.

I had awakened alone, but before I could panic, Damian appeared almost instantly, as though he were a genie I had summoned.

He sat on the bed, pushed back my hair, and leaned down to give me a brief kiss.

"You're dressed," I said. "That sucks."

He chuckled. "How do you feel?"

"Really good."

"No soreness?"

I took a moment to assess my body. Given our strenuous activity last night, I should have been aching and bruised. But I felt great. "Insta-heal, baby. I think I'm gonna like being a werewolf."

"It does have its perks."

"You want to take a shower with me?" I asked.

"In the future, the answer to that question will always be yes. However, I have duties to attend to. By phone," he clarified. "I'm not leaving."

I didn't realize I was holding my breath until he reassured me I wouldn't be left alone. I exhaled, relieved to know he was only a shout away. After what happened with Robert, I had never been comfortable being by myself, and for some reason, my connection to Damian exacerbated the fear. Maybe it was the simplicity of knowing that I felt safe with Damian. There was no else on earth who could protect me like he could. It was the kind of reassurance I'd never had—and I didn't want to be without it.

"C'mon, *Schätzchen*." He threw back the covers and scooped me out of the bed.

"I'm not thrilled that you can resist my naked charms," I complained as he strode out of the bedroom, down the hallway, and into the bathroom.

"Be assured I'm experiencing difficulties." He looked at me, and then I felt wrapped in a light blanket of his lust. My breath left in a rush and my entire body felt electrified.

"You're getting good at that," I said. My nipples were

tight and aching, and naturally, they drew the attention of Damian.

"So it appears." He put me down, and I clutched his arms, afraid my knees would buckle if I let go.

"I must make arrangements for your continued safety. Dante can't get through the Invisi-shield, but he is aware of Broken Heart's location." He kissed my forehead, then spun me around and patted my bottom. "I'll be in the living room."

The idea of Jarred finding us made me cold. But I wasn't going to give Jarred a second thought. I had cared about him in a way—at the very least he'd had my loyalty and respect. Now he'd been downgraded to a manipulative jerk.

I turned back around, just so Damian would see the front view. Was it wrong for a girl to want to inspire a man? "You're regretting this moment, right?"

"Definitely." He looked appropriately torn, but since he was sacrificing his sexual urges to take care of me in other ways, I could hardly be too upset. Besides, the faster I finished getting cleaned up, the faster I could seduce him. I didn't know if the constant, pulsing need to jump him was first-timer's excitement or the stirrings of werewolf libido. Either way, I couldn't keep my hands off him.

He escaped down the hallway, but he made it approximately two feet before he turned around and reentered the bathroom. He shut the door behind him, and then he dragged me into his arms and kissed me stupid.

Damian took up most of the space, making the small bathroom seem even smaller. He lowered his head to one plump breast and suckled the nipple. It hardened inside the warm cave of his mouth. I moaned as he laved the sensitive flesh.

With shaking fingers I tried to undo his shirt, but I

couldn't work the damned buttons. So I grabbed the top and pulled.

Buttons popped off and the material ripped, but then his massive, awesome chest was revealed, and I rubbed my hands over that warm, silky flesh. I was embracing my new lycan nature. No way could I have done that move if I were a mere human. It made me wonder, briefly, about the viability of Jarred's serum. It may have prevented the ability to shift, but it didn't seem to be affecting the other aspects of my transition.

Damian cupped the breast still throbbing from his attention and gently twisted the nipple. I gasped at the pleasure-pain invoked. As he pinched the still-wet nipple with his thumb and forefinger, he wrapped his lips around the taut peak of the neglected breast and sucked hard, nipping the end with his teeth.

I slid my hands into his pants and reached for his cock, which was already hard and straining. I couldn't get my fingers inside, so I went for the zipper, but Damian pulled back, laughing.

"I like these pants," he said. He shucked off his ruined shirt, and then removed his pants, boxers, socks, and shoes.

As soon as he was naked, I pressed closer to him, ravenous, needy. My hands glided over his chest. My fingers danced along the ridges of his stomach muscles, the firm skin of his thighs, and the roundness of his ass. One hand cupped his buttock, the other touched his cock pressed against my stomach. With one finger, I stroked it from base to tip. Then I encircled the head, gripping hard, before releasing it and sliding my hand down its firm length.

His hands drifted down my rib cage to my hips. Everywhere he touched made me tingle with heat. My heart was stuttering, and my breath rasping. I stroked his cock, reveling in the smooth, hard feel of it. Every time I reached the tip, it would jerk against my palm.

Damian growled.

God, I loved it when he growled.

He lifted me to the countertop, wedging me between the wall and the ceramic sink. I blinked at him, wondering at this new position, and watched as he got to his knees. Oh, baby. I held on to the edge of the counter with one hand while using the other to grab Damian's fabulous hair.

His tongue ravaged my clit, a too-brief torment, and I got so excited, I yanked his hair. He didn't seem to mind. Then he peeled back my labia and licked me with long, slow strokes. Every so often, his tongue would pause against my clit and flicker, causing all kinds of prickling sensations.

Then he planted his hands on either side of my thighs and pushed his tongue inside me.

I think I fainted.

Okay, no. I felt dizzy and weak, though. I abandoned my hold on the counter and grabbed his skull with both hands. My fingers were tangled in the dark strands of his hair, and my thighs were quaking.

Damian's tongue darted in and out of me, the strokes rough and fast. I sucked in oxygen, but there didn't seem to be any left in the room. Then Damian suddenly moved to my clit, drawing the pearl of tingling flesh into his mouth, sucking deep and hard. Just as an orgasm threatened . . . that rat bastard pulled away.

"Damian!" I yanked his hair, but he only laughed. He grinned up at me, his eyes sparkling, and I couldn't really be mad at him. He was having fun. And sex should be fun. However, the ache of unfulfillment settled between my thighs, and I kinda wanted to bash his head against the wall.

"I demand satisfaction, sir," I said.

"As the lady wishes." His head lowered and once again his mouth found my clit. He inserted two fingers inside me and curled them upward.

The pressure he exerted with his fingers in that odd position offered a strange intensity. If I had been panting before, I was gasping now. It seemed that breathing wasn't exactly an option when making love to Damian.

Then he started to thrust his fingers in rhythm to the thrusts of his tongue against my clit.

I shattered.

I was barely hanging on as waves of pleasure shuddered through me, but Damian didn't stop the movements of his fingers or his tongue. Seconds later, another orgasm built, released, and I'm pretty sure I left my body and floated up to the stars.

It's only a slight exaggeration.

Before I had fully recovered, Damian rose and placed himself between my legs. His gaze was all heat, and the playfulness was gone. He cupped my breasts, pinching the turgid nipples, and I squealed. They were aching and raw, feeling overly sensitive, but he was relentless.

"You need a break?" he asked.

I lifted a brow. "Do you?"

He offered me a smile, which wasn't the reassuring kind or even the you're-funny kind. It was more feral than that—more like a warrior would smile right before he slashed down with his sword to gain his victory. And yes, I understood the sexual connotations of my own analogy.

"Sword" was definitely an appropriate synonym for Damian's penis.

He kissed me, one hard, quick meeting of mouths. Then he left me sagging against the wall, my back digging into the frame of the mirror above the sink. For all my bluster, I supposed a little break from his majesty wasn't unwelcome.

Damian opened the glass shower door and stepped inside. He fiddled with the knobs, and the large shower head spouted a practical waterfall. That shower looked almost as good as Damian. I hopped off the counter and joined him.

He kissed me underneath the hot spray of water, his hands all over me, and then I felt him push that ever-present lust of his right into me.

Red-*beauty*-passion.

He turned me so that I faced the wall. Then he got behind me and lifted my hands, pressing them palm flat against the marble. My heart tripped over in my chest, my body trying to grapple with his lust and mine, but they were so intertwined, so much a part of the other, it was the same burning, bright flame.

He sniffed my neck. Then he clamped his teeth on my nape and parted my thighs. I was flattened against the wall, and my heart hammered, and I think I was sorta afraid. The smooth tile held a residual chill even with the steam of the shower filling up the stall.

Damian worked his cock inside me, nearly lifting me off my feet. I stood on my tippy toes. Once he was embedded, he adjusted our positions, and I was on my feet again, but not sure I could keep myself upright.

Then Damian squeezed his hand between my body and the wall. My nipples beaded, and there was this great rush of *soundlightfeeling* as he started to move.

He pinched my clit.

Electric fervor zinged me.

I was pinned too securely to fall, but it felt like I was at the edge of a cliff, and Damian was dangling me over the edge. The water sluiced over us as he pounded into me. And he kept pinching my clit.

His teeth were embedded at my nape. His free arm wrapped under my breasts. And he took me hard and fast.

I liked it.

Pleasure gathered in a tight, hot coil. Damian ripped his teeth from my neck, and for some weird reason the pain of that zigzagged to the riot of agony he was causing by tugging on my clit. It was the absolute intensity of the sensations, not pain, but awful, terrifying pleasure. It was like my body didn't care what he did to me because it would always interpret it as pleasurable.

He pressed his forehead against my shoulder.

"I'm coming, Kelsey," he admitted in a rough voice.

His words were the equivalent of shoving me off that proverbial cliff. Even as he stiffened and groaned with his release, I was falling into my own.

We reached the pinnacle together.

I don't know how long it was before I came to and realized I was being squished against the wall by a very satisfied werewolf, but at the same moment, he released me. I slid boneless toward the floor, but he caught me, and gently turned me around.

"You will never get clean until I vacate the shower," he murmured.

"I like getting dirty with you."

He grinned. He gaze dropped to the tattoo above my left breast and he swept his thumb across it. "I must admit that I like seeing my mark on you." He looked at me through his lashes. "How did you get it?"

"I was working as a *vaquero* in Mexico. One day, we were branding cattle, and I tripped. Landed ass over teakettle and *bam*—my shoulder hit the iron."

"Must've hurt," he said.

"Oh, it did, but I showed true grit."

He laughed softly.

He kissed my forehead, and left. I watched through the glass wall as he toweled off and got dressed. He waved to me, and I blew him a kiss. He pretended to catch it; then, still smiling, he left and shut the door behind him.

I got under the hot spray of water. The shower felt nice, but the being without Damian part sucked. I used the bath gel and the loofah (seriously, I couldn't imagine Damian using a loofah, but there you go) to scrub myself clean.

Then I went to work on my hair.

One minute, I was scrubbing the shampoo across my head and humming, and then the next I was standing in a moonlit glen that I immediately recognized. My hands were still clinging to my soapy skull, but the Moon Goddess had thoughtfully draped me in a silk robe. I was wet, though, so the material clung to me like a second skin.

Tark was in his human form, but at least this time he was wearing pants—though they were so tight, his impressive musculature and his genitalia were on display. I jerked my gaze away from him, and looked at the Goddess, who sat once again on her throne.

"Couldn't wait for me to fall asleep, huh?"

"I'm afraid my impatience has gotten the better of me. How is Damian? And Drake? And Darrius?"

"Um . . . okay, I guess. Damian's not too thrilled about—" I pointed to the mark on my neck. "But we're working through our issues."

Tark laughed. "Indeed."

My face went hot.

"Don't tease her, my love," said the Goddess sweetly. "I'm sorry I surprised you, but I miss them so much, you see."

"Why can't you just pull Damian here?"

"I cannot call forth a lycan. For now, you are human enough to cross the barrier, but that is changing rapidly." She shared a solemn look with her husband. "We hope that you survive."

"Thanks. Me, too."

She chuckled. "I do like you, Kelsey." Her gaze turned earnest. "We want to help you, but our resources are limited—at least until the Winter Solstice. Then we will be free."

"You're prisoners?"

"In a way." She studied my face for a moment, then appeared to come to a decision. "Nearly a century ago, I made a bargain. It was necessary, but part of the terms included my departure from the earthly plane."

"Forever?"

"Only a hundred years—and I could not reveal the details of the bargain. The moment it was struck, I was barred from your world. But though I disappeared, my wolves did not lose their faith. Then several decades ago, I failed my children when they needed me most. Damian stopped speaking to me. Almost all of them did. Before that terrible night, you see, when they said their prayers or whispered their hopes, I could hear them. It gave us succor." Tark clasped his wife's shoulder. She offered him a grateful smile. "It has only been bearable because of Tark."

"He took the bargain, too?"

"He was the bargain," she said softly. Her expression shifted like mercury, and I knew I would get no further information. My instincts told me that was a conversation she wanted to have with Damian. I had no idea why Damian and the other werewolves had chucked their religion out the proverbial window, but if I knew anything about the man, it was not a decision made without cause.

"Can you sense my emotions?" asked the Goddess curiously. "Or his?" She nodded toward her husband.

"I wasn't really trying." I lowered my shields and attempted to discern their emotions. Nothing. It was exactly like trying to read Jarred. "Is that a god thing?"

"In a way," she said. "You've known someone else you cannot read."

I nodded, unsure where my ex-boss fit in to the picture. "Jarred Dante. He's like you?"

"He is . . . and he isn't," she offered. She looked at me apologetically, obviously ill at ease with her non-answer. Then she said, "You must convince Damian to go home, Kelsey—to Schwarzwald."

I blinked at them. "You want me to convince Damian to go to Germany?"

"To the Black Forest, to the place and the hopes he abandoned there. You must both be at the temple on the eve of Winter Solstice—to prepare for our arrival. The few priestesses who still loyally serve me will know what to do." She smiled sadly. "I once had many names, but my favorite was Aufanie. You may call me that if you wish."

"Okay." My head was starting to itch from drying shampoo, and I felt chilled even though the air wasn't cold at all. I wrapped my arms around myself as I felt a sudden, awful foreboding. "I'm not going to make it, am I?"

"You were never meant to be one of us," said Tark kindly. He even looked a smidge sorry.

"But she will be," said Aufanie firmly. "Damian has chosen her. And we will not fail our son again."

Tark looked down at his wife, his gaze filled with tenderness. I didn't have to be an empath to sense the deep and abiding love they had for each other. I felt a soul-deep ache as I watched them. I wanted what they had. And I knew—the same as I knew the earth was round and the sky was blue—that I could have that kind of love with Damian.

You know, if I didn't die.

"Be well, Kelsey," said Aufanie.

Then, in the blink of an eye, I was back in the shower naked again, shivering under the now-tepid water with a crusty head and big wedge of foreboding lodged in my stomach. I guess Aufanie figured yanking me fully into her realm was better than leaving my body unconscious in the shower. I appreciated her thoughtfulness.

I finished in a hurry. After I got out of the shower, I grabbed a towel from under the sink and wrapped it around me. I heard Damian's voice—a one-sided conversation no doubt via phone—filter down the hallway.

I went into the bedroom and saw that Damian had placed Elizabeth's Louis Vuitton suitcase on the bed. I opened it and pawed through the designer clothing. Since Damian had shredded my bra and panties, I had no lingerie. I suppose going bra-less would be doable, but I needed panties.

I looked at the tumbled covers on the bed and saw hundred dollar bills. What the hell? Then I realized I'd left the five hundred dollars and my driver's license in the bra. Everything must've fallen out. Crud. I crawled into the bed, gathered up the bills, and looked for my license. I found it on the floor by the nightstand. I put the money and ID on the nightstand. I wondered where Damian had put my pants. At the very least I could wash and wear them.

I saw a peek of red underneath a gold blouse, and I tugged at it. A halter dress unfurled. Nice.

"Are you decent?" asked Damian. He strode through the doorway holding two sizable boxes. One was a pink rectangle, and the other a big white square.

"That's a loaded question," I said. "What are those?"

"Presents," he said, showing me the pink box. Then he lifted the other. "And this is breakfast."

I could smell chocolate. My stomach rumbled.

"Gimme!" I said.

He laughed, and moved around the end of the bed so he could lay the boxes there. In black scroll across the top of the pink box was Agent Provocateur. I forgot about food. I gaped at him. "Shut. Up. You did not."

"It's my policy to replace any undergarments I'm responsible for destroying."

I tore it open, and gasped. There were five bras and matching underwear, and underneath those a selection of silk stocking and garters. "Oh, my God. They're gorgeous, Damian! How did you know my size?"

He cocked an eyebrow.

"Never mind. How'd you get them here so quickly?"

"I'm persuasive." He seemed pleased with my reaction. His happiness unfurled like a flag snapping in a summer breeze. "There are more on the way."

I plucked out a red bra that had a scalloped edge and a thin black ribbon laced through the top. A tiny black bow graced the middle. I found the matching panties. "I can't believe you—" The rest of his words filtered through my bedazzlement. "More? I don't need more."

"I wasn't sure what you liked, so I ordered one of everything."

"One of . . ." I trailed off, astonished. "That's an insane amount of money to spend on underwear."

"Not if it pleases you." His smile widened. "You will need an extensive collection, Kelsey." He nodded toward the garments. "I can't guarantee I won't turn any of those into confetti."

"Good point," I said. I put down the lingerie, and opened the other box. Inside were a dozen chocolate frosted cupcakes. "This is breakfast?"

"Unless you want something nutritious and sensible."

"Hell, no." I picked up a cupcake and then looked speculatively at Damian.

He backed away, hands up. "We cannot indulge ourselves now, Kelsey. The queen wants to see us."

"The werewolf queen?"

"She rules lycans and vampires." Some of his playfulness disappeared.

"And she's your mom?"

His mouth dropped open. "What? No."

"But you're the crown prince."

"That's different. And irrelevant. At least for now."

I licked the frosting from the cupcake, and sighed with contentment.

Damian groaned. "I'm going into the living room to think about the natural beauty and wonder of glaciers."

"Are you afraid I'll smear you with cupcake and lick it off?"

"Damn right, I am." He crossed the room, pausing to kiss the crumbs off my lips. "And I'll do the same to you. Later."

He grinned at me, and then he left.

Then I ate my breakfast and got dressed.

"I don't have the boobs for this dress." I glanced down into my sad cleavage and noted the way the front of it sagged. Elizabeth had a bigger rack than I did.

"Please," said Damian in a pained voice, "do not mention your boobs. It makes me look at them and want to see them."

"And do things to them?"

He groaned.

We were walking down a lushly carpeted hallway to a meeting room where we had been summoned by the vampire queen. Damian had filled me in, somewhat, about a few things. Vampires and werewolves were under the purview of a lycan-vampire named Patricia March- and who ruled both species. Damian had not exactly clar- ified why he wasn't ruling the lycans, and it didn't exactly seem to be a sore point. But it did bother him.

Then he'd told me that the headquarters of a para- normal conglomerate named the Consortium was lo- cated here, and its massive compound held most of the official buildings and some residences. Damian's small, spare house was located within the compound. Most of the citizens lived in town like regular (if by regular, you meant were-cats, fairies, vampires, lycans, and dragons) people.

I was still trying to wrap my brain around it all.

"This dress was actually owned by Jessica Rabbit," I continued. "It's all boobs!"

Damian enchained my wrist to halt me, and then he swept me into his arms. "If you say boobs one more time, I will drag you into the nearest janitorial closet and fuck you."

Electric thrills raced through me. "Boo—"

He kissed me. Hard. I threw my arms around his neck and enjoyed the hell out of it. He pulled away, his breath harsh and his eyes glittering. "You're trying to kill me."

"Testing your resolve," I said. "You don't seem the type to issue empty threats. Honestly? I'm kinda disap- pointed." I opened my mouth and he put his forefinger against my lips.

"Don't say it. I'm already thinking about slamming you against a wall and pushing up that dress."

My heart started to pound. I was instantly wet. And hot for him. Oh, sweet mamma jamma. "Will you rip off my panties?"

"Yes," he said. He eyed me and then sighed. "I'm just giving you incentive, aren't I?"

"Pretty much."

"You are trouble," he said. "We must see the queen, Kelsey. And you should know that she will not be in a good mood."

"I'm a psychotherapist," I said. "I rarely meet anyone in a good mood."

Damian released me, and I didn't insist he hold my hand because I could feel that he was uneasy with our burgeoning relationship. He wasn't ready to display his affection for me, at least not in public. So I let him lead the way.

We entered a room that reminded me of a theater. The seating was angled and faced a small stage. On the stage was a long table and seated behind it were several people. I recognized Patrick and the brunette on the end. In the middle seat was a pretty blonde who wore a glittering T-shirt that read: QUEEN OF EVERYTHING. She looked grumpy. I could only surmise that she was Queen Patricia. Hmm. Wonderland's royalty. Was she the white queen? Or the red one?

Behind her was a big, tall man with moon white hair drawn back into a long ponytail. One hand grasped Patsy's shoulder. That must be her consort . . . um, Gabriel. Damian had told me a bunch of names attached to the people on the Broken Heart Council, but I had no real clue who was who.

A few people sat in the front row, one of them a lovely girl with violet eyes and a pretty smile. She was very, very pale and young—maybe seventeen, if that. On the other side of her was a woman with the same facial features and white hair as Gabriel. A twin? Huh.

As Damian and I approached the area in front of the stage (no doubt we were supposed to stand there for judgment) I spotted Damian's brothers. They stood off to the side of the stage talking to each other.

"The prodigal werewolf returns," said Patsy in a surly tone. "What the fuck were you thinking?"

I was immediately offended on Damian's behalf. My neck hair rose and I felt a snarl gather in my throat. *Oh.* That was different. I wasn't used to my rage manifesting in werewolf form. It was scary—and somewhat empowering. But mostly scary.

"Can you be more specific?" asked Damian. He had his serious face on—the mask he wore that displayed his ruthless efficiency and hid his pride. He was not a man who should be ruled. And yet he was. It felt wrong. Really wrong. He shouldn't be here. He was meant for something better. Something greater than a . . . a lackey.

I directed my gaze at the queen.

"You know," she said, her voice heavy with sarcasm, "disappearing like that and scaring the shit out of us. Fucking ETAC. Do you know how many tests Dr. Michaels is gonna have to do on your sorry ass? And why were you sneaking off to meet with Dante?" Her blue eyes zeroed in on me. "What's her story?"

"Kelsey Morningstone," I answered. "Damian rescued me."

"That's not what I hear," she said.

"Sounds like an inner ear problem," I said cheerfully. I turned on a high-wattage smile. "Maybe a visit to a physician would help."

She blinked.

Damian glanced down at me, giving me that one-arched-eyebrow expression he was so good at. I blinked up innocently at him.

"Damian," said Patsy, "what's going on?"

"There are prophecies concerning the lycanthropes," he said. He met her gaze. "It seems you are not meant to be queen of the werewolves."

Chapter 8

Patsy sat back in her chair, frowning. "Maybe you should start at the beginning and tell me the whole story. Then I'll decide how pissed off I am."

"A month ago I received a text asking that I meet a Vedere messenger in Tulsa. I arrived at the designated coffee shop, and the messenger recited a new prophecy about me—as well as a reinterpretation of the original prophecy about you."

"He couldn't send an e-mail?" I asked.

Damian glanced at me. "Vedere messengers must memorize every word of a prophecy and give it only to the person designated. When a prophet writes down a prophecy, those papers are locked away in a vault that only the elders can access."

"Got it," I said. Actually, I didn't know what a Vedere was at all, only that they seemed to be paranoid and secretive.

"A month ago," said Patsy flatly. "And you didn't tell me."

"I wanted to investigate the situation before reporting it." Damian pulled out a BlackBerry and started hitting the tiny keyboard. It amazed me he had any kind of accuracy considering how big his fingers were. He apparently found whatever file he was looking for. Then he read:

"A vampire queen shall come forth from the place of broken hearts. The seven powers of the Ancients will be hers to command. She shall bind with the outcast, and with this union, she will save the dual-natured. With her consort, she will rule vampires and lycanthropes as one."

"I'm familiar with the prophecy," said Patsy. "I've only heard it a gabillion times."

"According to the new information from the Vederes, the dual-natured refer only to the lycan-vampires—you and the other *loup de sang*," said Damian. "The last sentence should read: With her consort, she will rule vampires and lycanthropes *who are* one."

"I've had this gig for eight years," said Patsy. "Why the change-up now?" She paused. "Hang on. Am I hearing this right? I'm only supposed to be queen of the *loup de sang*? What the fuck? What's gonna happen to the vampires? And why do I have all the freaking powers if I'm not supposed to be the boss of the bloodsuckers?"

Wow. She was irate. And I didn't blame her. I knew very well what it was like to have the world suddenly, inexplicably crumble beneath your feet—and that didn't include my recent experience of werewolf bites and vampire rescues.

"Your highness," came a soft voice from the front row.

I glanced over my shoulder and saw the pretty, violet-eyed girl had stood up and was addressing the queen.

"Astria," said Patsy. "Don't be a dolt."

"Sorry, Patsy. I couldn't resist." The girl grinned. Then her expression went serious. "You know that my family's prophecies are truth, but our psychic powers are . . . limited. Sometimes it is like trying to view the world through a window smeared with Vaseline. I can see the image or the message, but it is fuzzy. Usually, this happens because it's not time to reveal the information. I would keep watching the window until what was outside it became clear. No doubt, they've been monitoring this situation for a while. It's always in the timing, you see." She pointed toward Damian. "Something has happened, or is close to happening, that has set new prophecies into motion. The trigger event prompted my family to contact Damian because now they believe their information will be useful."

"Terrific." Patsy waved at Astria to sit down, then turned her attention back to Damian. "What's your prophecy?"

Damian read in a strong, clear voice:

"To save the full-bloods and their cousins, a truth must be revealed and a secret finally spoken. The prince will choose his mate, and then his crown, and then his Pack. In the womb of the new alpha female is hope renewed. Only in forgiveness lies the redemption for the Moon Goddess, who is both Mother and Betrayer, and for her children."

Silence blanketed the room. Then Patsy said, "I think I understood all of it—except that last line."

"We're still trying to figure out," said Damian.

I had my shields up, but the weight of his lie sank right through them. He knew what the last line meant, but it wasn't my place to challenge him. I owed nothing to Patsy, and I wasn't sure I liked her anyway.

My loyalty was to Damian, the crown prince of werewolves.

"Well. This is the opposite of awesome," said Patsy. "Your prophecy says nothing about vampires. That's bugging the shit outta me." She glanced at Astria. "Should I expect a Vedere messenger, too?"

"I'm no longer the prophet," she said. "But I don't doubt there is a newer prophecy concerning the vampires. Damian's prognostication hints that things will undoubtedly change for you, and for those you rule."

"Terrific." Patsy waved at Damian. "Why don't you thrill me some more by explaining why you contacted Dante."

"I asked him to create a serum that would temporarily prevent transitions. It would essentially make a lycan . . . more human."

Patsy leaned forward, her expression a mixture of worry and confusion. "Why would you want to—" She sucked in a sharp breath. "Shit. You want to make babies with humans."

"It was an experimental solution," said Damian. "The last full-blood lycan was born three years ago. Even the Roma are not having as many children." He looked at me, an apology in his gaze.

Just when I thought he couldn't find anything else to feel guilty about, the man figured out a way to inject more poison into his soul. I couldn't blame him for trying to figure out how to save an entire race. It was the sign of good leadership to first experiment on himself. He'd done the very same thing when trying to breed with the Roma. Honestly? I wanted to be his mate and have his children, but I didn't truly know if that was in the cards for us. Yes, he'd bitten me, and yes, his former goddess approved of me, but I'd learned that wanting something was no guarantee of getting it.

"If I do not find a way to reverse the effects, my species will go extinct."

"Not according to the prophecy," said Patsy. "In your mate's womb is hope renewed." Her gaze turned to me. "I suppose that's you."

"Nope," I said so that Damian wouldn't have to issue

the denial. "I'm just a sailor on leave. Damian promised to show me a good time."

The brunette burst out laughing. She looked around. "What? That was funny. Jesus. You guys used to have a sense of humor."

"Knock it off, Jess," said Patsy without any real heat. She leaned back and rubbed her temples. "Okay. So, ETAC nabbed you on your way to Dante's."

"What's an ETAC?" Oops. I was just blurting out questions. I'd heard Jarred mention the name, too.

"A bunch of military assholes who hunt down supernatural creatures. They kill us, but only after they steal what powers they can to stick into their soldiers." Patsy eyed me. "I know it's hard to keep up, honey. Believe me, we've all been there."

"Dante knew ETAC was tracking down werewolves in the hopes of creating some sort of a human-lycan hybrid, so he was keeping tabs on them," said Damian. "They had me for two days before Dante managed to locate their facility and extract me. I had amnesia for the next three days. As soon as I regained my memories, Mari contacted you."

Then *I* woke up the next morning and tried to rescue a man who was already being rescued. And here we were—in a vampire and werewolf infested Wonderland. I hated that the lycans were going extinct. That was sad. Awful and sad. And now I knew that Damian remembered everything, including the torture and pain of those days within ETAC's grasp.

"You might as well tell me about the bite, too," said Patsy. Her gaze went to my neck, but I'd left my hair down and it covered up the mark.

"I broke out of my patient room, tracking Kelsey to her apartment, and claimed her," said Damian in a clipped, professional tone. He kept his gaze on the queen, and stood very, very still. Inside, though, his emotions churned.

"But she's not your mate."

"I'm really a stripper," I said pleasantly, annoyed that she kept trying to force Damian into a corner. The whole mate issue was ours to worry about, not hers. "He pried me off that brass pole and swore I would never have to wear a sparkly thong again."

Chuckles rolled through the room, and even the queen flashed a smile, brief though it was. "And in your spare time you're a psychotherapist?"

"I was. I've decided stripping pays better."

"Ah."

"Oh, my gawd!" The exclamation came from . . . hmm, what was her name? Jess. Yeah, that's what the queen had called her. "You're that chick." She waved her hands around. "Last year, on the Leo Talbot Show. There was that serial killer—Robert something. You took him out with his own knife." She stopped gesturing wildly, which was a good thing because her husband kept having to duck her flapping hands, and stared at me. "Your mom is a real bitch."

"Mo chroi," said Patrick in a patient voice. "Perhaps this is not the time for this particular topic."

"You think my mom is a bitch?" I asked, amazed. "Really? You do?"

Jess blinked at me. "Uh . . . *yeah*. She shish-kebabed her own kid on a daytime talk show. I wanted to throw her in an alligator pit. See how she liked being attacked." She grimaced. "And then to go and write that tell-all book. Alligator pit is too kind. Maybe piranhas."

Tears pricked my eyes. No one had ever called Margaret Morningstone a bitch—at least not within my hearing. I'd always been on the other side of the equation—the figure with the minus sign—and I'd never met anyone who'd taken my side in that awful debacle. "That's one of the nicest things anyone's ever said to me."

"Wow. You need new friends," said Patsy.

I sniffled. Then I pivoted toward Jess. "What book?"

"The book she wrote about you and the serial-killer dude." She frowned. "I think it was called *A Mother Betrayed*, or something. It came out a couple of weeks ago. It's been all over the news." She looked at me, and blanched. "Shit. You didn't know."

I felt woozy. And my tears kept falling. How annoying.

"Tell me about the werewolf bite," said Patsy, barreling right past my personal drama. "What do you—"

"No more questions," interrupted Damian. "I'm taking Kelsey home."

"What?" I cried. "I don't want to go home. I want stay with you!"

He looked down at me, his brow furrowed. "What are you talking about?"

"What are *you* talking about?"

"You are crying," he said in strangled tone. "I wish to take you home."

"Oh. Your home. Okay, then." I blinked away the moisture in my eyes. Then I sniffled. I had the sudden urge to start sobbing. Granted, I had plenty of reasons to cry (my mother wrote a goddamned book about the ugliest experience in my life), but this new urge felt foreign. Someone else in the room was feeling weepy, and I was getting the brunt of it. And it was contributing to my own unsteady emotions.

"Look, wolfie, I don't want to be here, either," said Patsy. "So let's just get the whole thing over, all right?"

"We're done now," said Damian.

"No, we're not. Your girlfriend can go . . . all the way to Dr. Michaels. We need to make sure she's not dangerous."

"Me?" I squeaked.

"We don't know how the werewolf DNA will manifest," said Patsy. "It's better to get you both tested. I'll figure out what to do once we get the results."

"The lycans are no longer your concern," said Damian coolly. "I believe I made that clear." My shields misted away under the onslaught of his anger. His emotions battered me: He was the royal alpha, and he would claim his place again. He was her equal, not her servant. The sooner she realized it, the better.

Oh, boy. My tears dried up, and I was used to enough of my mother's shocking actions (don't get me started on the sex talk I received at the tender age of eight titled "Whores and Other Demeaning Female Roles to Avoid"), that I could file away the book issue.

Damian needed me.

I tugged on his shirtsleeve, but he ignored me.

"Don't get all persnickety with me," snapped Patsy. "I don't care if you think you rule the pack or not, right now everyone is my responsibility and I'm still the goddamned queen of you all!"

Damian growled.

I watched his brothers take up positions on either side of us. The room went very quiet, and horribly still—the kind of static moment right before a storm unleashed its fury.

I grabbed his arm, and he looked down at me, rage in his eyes. They had gone wolf, I supposed, which is why they looked so strange. His nostrils flared. "What's wrong with you?" he asked, his gentle tone belying his simmering anger.

You know, it seemed like he was always asking me that question.

I felt very strange. Like I wanted to laugh and cry at the same time. And I was craving a rare steak and choc-

olate ice cream and feeling *crabbyandweepyandstupid-
andfatandboredandhorny!*

I swayed, feeling suddenly boneless, and Damian
steadied me. "Kelsey?"

"Don't be mad at her," I said softly.

His anger receded—a little. He understood that I
sensed her emotions, and he was taking my opinion seriously. I felt good about that.

Patsy shoved the chair back and got to her feet. "I've
had enough of this crap—"

"You're pregnant," I blurted.

I didn't think the woman could get any paler, but she
did. She plopped back down in her seat, looking stunned.

"Oh. Um. Was that a need-to-know?"

"We would know if she was pregnant," said Gabriel.
His gold gaze accused me of being a liar. I didn't really
take much offense, though, because (a) I was a really
good liar and (b) they had no reason to trust me.

Damian released my arm and then tapped the side of
his nose. "We would smell the change in her."

"How soon?" I asked.

"Within two weeks of conception," answered Gabriel.

"Well, I guess it just happened," I said.

"How do you know?" asked Patsy. All the fight had
gone out of her. She was rubbing her belly and staring
vacantly.

I looked at Damian. His gaze offered me support—
and I knew he would honor whatever decision I made
about revealing my empathic abilities. I drew in a deep
breath and released it slowly. I could hardly worry about
what these people would think about my gift. Some
were undead, and others could shift into wolves. So my
little quirk was hardly a blip on the crazy radar here.

"I can sense the emotions of others. Yours are scrambled and intense. I've learned that pregnant women have an echo ... sorta like your feelings are miniaturized and felt by the baby. At least until he gets big enough to have his own emotional resonance."

"You know what?" Patsy smacked her hand against the table. "Meeting adjourned." She pointed at Damian. "Go to Dr. Michaels. We'll resolve our 'who has the bigger crown' issues later. I want to know what those ETAC bastards did to you."

"Very well," said Damian.

He might as well have been carved from stone. At some point, he'd managed to fold away every single niggling emotion, including his impressive fury, except for a very vague irritation that he'd lost control—and he didn't like losing control. Not ever. I could feel his resolve hardening inside him like cement, and I knew that I couldn't allow him to retreat into the armor of logic and duty.

So I leaned very, very close, got up on my tippy toes, and whispered, "Boobs."

He sucked in a shocked breath and looked down at me. I smiled beatifically. "I dare you to make confetti outta my panties," I whispered.

He laughed. It was a deep, bold sound and it echoed into the room and right through me, and, more important, it swept open the door to his emotions. Even though he was still upset and angry and everything else, his humor won out.

I realized then how quiet the room had gotten. Everyone was staring at us, well, mostly at Damian. It's like they'd never heard the man laugh before. Sheesh.

"What's their problem?" I asked in a low voice.

He leaned down and tapped my nose. "They have no sense of humor."

"That's a shame."

"It truly is," he agreed. He nodded to his brothers, who looked at him with stunned expressions, and then turned their gazes to me. I wiggled my fingers at them; then I grabbed Damian's hand and we walked out. As the doors shut behind us, I heard Jess say, "Holy shit. Did you see that? Damian laughed! Take cover, people, it's the fucking apocalypse."

Then we were in the empty hallway.

"Not many people in this place."

"It's Sunday. Usually no one is here, unless Patsy calls an emergency meeting." He was still chuckling, his eyes sparkling, which made me happy. Because no matter how awful life could be (and it could be really, really awful) one tiny light could melt the darkness.

I started opening doors on either side of the hallway. Wow. This place had a lot of conference suites. "Good thing I rescued you." The third door on the right offered exactly what I wanted. "C'mon."

"I believe this was my threat," he said. "You're being far too amenable."

"Get in, Skippy. And I'll show you all kinds of amenable."

I had the light flipped on and the door shut and locked behind me before he'd even turned around. He glanced at the shelves filled with cleaning equipment. "I'm obligated to fulfill my threat. I never say anything I don't mean."

"I figured that out," I said sweetly. "And really? You were thinking about screwing me in a janitorial closet? You, sir, are a romantic."

"I was thinking about screwing you anywhere. Wanting you is like breathing, except I can't breathe when I'm around you."

His ragged confession did me in.

I reached behind me and unzipped the dress. It fell in

a pool of red at my feet. My life had changed immeasurably—in ways I could not control. I might well be dead in thirty days, but I could've been dead more than a year ago with Robert's knife plunged into my heart. Maybe my second chance was already up, and I could hardly hope for a third. I wanted Damian. I want to live every second possible. And I was sick of worrying what other people thought of me. I was tired of not feeling worthy enough to still have a heartbeat.

He took in the red bra and matching panties. "I like those."

"Enough to keep them intact?"

"Enough to replace. I'll buy an extra set . . . or five." He stalked toward me, which took all of three seconds, considering he was less than two feet away. He pressed me against the door. "You're impossible."

"Flatterer." I yanked up his shirt and splayed my hands across his muscled abdomen. "Whoa, mama."

He kissed me, hard and unrelenting. I bit his lower lip, and he growled. And that noise, both fury and possession, singed me to the core. I pushed my hands all the way under his shirt and scored his nipples.

His hands stroked my flesh. And his lips marked me. Everywhere. He was ravenous and feasting, a starving man. A starving wolf. Oh, my God. Me and my red dress. Little Red Riding Hood. It was ridiculous.

I was touching him, too, scraping my nails over his muscles, and then trying to tug open the buttons of his jeans. I couldn't quite catch my breath, and my heart was racing. My body shook under the assault, and I wanted more. To take all he would offer. To give him whatever he wanted. Needed.

He paused long enough to pull the bra apart. It snapped in the middle; then he peeled it away to reveal my breasts. He cupped them and leaned down to suck on my nipples. Sharp pleasure sliced me, and my lust exploded, shattering what little of my psychic shields were left.

Then his feelings washed over me. Primal and strange and raw. Emotions weren't exactly easy to disseminate—and like always, his came with colors and with words. A blast of red, which was passion, so much of it, because of me. *Beautiful. She's so beautiful.* Pink burst through that fabulous heat, and offered tenderness. *For her, all for her.* And green, the jade of his eyes, filtered through, and then *mine, she's mine, always mine.*

"Damian," I whispered.

He looked up, his hands clutching my waist, his lips swollen and wet from pleasuring my breasts. His eyes were glazed and he was breathing unsteadily. His adoration flowed over me with the same sensual acuity as his fingertips, his mouth, his cock. All at once. It was . . . intense.

"Oh!" I clutched at his arms as I felt something wonderful twist tighter and tighter. I moaned as the sensations coursed through me, waves of anticipation edged with such aching pleasure, it impaired my ability to think, to breathe.

Damian was doing nothing more than holding me now.

"It's . . . y-your . . . feelings." I sucked in a breath as another wave of red, of heat, of passion rolled over me. I was trembling now, my toes actually curling. I was barely holding on here.

One corner of his mouth tugged up, and male satisfaction stirred in his gaze. "You're going to come, aren't you?"

"If you would tone it down," I offered in a raspy voice, "I wouldn't."

"Hmm." He splayed his hands over my stomach.

"You have scars. Like I do. Lycans appreciate the marks of a warrior."

"You like my flaws?" I asked. "Those are ugly."

"Symbols of your courage." He traced one of the thin white lines where Robert's knife had sliced me open. "This is beautiful." His gaze flicked up to mine. "*You* are beautiful."

The truth of his words splashed right in with his lust, which he wasn't trying to tone down at all. In fact, the more he looked at me, at those reminders etched on my skin, the hotter his passion, and therefore, the hotter my passion.

"Damian!" My nails were digging into his forearms, but he didn't seem to care. He was staring at me intently now. I couldn't look away from his eyes, and he didn't want me to—he wanted to witness my pleasure. He held me at the waist, but his gaze pinned me more effectively than his body. In fact, he wasn't really touching me anywhere else.

I don't know what he was thinking. I did, however, know what he was feeling.

The need for *me* burned through *him* like wildfire. He sent it all to me, all that aching, endless wanting . . . it rained over me like a waterfall, soaking into my skin, burrowing into my nerves, striking like lightning into my very core.

Pleasure shattered me.

I squeezed my thighs together, my hips jerking as the orgasm claimed me fully. I was clutching Damian's arms, trying to stay upright. And the whole time, my bliss was winding around me like sparkling ribbons, and then his, too, because he enjoyed what had happened, and he wanted me, and he wanted more.

I couldn't draw a proper breath. Damian's gaze held mine hostage. He ripped off my panties. Then he was pushing me against the door . . . and dragging down his jeans . . . and he grasped my buttocks and lifted . . . and I clasped my legs around his waist, and then he was . . . he was . . .

"Damian."

"You're going to come again."

His cock teased my entrance.

"Yes," I said. I licked my lips. "Right now, if you like."

He slid inside me, going slow, watching me carefully, until he was fully sheathed. He waited, panting, trembling, barely hanging on to his control, wanting me to get used to his penetration.

I squeezed my inner muscles around his cock, and he growled. My heart skipped a beat, and my womb clenched. I clutched at his shoulders, riding the waves of his lust, grabbing on to his pleasure and weaving it with my own.

"Kelsey."

"Keep your threat," I said. "Keep your promise."

He started to move.

I was consumed all over again.

Burning. Red. Burning. Pink. Burning. Green.

Control. Control. Damn it. Con—

He slammed into me, over and over, and his lust was feral and raw and glittering. I couldn't help myself . . . I wanted him to feel me, too . . . and so I sent my own passion, my own tenderness to him.

He gasped, his back arching, and he pierced me deeply.

I tipped over the edge, falling, falling, and he followed me, saying my name like a mantra, like a prayer, as he emptied his seed inside me.

"I think we should do it again," I said.

We were in Damian's very nice black BMW, on our

way, presumably, to see Dr. Michaels. However, I was far more interested in exploring the sexual options available in the BMW. Damian hadn't really said much since he helped me put back on my dress. My murdered lingerie he stuck into his pockets. Then he hustled me out of the building and into his car before we attacked each other again. Or someone caught us. Or both.

"Kelsey."

I glanced at Damian and noted his stony expression. I had my shields up because the intensity of our sexual encounter had wrung me dry. But I didn't need my gift to know that Damian was in a snit of some kind. "What?"

"I do not wish to discuss our sex life."

"Oh," I said. "Then I guess I'll just shut up. Because your life should be as uncomplicated as possible, right? I mean, why should *I* discuss one of the most exciting, awesome events of my entire twenty-eight years when it makes *you*, the reason I had such an exciting, awesome—"

Damian pulled the car onto the shoulder and put the Beemer into park. We were on a narrow two-lane road in a heavily wooded area. There weren't any streetlights, and the moon was hidden behind thick clouds. Snow dotted the trees like whipped cream. The only illumination was provided by the dashboard.

"First of all," he said in a no-nonsense tone, "I don't think—" He paused. Then he looked at me. "The most exciting, awesome event of your entire twenty-eight years?"

"Yes. And I would know. Because I was there for the whole time." I leaned over the console, grabbed his shirt, and pulled him close. Of course, he allowed me to do this because no one could make Damian do anything. I kissed him. "I want to do it again."

"We should go see Dr. Michaels."

"Don't you think if ETAC did anything to you, and

your bite did anything to me, okay anything *else* to me, we'd know by now?"

"That assumption does not negate the need for Dr. Michaels's examinations."

"Will I have to wear a paper gown?"

He narrowed his gaze.

"I don't really like the paper gowns. I'm not wearing a bra or panties, and my dress doesn't fit. Anyone can see my cleavage. Of course, I'm not shy, I could just be naked. I was naked a lot in the hospital last year, thanks to the varied locations of the knife wounds. Doctors examined me a lot."

"You will not be unclothed."

"Are you sure?"

"You are trying to rouse my jealousy so I will not take you Dr. Michaels," Damian said in an even tone. "It's childish."

"True. And not one of my better manipulations," I admitted. "But really, do you want him to see my boobs?"

His lips thinned. "No one but me will ever see you naked."

"You know that's not true," I said. "I'll see myself naked. And if this werewolf thing works out, and you don't mate with me, I'll have to—"

"Do not finish that sentence," he said through gritted teeth. "You are mine."

"You gonna put a brand on me?" I asked. Then I realized it was the wrong thing to say. I just wanted to rile him, to keep him from disappearing behind his cold facade, but instead, I'd reminded him about my goddess-given tattoo.

He pushed down the shoulder of my dress and touched the weird mark. "Where did you get this?"

"Prison," I lied blithely. "Big Betty gave it to me so everyone would know I was her bitch."

His lips curled upward, even though I could tell he didn't want to smile. "This is my mark," he said. "So, in effect, you already wear my brand."

"Neat." I trailed my fingers along his jaw. "You know how I got it."

"She gave it to you. It's a sign that she approves of my recklessness. It is, unfortunately, a quality she admires."

"I think she loves you."

He closed up immediately. I hadn't even realized his emotions were floating around, like friendly ghosts, until he yanked them all away. I felt chilled by the suddenness of his withdrawal, and rubbed my arms. "Soooo . . . not something you want to discuss."

"No." He tugged up the dress, and sighed. "You're very frustrating."

"I know." I patted his knee. "It's a testament to your fortitude that you've been able to put up with me for this long."

"It is not my fortitude you should be worried about," he said. "It is my patience."

"Oh, I'll piss you off eventually. It's a talent of mine." I glanced at the backseat. "Since we're stopped and everything, we should do it in the car."

He closed his eyes and rubbed his temples. Then his eyes snapped open. He frowned as he reached over to feel my forehead. "You are warm."

"I am?" I didn't feel warmer than usual. I did, however, feel like having sex. "You're making that up so I won't attack you."

He glared at me.

Okay, he wasn't lying, and frankly, he was the kind of guy who didn't fib. Yep. He definitely fell in the category of: *The truth is better no matter how much it hurts.*

"Aren't you ever impulsive?" I asked.

"No."

He was struggling with his loss of control again, with how I could circumvent his sense of duty. And he was worried about me. He was trying to file everything away. He hated the mess of feelings, how they tangled together and made him want things. Want me.

I was, of course, interpreting the riot of his emotions. I had plenty of time to practice over the years, especially as a psychotherapist. He was trying to go cold on me again, to push me away, to push everyone away. Something had happened to break his confidence, his faith in himself, and he'd coped by separating himself from pesky emotions. That was no way to live. In fact, it wasn't living at all. And he needed to know the value of joy, of laughter, of singing, of spontaneity.

"Don't," I said. I took his face in my hands. "I told you, Damian. If you have to put on that mask for everyone else, then okay. But not with me."

He stilled, his expression going carefully blank, his eyes displaying distant curiosity.

"If I only have a month to live," I said, "then I want every day to be filled with wonderful things. With you. With sex. And cupcakes."

He cracked a smile, and then seemed surprised that he'd done so. He turned his head and pressed a kiss to my palm. "I will give you everything within my power," he said. "Including all the cupcakes you can eat."

"And you won't turn into Statue Man?"

"Not with you," he promised.

"And you'll have sex with me whenever I want?"

"I shall try to live with the inconvenience of servicing you."

"Sweet. Then let's go see Dr. Michaels."

Chapter 9

The visit to Dr. Stan Michaels was anticlimatic. We met him and his wife, Linda, at their house, which was sorta out by itself in the middle of nowhere. They did, however, have a killer pool—with a rock waterfall and everything. And get this—it smelled like lavender.

Anyway.

We ended up going to the basement laboratory, which was filled with shiny tables and fancy equipment and a number of machines I couldn't begin to identify.

He took blood, scraped off some skin, and even plucked some hair. He did the same to Damian, told us it would be a couple of days before he got back any results, and then we were on our way home.

Well, almost.

"She's too warm," said Damian. "And she's—"

Dr. Michaels stared at Damian, waiting for him to continue. And I stared at Damian, too, and smirked. My poor lycan pressed his lips together, unable to verbalize that I was too horny for his own comfort.

"I'm what?" I goaded.

"Can you just check her temperature?" asked Damian.

"I did," said Dr. Michaels. "She's running a little hot, but lycans have a higher body temperature. It's nothing abnormal."

"So I am officially a werewolf?"

"Given your pupil dilation, your higher body temperature, your increased strength, and heightened senses . . . I would say you are. But the blood work will confirm."

"You think I'll survive my first shift?"

He looked away, studying the wall for a few seconds, and then he sighed. "I don't know. Lycanthropes are a different species, and their bodies are designed to shift. You are a human. It's unclear if your body will accept all the changes necessary to become a full lycan."

"Like a patient who gets a new heart, or a kidney," I mused. "I could suffer a transplant rejection."

"In a way," agreed Dr. Michaels. "Lycans and humans cannot procreate because lycan DNA essentially destroys anything perceived as foreign matter, including human eggs or semen."

"So the fact I'm alive means my body has accepted the lycan DNA?"

"Or it means that the serum is combating the effects and once it runs its course, you will be vulnerable again."

"And yet I'm manifesting werewolf characteristics."

"Yes," he said, offering a small smile. "That does seem to indicate a positive outcome."

I beamed at Damian. He arched a brow, his expression serious, but I detected a sliver of relief that managed to wiggle through his weighty concern. Aw. He was so cute.

"I still recommend quarantine," said Dr. Michaels.

"At least until I get the test results back and can determine the extent of your condition."

"You think I could be dangerous?" I was completely flummoxed by this idea.

"This is a rather historic situation," he said. "There is no one else like you, Ms. Morningstone. We have no idea how the changes might manifest. Not even the blood work will tell me that. It's safer to keep you contained until we have more information."

"That makes sense," I said. "I don't want anyone to get hurt if I accidentally go all furry and fangy."

"I will take care of you," said Damian. He nodded to Dr. Michaels, and then grasped my hand and led me out of the doctor's house.

Damian drove us back to the compound—and to his little white house at the end of a whole row of little white houses. They even had picket fences. His was tidy, but boring. No flowers, no paint, no color. Everything was neat and in its place, no comfortable messes in the yard, not even a carelessly tossed hose or a pile of rust-colored leaves. The only incongruity was the snow-spattered grass. The porch was too small for a rocking chair, which was too bad because I liked to imagine owning a house with a wraparound porch and space for a couple of old-fashioned rocking chairs. Somewhere in that fantasy was a table that held a bouquet of spring flowers and freshly made lemonade. Or mint juleps. I'd always wanted to try a mint julep.

Damian didn't even have a welcome mat on the tiny porch, which seemed sad to me. Not even in that small way could he invite people into his life. It was another symbol of his attempts to keep everyone in their places— far away from him.

Damian's cell rang as we walked inside. He shut and locked the door, then plucked the BlackBerry from his pocket and continued into the kitchen. While he had his conversation, I went into the living room and studied the bookshelves. Talk about eclectic. Louis L'Amour paperbacks were squeezed next to science textbooks; there was a whole section of Charlaine Harris novels and underneath those, leather volumes of Shakespeare. Then I spotted a series of slim hardcovers with titles like *Vampires Are Real!* and *Aliens Are Real!* and *Werewolves Are Real!*

I grabbed the werewolf one and settled on the couch to leaf through the pages. A few minutes later, Damian walked into the living room.

"I've updated Patsy on your condition."

"What about her condition?"

"It appears you were correct about her pregnancy."

"Yay, me." I looked up from the book. "And where will I be quarantined?"

"Here," he said. "I will watch you for as long as necessary. My brothers will take over my duties until I can resume them."

"What duties?"

"I head up the security for Broken Heart and for the queen."

"I thought you were the crown prince of the lycans."

He gave a short nod. "Yes. I suppose I will not have to worry about Broken Heart for much longer."

"Where are your parents?"

For a moment, Damian looked as though I'd struck him. He went pale, his gaze opaque. I shut the book, alarmed. "What?"

"Why would you ask about my parents?"

"Other than it's a typical 'getting to know you' question, I assume that the king and queen of werewolves have to be alive somewhere, otherwise you wouldn't be a crown prince."

"Oh." He crossed his arms. "It's complicated. I do not wish to discuss it."

"Okay."

He narrowed his gaze. "You are not going to harangue me about this issue?"

"Good use of 'harangue,'" I said. "And no, I won't. If you want to tell me, you'll tell me." I smiled. "Do you know you speak formally when you're in Statue Man mode?"

"You are psychoanalyzing me," he accused.

"Making an observation," I corrected. "Do you want to fight? Because we can do that if it'll make you feel better."

"Did I say I wanted to fight?"

"Why would you say that?" I rose from the couch and walked past him. "You're too much a warrior to give away your strategy."

He seemed disconcerted by my sudden exit, and turned to follow me down the hallway. I opened the bedroom door, flipped on the light, and stepped inside. "Is this the only bedroom?"

"Yes," he said in tight voice. "I'm sorry if it displeases you."

"Are you?" I asked, amused at his continued irritation. "Then you should probably do something about it so that I'm no longer displeased."

"It's my house. I decide if anything should be changed." He made a show of looking around. "I like it."

"Okay." I unzipped my dress and stepped out of it. Then I went to the still-unmade bed, and started removing all the items piled on top of it. Damian watched me in frosty silence—even when he muscled in to take the suitcase, which he heaved over to the closet and stuck inside. I put the lingerie box on the dresser, and then pushed the cupcake box close to where I planned to tuck in. Oh, yeah. I was gonna eat cupcakes in bed. I needed a nap, and probably some real food, but what was the fun in that?

I stood up and half turned. "I forgot my book."

Damian's gaze jerked up to meet mine. He'd been examining my backside, and I knew he wanted me again. I knew because I wanted him. However, he was trying very hard not to desire me. Something had spooked him—perhaps the reminder that I was almost lycan, but mostly human. Or that he cared about me, and that scared him, or maybe he didn't like that he couldn't hide his feelings from me. That tended to irk everyone, not just big grumpy werewolves. I could probably drop my shields and cull through his emotions, but I was feeling a little vulnerable myself. Damian's feelings were powerful, so much so I was absorbing and reflecting them as easily as my own. I didn't want to repeat past mistakes—but the circumstances were not completely under my control, especially during lovemaking.

"I will retrieve your book," he said. He returned a minute later and handed me *Werewolves Are Real!*

"Thank you." I put the book on the bed. Then I placed my hands on his chest and reached up on tippy toes to brush my lips across his.

He didn't step away, but he didn't touch me back, either. "I have ruined your life," he said. "I may have even killed you."

Ah. So that was it. He was feeling guilty. Our visit to the good Dr. Michaels had reminded him that all was not well. It was difficult for anyone to stop using the coping skills that had served them in the past. It took patience and time and a willingness to replace the old behaviors with new ones. Getting Damian to stop retreating behind his stone mask would be difficult—and only possible if he wanted to discard it.

"We may have limited time together, and I don't want to spend it in recrimination." I cupped his cheek. "I know better than anyone that feelings are complicated, and it's not easy to deal with them. You do what you have to, okay? If you want to talk, I'm here."

He studied me for the longest time, and then he cracked. The tension went out of his body, and he gathered me into his arms. "You are not like anyone I've ever known. You're not scared of me. And you react to situations oddly."

"Is that a compliment?" I asked.

"An observation," he said, grinning.

I kissed him, and started tugging at his shirt, but he stilled my hands. "It may be wise to refrain from sex until we know more about your condition."

"No backsies," I said.

"What?"

"You can't undo what we've already done. And therefore, we should keep doing it."

"That made no sense."

I sighed. "All right, Damian. If you think we should refrain, then we'll refrain." I gave him my most pitiful look. "But it makes me very, very sad."

"I bought you cupcakes. They are the antidote to sad."

"Well, I do love a good cupcake . . . especially if I can smear it across you and lick it off."

"You know," said Damian hoarsely, "refraining may be overrated. Perhaps only a precaution is necessary."

"What kind of precaution?" I asked, suspicious.

"Condoms." He brushed my hair away from my face. "If Dr. Michaels is right, and you are already turning into a lycan, we cannot risk pregnancy."

"But we already have, haven't we?"

"Yes. It was foolish of me to risk it."

"Why did you?"

A flush of red crawled up his neck. "When I make love to you, I cannot think straight."

"That's a good thing." I hadn't thought about the possibility of children. I could see why Damian would be concerned. If I got pregnant, but didn't survive the initial shift, I would destroy two lives. My physical need for Damian was weakening my emotional barriers. It appeared that I wouldn't be able to keep my walls strong and steady around him.

And that was a tad discomfiting.

There was something else bothering him—the echo of a past decision, a past shame that mirrored what was unfolding between us. Him and Anna. The lycans and the Roma. Second chances—or grievous loss.

"I broke my promise," said Damian.

"You would never break a promise."

"I promised not to be Statue Man with you."

"I understand your fears about getting close to people, Damian, perhaps better than anyone. Especially if you feel like they might be taken away. What's happening with us reminds you of Anna, doesn't it? It's easier to have no expectations at all. Better really, than to have even the tiniest happiness so brutally ripped away."

"Yes," he said. "But I do not want to keep you out."

"I know. Hey, life can really suck." I kissed him. "But most of the time, it doesn't."

"You're talking about the cupcakes again, aren't you?"

"Yep." I wiggled out of his grasp, and tucked in to the bed. He watched me hungrily, and I felt his need rising again (and saw it, too, given that I was looking at his crotch).

"I have to tell you something."

Wariness immediately chilled his ardor. "Your tone suggests this will not be a topic I like."

"I saw Aufanie and Tark again."

"Aufanie." He said the name slowly, as if he hadn't

uttered the word in a long time. He probably hadn't. "She told you to call her that?"

"Yes." I looked at him. "They want you to go to Germany. They said we should both be at the temple on the night of Winter Solstice."

"What the hell for?"

"I think they want to see you," I said. "And they want to help me. I get the feeling that maybe things aren't gonna go my way once it's time to go full lycan."

Damian sat on the bed and gathered my hands into his. "She is a liar, and he . . . he is a fool. It's been almost a century since she's talked to anyone, and when she does, she calls on you. You have no connection to her."

"You're my connection. She says she can only call me because I'm still human enough to go through the barrier." I traced his knuckles. "I think they're trapped."

"And yet they can port into the temple two weeks from now?" He snorted in disbelief.

"She made a bargain, and the terms are nearly done."

"Bargain," he said sharply. "What do you mean?"

"That's all I know. She was reluctant to share details. She made whatever this bargain is and got sucked in to this other place, which FYI, looks like the woods in the dead of night. She said she couldn't tell anyone—it was part of the terms."

"And what could've been so important that she left us all without a word?"

I brought his hand up and kissed his fingertips. "Tark," I answered. "Whatever she did . . . it was for love."

My words didn't nullify his anger, but I could tell he was mulling over all that I had said. He nodded. "It's worth considering, Kelsey."

"I think so, too."

He tilted his head, and studied me. "Something else is bothering you."

"Very perceptive. It's like you're a werewolf or something."

"Maybe I'm an empath."

"Hey, no horning in on my territory."

He laughed. Then he said, "Tell me, *Schätzchen*."

"I want a copy of my mother's new book. I need to know what she wrote."

I felt the shadow of his fury. He hadn't been thrilled at Jess's news, either, but he'd been much better at compartmentalizing it. "She had no right."

"Oh, she thinks she had rights out the wazoo, believe me. I think it's a side effect of being an advice guru. You tend to think you know what's best for everyone. And it doesn't hurt that she knows how to spin gold from straw—me being the lucky, lucky straw."

"I will get you a copy."

"Thank you."

He brushed his lips over my temple. Then he pushed me back onto the bed and murmured, "You said something about smearing cupcakes all over me?"

Yes. Yes, I did.

The next two days, while Dr. Michaels ran his tests, I enjoyed the limitations of quarantine. Damian and I couldn't keep our hands off each other. We'd be doing something mundane like making sandwiches in the kitchen and in the next moment, we'd be tearing off each other's clothes and having hot monkey sex on the floor. Or table. Or couch. Or in the backyard underneath the branches of an old pecan tree. Damian kept several condoms in his pockets for these occasions. I didn't mind the protection, but it made me wonder about the first times we were together, and whether my lycan DNA had been strong enough to accept his. Or maybe I'd been too human and the potential of making a baby had been nil.

I couldn't stop thinking about children, and how very much I wanted to have them with Damian. But he was skittish about the idea, and I couldn't blame him. We didn't know if I would become a full-blood, much less have the ability to make babies. There were lycan females who could not conceive or worse, carry to term—what chance did I have?

Damian talked to me about werewolf basics, and he fed me rare steak and wine and cupcakes. He was always touching my hair or rubbing my back or kissing me. His emotions were as full and open as mine. It was almost like he could read me, too. Maybe it was the werewolf in him, or he was just a good man who paid very close attention.

On day two of quarantine, my mother's book arrived. I left it in the living room and ignored it, even though I knew I would have to eventually confront all that she had written.

She never once asked me about what happened. She knew some of it, because she'd sat in on several police interviews. She'd written an entire book about me and my infamous patient, and hadn't bothered to interview me. Or mention she was going to profit off one of the worst episodes of my life. It made me wonder if she'd cut me out of her life because I'd shamed her, or because she didn't want me to interfere with her research.

But I had Damian, so I left the book and I turned to him. He was funny and kind, courtly in some ways, and barbaric in others (of course I'm talking about sex). Damian was the perfect blend of gentleman and ruffian.

Broken Heart ran on an evening schedule due to all the vampires and other creatures who appreciated the dark. So we slept all day, stayed up all night, and created our very own love cocoon.

Then, on the third evening, we got a visit from Dr. Michaels.

We sat on the couch, the doctor on one end and me on the other. Damian perched on the couch's arm behind me and massaged my shoulder.

"It seems that Kelsey might have successfully transitioned to full-blood lycan," said Dr. Michaels. "However, Dante's serum has complicated the process."

My heart dove to my toes. "You mean if Jarred hadn't injected me with that crap, I'd be okay?"

"There are no guarantees, of course," he said. "But yes, I believe that would be case."

I shared a look with Damian. I could feel his concern wrap around me, and put my hand on his thigh because I needed the extra contact.

"You have an interesting genotype," continued the doctor. "One that would've no doubt remained inactive your entire life. But with the introduction of Damian's saliva into your system, this genotype was, for lack of a better word, awakened. It absorbed the new DNA and attempted to . . ." He paused, obviously searching for a word that wasn't ten syllables long. "Um, replace it. Well, part of it."

"I know that DNA strands are made up of forty-six chromosomes," I said. "And that genetic material is donated from both mother and father—twenty-three chromosomes each."

Dr. Michaels brightened. "Exactly. Half your DNA was human. The other half, too, but only as mimicry, if you will. The minute new DNA was introduced, the nonhuman chromosomes took on the characteristics of lycan."

"Changeling DNA," I blurted. I absorbed the enormity of what he was saying. I'd been only half human, which meant either of my parents had to be . . . well, something else. I could totally buy that my mother was the daughter of Satan. "But that would still make me only half werewolf."

"Well, it does now," said Stan. "My theory is that the ... er, changeling DNA would have completely reworked both sets of chromosomes. You would've been lycan."

"But the serum has interrupted the process," said Damian. Fury was building within him, and I knew it was directed at Jarred. I wanted to be angry, too, but mostly, I was scared.

"Corrupted is a better word," offered the doctor.

He was uneasy now, and I knew whatever he said next was not going to be good. For all my blithe thoughts and words about dying and living in the moment, I didn't want to face the reality that I wasn't going to make it. I wouldn't be Damian's mate or bear his children. I wouldn't be lycan. I wouldn't be *alive*.

"Whatever element was used to prevent shifting has ... I suppose 'confused' is the best word here ... the genotype. It's trying to compensate, but in ways that further disrupt the process. It's almost if it's getting conflicting information—one set of instructions from the lycan DNA and one set of instructions from the serum."

"Then it's only a matter of the serum dissipating," said Damian. "Unless you can extract it from her system."

"I can't," said Dr. Michaels. "I've tried to figure out any number of ways to help her, Damian, but the truth is that her chromosomes are a mess—and they're in a big fight."

Hope leapt inside me. "You mean the lycan DNA might win?"

I could tell he wanted to reassure me, but his integrity was too solid. He shook his head. "The process is accelerating. My estimate is that you have two weeks or less before your system overloads."

"Dante said the serum lasts thirty days," said Damian. He was grasping at straws. His fingers dug into my arm. He radiated a rainbow of emotions: anger, fear, hope.

"She doesn't have until the end of the month," said Dr. Michaels. "I'm sorry, Damian. I promise I will work night and day on a solution, but . . ."

"You don't think it's going to end well," I said. He looked so helpless that I leaned forward and patted his knee.

"A blood transfusion," said Damian. Desperation tinged his voice. "Our royal blood conquered the Taint, so why not this?"

"It conquered the Taint for a few vampires, and all of them very old. Adding more lycan DNA to her system might make her cells implode. I don't suggest we risk it."

"Then the vampires can Turn her," he said. "If Lorcan and Eva and the *loup de sang* can be both wolf and vampire, why not Kelsey?"

"Um, Kelsey isn't groovy with becoming a blood-sucker," I put in. "In case I have a vote this time."

Damian looked at me reproachfully. "The choice is yours, of course. But *loup de sang* is better than dead."

"You have a point."

"I already considered that possibility. Unfortunately, she would be toxic to a vampire," said Dr. Michaels. "It appears to be a defense mechanism of the genotype. Once the change has begun, anything interfering with it is attacked and killed."

"Like the serum," said Damian.

"Except the serum has properties that are similar enough to the genotype to make it believe its part of the process. It's why everything is screwing up," said the doctor. "The lycan DNA fights off any foreign matter, and the activated genotype fights off anything it perceives to be not lycan DNA."

"Then there's shifter DNA in the serum," I said. "It would have similar properties, but be different enough to confuse the new coding."

"It's possible," said Dr. Michaels. "But if there is shifter DNA in the serum, it's unlike any I've ever seen. And I have collected samples and information about all known shifter species." He turned his gaze to Damian. "Even if we were to drain her manually and allow a Master to perform the blood exchange and spellwork—it could have dire consequences for both the vampire and Kelsey. And that's not including the consideration that only one in ten humans can be Turned."

"You are saying we cannot help her," said Damian.

"Not yet. And maybe not in time." He stuck his hands into his jacket pockets. "I think continued quarantine until . . . um, this is over would be advisable. We don't know how it will play out. You could get more aggressive, Kelsey. Unable to control your impulses or your temper."

An uncomfortable silence fell, and the weight of it pressed on me until I wanted to scream.

"Thank you, Dr. Michaels," I said, needing the conversation to be over. Facing my own mortality, the inevitability of dying, was freaking me out.

He took the hint, offering a tepid smile as he rose from the couch. He was halfway to the door when he paused and turned around. "Not that it matters, but I should also tell you that you're in heat."

My jaw dropped. "What?"

"Elevated hormones and—" He glanced at Damian, and visibly swallowed. "Er, other factors," he said. "It's a lycan female characteristic. Every month, females have a heat cycle. You're in one."

"How long does that last?"

"Seven to fourteen days."

"Oh. Well, like you said," I responded, "it doesn't matter." And then I thought: *Lycan females are in heat two weeks every month? Sheesh.* Not that it was a hardship, mind you. At least it explained why I was so crazy to jump Damian's bones all the time.

After the doctor left, I looked up at my very worried lycan boyfriend. "I'm in heat," I said. "What's your excuse?"

"Kelsey." My name was recrimination and sorrow, and hearing the grief in his voice broke me.

"Take heart," I said, as my throat knotted and tears escaped. "You didn't kill me after all."

"No," he said, wiping away the moisture from my cheeks. "Dante did."

"And you will, no doubt, try to kill him back."

"I would," he admitted, "if he could be killed."

"Oh." Well, that explained a lot. Except the part where he wanted to claim me for himself. What would Jarred want with a woman with changeling DNA? It wasn't a question I intended to ponder, especially given my current life expectancy. I literally didn't have time to waste on answering questions that no longer mattered.

Damian stared at me, his jade eyes glittering with anguish and fury. "Would you beg for his life, Kelsey?"

"No," I said. "I would beg for my own. In fact, I have. It's not as difficult as you might believe." Then I hiccupped a sob, and let loose with a full torrent of tears.

Damian slid onto the couch, drew me into his lap, and held me tightly while I wept.

Chapter 10

The nightmare began as it always did.

Robert knew how much I liked candles because it was part of my therapeutic approach. Curtains shut, lights dimmed, candles lit. The scents of lavender and vanilla and, sometimes, sandalwood filtered into the air, mixing with the words—words filled with pain, with suffering, and when there were breakthroughs, victory.

He liked sandalwood best of all, and he'd brought a dozen thick brown candles. While the drugged girl lay in languid surrender on my couch, he put a knife against her throat and directed me about where to place his scented offerings.

It was nearly August, and the Oklahoma nights were hot and moist. Venturing outside often felt like falling into a vat of simmering water. It was a misery, but beauty was out there, too, once you learned how to breathe. Then you could see the lightning bugs mimicking stars, and the trees reaching toward the velvet sky, and mixed in with this palette was fragrant sweetness of honeysuckle blooms and the music of crickets and windswept grass. Brushes of color and scent and sound. Green

Country, as they called this part of the state. It had been my home, my sanctuary.

And he took it away. The meaning of it. The security. Worst of all, the hope.

It was a difficult thing to watch evil bloom, to see it triumph over the meagerness of prayers, of begging deities for a single, pure miracle. Mercy was a gift, and neither God nor Robert had been in the mood to bestow it.

It was true that Robert had not broken me. But that night, something inside me was lost, locked away into the dark, still corners that even psychotherapists dared not tread.

He'd wanted to unleash the beast he felt lurked within me, but instead, he had imprisoned it. It wasn't the creature of his fevered imagination—it was instead a monster of discontent and fury and fear. I had known my whole life that I was not the daughter my mother wanted. In fact, no matter where I turned or what I tried, I did not seem to be a girl that anyone wanted. I was different, and people seemed to know that, even though I looked the same as they did. I was human . . . and yet I was not.

Blood will tell.

He'd said that, but he'd said a lot of other things, too. Given that my definition of crazy had been turned upside down and shaken vigorously, I couldn't say now if Robert was truly insane, or had been touched by the paranormal. He'd seen in me what others reacted to on a primitive level—but he hadn't shied away from it. He had embraced it. He'd wanted to draw it out. Make it his friend. His partner.

The inner me. The outer me.

One must die, so the other can live.

After I watched Robert murder the girl, after I fought for my own life and took his, I had a revelation: I did not belong in this world.

It's funny how the serial killer and I now agreed on that singular point, though for entirely different reasons. I fought a sense of doom from the day I woke up in the hospital. I plodded forward—through the physical and mental recovery, the police and FBI interviews, the lawsuits, the public condemnation, my mother's abandonment and betrayal, the bad job and crappy apartment. Every day that I got to wake up and take a breath felt undeserved. And I wanted so badly to deserve my second chance.

And now, while I stood in my own living room with its leather furniture and glass tables and chrome accents, lighting candles so Robert could begin his sick ritual, I felt the beast stir.

I was awakening.

"You feel it now, don't you?" asked Robert. The knife dug into the girl's throat; blood beaded at the tiny wound, then fell like a teardrop.

"Yes," I said. "You were right."

"It's too late for me to help you. I tried, you know. But you're stubborn."

"I didn't want your help. And I'm not sorry you're dead, either."

"That's the beast," he said, his voice thick with satisfaction. "Have some gratitude, Kelsey. If it wasn't for me, you wouldn't know about your father's little indiscretion. You wouldn't have discovered your true path."

I jolted. "Indiscretion?"

He gave me a long look that I interpreted as "yeah, right, like you didn't know." "Duh. You're only half human. Your mother is a bitch on wheels. You ever think she has a reason to resent you?"

Cold sweat slicked my spine. "This isn't about my mother."

"Oh, but it is."

I lit the last candle, then carefully put down the

lighter. I stood on the other side of the coffee table, watching him huddle against his victim, the knife sharp and wicked against her quivering flesh. "Why didn't you let her live?" I asked.

He flashed me a sunny smile. "Why didn't you?"

Then he slashed her throat in one big, vicious jerk

The blood sprayed over us both.

It hadn't been like this in the reality. He'd tied me to the chair, placing me at an angle so I could see her face. He used the coffee table like an altar. He'd stripped her bare and made little Xs on her body—the points, he said, where the essence flowed from. Then he waited for the drugs to leave her system, just enough to realize she was being murdered.

But now, in the dream, Robert sat on the couch, his hands wrapped in her long blond hair, his gaze on mine as we endured the gruesome baptism. Its foul warmth covered us both until all I could see and taste and feel was the blood of an innocent.

Sacrifice is necessary.

In the blink of an eye, my living room disappeared. I stood in a circular clearing caged by tall trees. Above me, the full moon gleamed like a pearl tucked into black silk.

Aufanie and Tark's glen now held a stone altar—but not them. They were gone, and with them, the hushed sense that this place was sacred.

Robert had defiled it.

On the altar lay a naked, unconscious woman. Robert, dressed in a gray robe, stood on the dais, his features harsh as he used a dagger to carve on her stomach.

"Come here," he demanded harshly. "This is the path to understanding."

I was drawn to Robert, and to the altar. I didn't want to go, but my feet moved anyway. In moments, I stood next to him, yet again his unwilling, chosen victim. Anger pulsed hotly through my veins. *You shouldn't be here,* I wanted to yell. *You've ruined it! You've ruined me!*

But I couldn't get my lips to move, or my throat to work. My protests remained locked inside, and so, too, my unfurling rage.

"Do you see?" he asked.

Reluctantly, I looked at the symbols he'd etched into her flesh. One looked like an upside down cross with circles on three ends. At the top was a bigger circle. Flaring out from the intersection were two curved lines. The other mark was a three-pronged arrow with a small triangle base.

"Nature. Wolf. Silver. Moon." He pointed up toward the woman's chest. "Mate."

My gaze locked on to the symbol above the woman's left breast, and the air left my body in a whoosh. Damian's symbol.

Oh, God.

The face of the sacrificial victim was mine.

"One must die, so the other can live," said Robert.

I heard chanting, but the words had no meaning. The thrum of the voices, though, wound through me like serpents, hissing and coiling. I watched as he slit the victim's wrist and held a silver chalice underneath to catch the stream of black blood.

When it was full, Robert cawed and held up the silver cup. An image of a raven was engraved on it, along with the symbols I'd seen carved into the woman's—into *my*—stomach.

"To the beast within," he shouted, and then he drank.

Inside me, beyond the shadows of my soul, something awful stirred.

I felt my bones crack and my muscles peel away. The beast nestled inside me, the one that felt like shame, like regret, clawed its way to the surface. A voluminous blackness burst around me, and there was pain, so much of it. I fell onto my side, screaming in agony. My skin flaked off, my hair shed, and then . . . I felt everything shift back together, but in a completely wrong way.

I was reborn.

I lifted my snout to the sky, and howled.

"Take what's yours," shouted Robert. "Wolf of Silver!"

Stupid human. I felt the power, the strength in my muscles, the fury that beat within me with the same ferocity of my pounding heart. I leapt and knocked him down. The chalice flew out of his grip and bounced on the ground, the blood splashing onto the soil.

He looked at me, and laughed and laughed.

My jaws snapped down.

I easily ripped out his throat.

I woke up, heart thudding as I bolted upright. Damian came instantly awake, sitting up and putting his arms around me. He nestled his chin on my shoulder.

"What is it?" he asked, his voice thick with sleep.

"Dream," I said in a hushed voice. "A really weird one. And considering my track record with nightmares, that's saying a lot."

"I'm here," he said. "You're safe."

"I know." I leaned against him, taking comfort in the solidness of his embrace. "Does silver kill werewolves?"

"Not usually," he said. "Unless there's a lot of it. Even a little burns like a son of a bitch, though. Silver has magical properties. Most metallic substances do. And any of them can be used to hurt or imprison paranormal creatures." He kissed my neck. Then he yawned. "Except vampires. Nothing kills them except extreme exposure to light and beheading."

"I'm sure anything dies if it's beheaded."

"Not necessarily."

"Really? Do I want to know?"

"Nein." He fell back and dragged me with him. I snuggled against his side, my head resting on his chest. "You dreamed about silver? Is that a hint for jewelry?"

I smacked him on the pectoral. "No." Then I peeked up at him. "Maybe."

He chuckled. He hugged me closer, which caused a flurry of warm fuzzies. "Tell me about the dream, Kelsey."

I told him everything, and when I was finished, he was silent. While he was getting his thoughts together, I let my hand wander over his chest. I trailed my fingertips over his stomach, heading right for the goods, but he stilled my fingers and folded them within his hand.

"I wasn't going to hurt you," I said petulantly. What can I say? This being in heat thing made me grumpy.

"There are different kinds of pain, *Schätzchen*," he responded softly. "Do you believe dreams are portents?"

"I believe dreams can be important."

"Will you remember these symbols tomorrow?"

"Yes," I said.

"And you are sure you saw a raven on the chalice?"

"Well, I'm not familiar with every bird species on the planet, but I'm pretty sure it was a raven."

"I feel certain this dream was a message—one meant to help us."

"You think Aufanie sent it?"

He tensed. "Perhaps."

"Why do you hate her so much, Damian?"

He let my hand go, and I flattened it against his spectacular abs. I was trying to resist the buzzing need in my body, which insisted I stop talking and start grooving. Damian rolled on top of me and nuzzled my neck.

"We're not gonna talk about it, are we?"

"Nien."

He started doing some very interesting things with his hands, all designed to distract me, of course, and I let him.

I was an official werewolf slut.

When I awoke, I was alone. Panic seized me for all of a minute, until I realized that Damian had left on the bed-side lamp and the door to the bedroom was wide open, allowing the hallway light to spill inside.

After I killed Robert, I hadn't had a single full night's rest—at least not until I had gotten the job at the Dante Clinic. I'd been so reassured by the security that I'd been able to relax enough to take a sleeping pill. When I lived alone in my tiny, crappy apartment, I hadn't dared to take even a Tylenol PM. I couldn't dampen my alertness. Between the nightmares and panic attacks, I never slept more than a couple hours at a time.

And now, with Damian, I felt secure, too. But I was still dealing badly with being alone for any length of time. I felt like a wimp, and even though I knew, not only from a human perspective, but also from a therapist perspective, that my feelings and actions were normal responses to the trauma I'd suffered—I couldn't quiet the voice that whispered incessantly about my cowardice. I had killed Robert. I had survived. And I was still hostage to the terror he'd invoked.

I sat up, and before I had shoved off the bedcovers, Damian appeared in the doorway. He was dressed in a T-shirt that molded to his sculpted chest and a pair of faded, tight jeans. He wore black boots, too. His hair had been tied back, making his gorgeous face look even gorgeous-er. Damn, the man was sexy.

He held a cup of coffee in one hand and a cupcake in the other. "Breakfast?"

"Is it the cupcake?" I asked. "Or you?"

"Ravenous creature," he said, chuckling. "As much as I want to be your breakfast, we are expecting a guest."

"Oh." My disappointment was keen. "In the next five minutes?"

"Five minutes will not be enough time," he said, putting the mug onto the nightstand and offering me the chocolate cupcake.

"Is that a challenge?"

"Hmm." He considered me for a moment, then sighed deeply. "No. However, I reserve the right to rechallenge you at a later time."

I grinned. As I licked off the frosting—much to Damian's consternation—I felt the faint edges of his anticipation and impatience. I frowned up at him. "What are you expecting?"

His brows winged upward. Then he shook his head. "Ah. Your superpower is tingling, *ja*?"

"Ja," I said.

"My brothers may have tracked down Dante. I am waiting to see if they've been successful in . . . ah, acquiring him."

I almost dropped my cupcake. Instead, I put it on the nightstand next to the coffee cup. "You went after Jarred?"

He peeled back his lips and gave a little growl. "I do not like your familiarity with the man."

"Jealousy suggests insecurity," I said. "And you are not insecure."

"It is not insecurity," he said, obviously affronted. "He hurt you. He lied to you. And he wanted to mate with you. You are mine. I cannot tolerate . . ." He trailed off, apparently trying to find the right word. Then he gazed at me and said, "Competition."

"If I only want you," I pointed out gently, "then how can anyone else be competition?"

He blinked at me. "That's very a logical approach. But werewolves do not use logic when it comes to their mates."

I stopped short of saying that I wasn't his mate, not officially. But I didn't want to put that out there between us, not when the clock was ticking down on my life. We were for each other, as he'd once said, and that had to be enough.

"When did you decide to go after Jarred?"

"The moment we got back to Broken Heart. A team was dispatched immediately to the clinic, but it was cleared out. Dante, his staff, and all the patients had disappeared. My brothers have been tracking him since."

"So the whole time that I've been in quarantine with you . . . your brothers have been trying to find Dante."

He looked at me questioningly, studying my expression. "Is this something I should've discussed with you?" he asked.

He sounded genuinely curious, and his honest inquiry checked my growing irritation. Was it really my concern if anyone from Broken Heart wanted to chase down Dante? I hadn't been the only one affected by the man's manipulations and lies. I wasn't as angry at him, but I did have to wonder about his motives. What was the point of his clinic? Why had he chosen those patients? And how had he found me—the woman with changeling DNA?

"I don't know," I said slowly. "Probably not."

"Yet you are upset that I did not tell you we were trying to bring him in."

"If you're worried that I care about him, then—" I stopped, surprised to realize that I did care about Jarred. I'd never been able to read his emotions, but up until the night he'd admitted he wanted to seduce me, he'd done nothing but offer kindnesses I could never repay. I couldn't discount the job, the money, or the security—yes, all payment for his grand hope we would be together. But I knew that Jarred was a wounded creature, in search of something—or someone—that he might never find. He'd mistaken me for his answer. I pitied him. And now that I could examine what had happened, I realized he'd given me the serum to save me. Although it could be argued the gesture was selfish. After all, he'd wanted me, and he was beyond pissed off that Damian had gotten to me first.

"You do care about him," said Damian stiffly.

"Yes," I admitted. "But he made his bed. He'll have to lie in it. I don't want to save him. Or plead his case. He's an attractive man, but I'm not attracted to him." I put my hand on Damian's arm. "And if you dare say that I only like you because you bit me, I'll . . . I'll . . . punch you in the head."

"I tremble at the thought," he said dryly. He picked up my hand and turned it, kissing my wrist. It seemed to be his signature make-Kelsey-melt gesture, and it worked every time. "I will try to control myself better."

"Well," I said. "Not too much."

He laughed. "Come, *Schätzchen*. Brigid will be here soon. You must shower and dress."

"I'm showering alone, aren't I?"

"To my great regret."

"Fine," I groused. "But I'm eating my cupcake first."

A half hour later, I was showered, dressed, and tucked onto the couch in the living room to await our guest. Damian joined me, and put his arm around my shoulders. I snuggled close.

"Who is Brigid?" I asked.

"Patrick and Lorcan's grandmother," he said. "The mother of Ruadan."

"Our rescue vampires."

"*Ja*. She is a revered goddess of healing. You will like her."

"Goddess. A real goddess? And she's just coming over like a regular person?"

Damian chuckled. "There is nothing regular about Brigid. She has a soft spot for Broken Heart and its residents. She is immortal, one of the beings, like Aufanie, who was worshiped in ancient times."

"Wow." Nerves plucked at my guts. Technically, I'd already met a real goddess and god, but that had been too surreal, and it was not the same as one popping by in real time. *Hello, I'm Brigid, your local goddess, here's a welcome-to-the-paranormal-world gift basket.*

"You think she can work some magic on me and fix the DNA issues?"

"I don't know," he said. "But it's worth a try."

I felt a shift in the air, a tingling sensation, and there was a pop of gold sparkles. Damian was on his feet, pulling me up with him, before the glitter had faded to reveal a very tall, very beautiful redhead with the strangest tattoos I'd ever seen. She wore a long green dress that matched the shade of her eyes. Her hair was streamers of red curls that reached her hips. And she wasn't wearing shoes.

"Damian," she said in an Irish-tinged voice. She stepped forward and bussed his cheek. Then she turned to me. "And you must be Kelsey. Oh, you're lovely, you are."

"Thanks," I said. "Nice to meet you." I wasn't sure if I should curtsy or something. I could feel the power emanating from the woman. It wasn't emotions—like all the immortals I'd met thus far, her feelings were inaccessible. No, this was raw, pulsating power.

Brigid took my hand and squeezed. "Shall we take a look, then?"

Damian moved away so the goddess could sit with me on the couch. Her dress revealed impressive cleavage and left her arms bare. The swirling gold symbols on her skin shifted into different shapes—none of which I recognized. I was utterly fascinated, and it took all my self-control not to poke her.

"It's my *draíocht*," explained Brigid. "Magic. The symbols change to accommodate the needs of the one to be healed." She took both my hands into hers and closed her eyes. I felt my whole body prickle, as though I had a bad case of static electricity. I glanced at Damian, who'd remained standing and watched us with worried eyes.

"Aiteacht," she murmured. She opened her eyes and shook her head slightly. "This is a wrong that I cannot right." Her gaze was sympathetic. "I'm sorry."

"So it's not like you're a genie who can grant wishes, right?"

"I have limitations. All power must have its checks and balances, and your problem does not fall within my domain. You are Aufanie's child now."

"Tell her about your dream," said Damian tightly. "Tell her about the symbols and the raven chalice." His gaze had gone hard. Ah, he was invoking Statue Man. Well, I was upset, too, though it hardly helped to rail against fate. Maybe I'd fall apart later. Or have a cupcake. And sex with Damian.

"You dreamed about a raven chalice?" asked Brigid in surprise. "'Tis one of my mother's tokens."

"And she would be . . ."

"The Morrigu," said Brigid.

"We're talking an Ireland connection?" I knew bupkus about the Celtic pantheon. The psychiatric community preferred to use Greek tragedies as analogies. (I'm looking at you, Oedipus. You, too, Electra.)

"The crow queen. The Goddess of Battle and Discord. She likes to stirs things up, she does. Everyone has a purpose, Kelsey, but not everyone's purpose is nice."

"Chaos needs order and that kind of thing."

She nodded. "Your dream was an augury, to be sure. Show me the other symbols."

Damian retrieved pencil and paper for me, and I drew the two images Robert had carved into flesh. The third one belonged to Damian. I looked up at him, a silent question in my eyes. He nodded, so I drew the tattoo as well. Brigid studied them for a long moment. "These two are alchemist's symbols." She pointed to the three-pronged one. "This one means silver. And its astrological meaning is moon. And this," she said as she tapped the other one, "represents antimony. It symbolizes the wildness of nature and it's also associated with the wolf." She gazed up at me, smiling. "And you know this one, do you not? It's a very old symbol used by the Germanic peoples. If you turn it vertical, it's called *Donnerkeil*."

"Thunderbolt," said Damian.

"But used horizontally, as it is here, it is *Wolfsangel*. The wolf's hook." She glanced at Damian. "It means werewolf."

"The *Wehrmacht* stole many lycanthrope symbols," said Damian. "Including mine."

His voice was flat and emotionless, and I ached for him, for the losses he'd suffered. Though I wasn't a math genius, it wasn't difficult to add it all up. Sixty years ago, Damian lived in Germany, in the very country that started World War II. Oh, crap. What had happened to Damian's village? Who had attacked the werewolves? And who had killed his pregnant wife? Were they also the ones who had taken his sister and then killed her?

"What about Morrigu?" asked Damian.

"Ah, yes. Perhaps we should call her in for a consultation." Brigid settled herself against the couch and closed her eyes. Within moments, the air felt electrified. I could feel the hair on the back of my neck stand on end . . . then *bang!* A gray mist roiled up from out of nowhere, and when it dissipated, a tall, willowy woman stood on the other side of the coffee table. She wore a hooded green robe and held within her bejeweled grasp a gnarled, polished wood staff. At its top sat a gleaming silver crow.

She pulled back her hood. Her ink black hair hung in long, silken ringlets around a pale, unlined face. A thin silver crown nestled on her head, a single red stone glittering from its middle. Her dark eyes fastened on me, and for a scary moment, I could see rivers of blood bisecting a muddy landscape, the cries and grunts of soldiers as they fought with swords and pikes, and above it all, the screech of crows. Then she turned away from me and inclined her head toward Brigid. "Daughter." Her gaze flicked toward Damian. "Child of Aufanie."

Damian offered a curt, courtly bow, but it didn't take my empath abilities to see he didn't like being addressed that way. And though I couldn't read Morrigu at all, I could see she found amusement in both the term and in Damian's irritation. Queen of Chaos, all right. Sheesh.

"So," she said, her gaze once again swinging toward me. "You are the one who will save the lycans." She cocked her head in a birdlike manner, looking very much like a raven. "Hmm. You're dyin'. If you breathe your last before the Winter Solstice, you won't fulfill your prophecy."

"I can tell you're all broken up about it," I said.

She smirked. "Ask me your question."

I explained about the symbols, showing her the paper on which I'd drawn them. Then I told her about the part of my dream that featured the silver chalice with its raven engraving—and how Robert had filled it with my blood. "What does it all mean?"

Morrigu pursed her lips as she stared at me, obviously trying to decide how much information, if any, she wanted to share. "You've been given instructions about how to save yourself. Aufanie can't contact you anymore, can she? Seems you're more lycan than human already."

That also meant my DNA was going to go postal soon, too. Not a happy thought.

"She told me about the bargain," I said. "And how she can't talk to the lycans." I considered the implications of that chalice, and made an intuitive leap. "What did she promise you in return for Tark's life?"

Morrigu chuckled. "I won't deny my part." She shook her head. "Aufanie's always been too softhearted. Always looking for a cause, that one. Do you know how werewolves came to be?"

Damian opened his mouth, but Morrigu pounded the staff on the floor. "Don't repeat that drivel the temple priestesses spout. Neither Aufanie nor Tark created the full-bloods or the Roma. Zeus did."

We stared at her. I was fascinated, as was Brigid, but Damian looked as though someone had just stuck a knife in his heart. I wanted to leap off the couch and comfort him. But he must've sensed my intention because he gave me a look that basically said: *Please, don't.* So I stayed put. And if I was hurt by that rejection, I tamped it down. I was a tough werewolf now, damn it.

"In ancient Arcadia, there was a village called Lycosoura. Fools got it into their heads to worship Zeus as a wolf. Called themselves the Cult of Zeus Lycaeus and every nine years, they hosted a festival. When Zeus heard there were orgies, he couldn't resist a visit." Morrigu rolled her eyes. "He's the horniest bastard you'll ever meet."

"Mother," said Brigid in a choked voice.

"Well, he is," said Morrigu tartly. "So he disguised himself and joined some Romani who'd been summoned as entertainers. Spent the whole day and evening drinking and feasting and whoring.

"Midnight came, and everyone gathered in the town square and drew lots. Zeus, who was drunk and oversexed, believed he was playin' a game. He lost the draw. He was taken to the makings of a bonfire and tied up as the sacrifice. Not only did they plan to kill him, in his own honor"—and here, Morrigu snickered—"but they wanted to cook and eat him, too." She paused, as though considering the perks of humans eating humans (or gods disguised as humans). If she said, "What's the big deal? Humans taste like chicken," I would hurl—on her and her fancy robe. But she shrugged and continued the story. "Everyone started dancin' around and howlin'. Zeus was so furious that he took his god form and started throwin' around those fancy lightning bolts of his. Then he cursed the whole town. Turned everyone into lycanthropes. Not even his Romani friends escaped his wrath, but they received a lesser punishment, only turning into wolves on full-moon nights."

"Donnerkeil," said Brigid. "Thunderbolt."

Morrigu nodded. "Tark was the one who turned the symbol sideways and gave it a new meaning."

I saw Brigid looked at Damian, her expression seven kinds of worry. "Did you know any of this?" she asked.

He shook his head. His hands were fisted at his sides. He kept his emotions buried, but I could feel the whispers of his shock. He'd never heard this story before. Everything he'd known about his origins was a lie. I opened up my ability and reached out to him, wrapping him in empathy. He visibly relaxed, and sent me a grateful look.

"If Zeus is the reason lycans exist, then why is Aufanie our goddess?" asked Damian hoarsely.

"Once Zeus spent his ire, he forgot about the creatures. They roamed everywhere, hunting whatever, or whoever, they could find. Over the years, humans killed many of them. Then Tark was born. He became the first alpha. He banded the full-bloods together, led them all to Schwarzwald. To Aufanie's territory."

"What about the Roma?" I asked. *What?* I didn't like stories with loose ends.

"They had smaller populations, and like their human ancestors, they preferred travelin' to settling down. They became mercenaries, hired by villages to hunt and kill vampires, and other creatures who menaced humans."

"Aufanie fell in love with Tark," said Brigid. Her expression was tinted with surprise. She hadn't known the true lycanthrope history, either. It appears no one had. "But he wasn't immortal."

"Not then," agreed Morrigu. "He was just a werewolf. Long-lived, to be sure, but what was eight hundred years to a goddess? She couldn't bear the thought of living without him, especially after she realized she was pregnant."

"Nein," said Damian. "Stop."

We all looked at him. He'd gone pale, and this time, I couldn't stop myself from getting up and going to him. I wrapped my arms around his waist and gave him all the support I could. He put his arm around me and held me tight, but his tortured gaze was on Morrigu.

"You don't want to hear the truth?" asked Morrigu coyly. "Or you don't want her to hear it?"

"Mother," admonished Brigid. "What are you trying to do?"

"I'm answering the girl's question," she snapped.

"In the most roundabout way possible," I said, irritated with the woman's dramatics. "And you're trying to hurt him."

"He caused his own pain. His choices have naught to do with me," said Morrigu. The gleam in her eyes was not reassuring. "I offered to give Tark immortality, but the price was a hundred years banishment for them both—to be taken whenever I chose, without question."

"You banished them." Damian's fury was building, the impetus, of course, his own grief, guilt, and years of resentment, all because Morrigu was fulfilling her purpose of chaos.

"World War II. Hadn't had a good battle in a while, right?" I asked softly. "Afraid the lycans might interfere?"

"Not in the way you believe," offered Morrigu coolly. "Perhaps there were other bargains to fulfill—other prices that needed payin'."

"Back to riddles, are we?" I asked.

Morrigu shrugged. "Aufanie got what she wanted—an immortal husband. And then she bore him triplet sons." Her knowing gaze latched on to Damian, and I heard Brigid's breath go out in a soft rush.

I stared up at him, my heart in my throat. *Sweet mamma jamma.* "You're the son of a goddess?"

Chapter 11

Damian met my gaze, and I saw within those strange green eyes the silent plea for understanding. "Yes," he admitted. "My brothers and I are the true sons of Aufanie and Tark. But we didn't know. They lived as the alphas of the governing pack. We were raised as royal heirs, not knowing that our mother was the same goddess we worshiped."

"She never told you?" asked Brigid, horror in her words.

"A century ago she told us the truth," he said bitterly. He glanced at Morrigu. "One truth, it appears. Then she and my father disappeared. Our world was crumbling. More and more lycans were diagnosed with sterility, and nearly half of those who did conceive buried their children a year later. Many left the safety of Schwarzwald. It took forty years of bridging the gap between us and our cousins, but we managed to build a new village, and a new pack with Roma."

I had so many questions buzzing around in my mind that it felt like a hive. I couldn't grab on to just one inquiry, but that might have had something to do with the fact I was in shock. I'd been sleeping with a guy who was, for all intents and purposes, an actual god. Well, a half god. I could read no other immortal's emotions but Damian's. What did that mean?

Morrigu had known the truth. Why would she keep such knowledge to herself for so long? Had it been part of the bargain with Aufanie? Or had she just been waiting for the right moment, such as this one, to offer it up so that she could gain something for herself?

I looked at Brigid. "Why didn't you know? Why didn't anyone else know?"

"No one can know everything. Not even the gods," she said. "Zeus would not have told the tale, not when he'd have to admit being imprisoned by his own worshipers." Her gaze flicked to her mother's stoic expression. "My mother is very good at ferretin' out secrets."

"That I am." Her gaze zeroed in on me. "And to be sure, there is a price to be paid for everything."

I'd heard the same spiel from Jarred, although he'd said everyone had a price. I knew both sentiments to be true, but I think Morrigu was trying to warn me about upcoming events. Either that, or scare me. And let me just say: mission accomplished.

Morrigu gestured to the papers scattered on the coffee table. "There's your answer, girl."

We all looked down at the table. Brigid was the first to understand. "It's an equation. A formula."

Comprehension dawned as I fit all the pieces together. The dream. The symbols. *The blood.* I glanced at Morrigu. "I need your blood to make it all work, don't I?"

"And the chalice."

I studied her. Her expression offered no clues about her emotions or her intentions. Only her dark eyes hinted at what she hoped I would do. But I'd been raised by a master manipulator, and I'd learned a thing or two.

"Do you have the chalice?" I asked.

Her lips thinned. "No."

"But you know where it is," I conjectured. "And we'll have to retrieve it in order to perform whatever ritual will complete my lycan transition."

"If I decide to help you," said Morrigu, raising her chin and looking down her nose at me. "What use are you to me, or to the world, if you are dead? The risk may be too great." She sniffed. "Destiny is as malleable as clay."

I wasn't interested in playing games. Or being reminded that I was dying. I was sick of portents and dreams and the whims of immortals. I raised an eyebrow. "Is it that you're incapable of speaking plainly ... or do you just like fucking with everyone because you can?"

Brigid sucked in a shocked breath, and even Damian looked at me in alarm. Morrigu's gaze narrowed. "You dare speak to me in such a manner?"

"Do you know it's the twenty-first century?" I responded. "Maybe you should consider updating your language database." I eyed her. "And your style. It's hard to look like a badass when you're stuck in medieval fashions." I sent an apologetic glance to Brigid. I was trying to rile her mother, not insult her.

Morrigu's eyes flashed, with what emotion I couldn't begin to discern. Fury. Sadness. Boredom. Who knew?

Then she laughed.

It wasn't even an evil I-will-smite-you laugh, either. It was more in the oh-you-funny-girl category. She leaned the staff toward me. "You are a fool, Kelsey Morningstone, but you have balls." She looked at me smugly. "How's that for updated language?"

"Meh," I said. "You'll learn."

Morrigu looked shocked for a moment, and then she

slowly smiled. "You have much to learn as well. Perhaps we can come to an agreement. However, for your rudeness, the price is higher now."

"Forget it."

A speculative gleam entered her eyes. I pulled free of Damian and crossed the room to stand in front her. She understood I was putting us on equal ground, and while she didn't like it, she seemed *almost* to respect the action. Of course, this was guesswork based on the quicksilver expressions I saw cross her face.

"You cannot save yourself without my blood."

"Aufanie will gladly make the offering," said Damian.

Morrigu laughed. "It's my bargain, boy. And my chalice. No other god's essence will work the needed magic. And I will not give it to you unless you agree to my terms."

"No. I won't let you dangle your 'higher price' like a guillotine over our necks," I said. "We get you the chalice. You make the formula with your blood and let me drink it from your fancy cup. We'll do the exchange on the Winter Solstice in Aufanie's temple."

Morrigu stepped into my personal space and stared daggers at me. "I do not accept."

"Fine." I shrugged and turned away. Damian stood rock-still, his face ice white. The fear slivered in his gaze staggered me. What the hell? Had no one ever stood up to Morrigu?

"You're not afraid of me," she said in wonderment.

"I'm terrified of you," I corrected. "But I won't let fear guide my actions. Not ever again." I whirled back around and put my hands on my hips. "Admit you sent me the dream."

Her mouth dropped open. She quickly closed it, and huffed. "You are too clever for your own good."

"No, I'm too clever for *your* own good. For some reason you need us, and you're trying to play it the other way." It was my turn to smirk, but I kept it quick and light. No need to push the woman to the point she decided to aim that staff at my head. "Do we have a deal?"

She said nothing for a long moment. Tension threatened to suffocate the whole room. Finally, she nodded. "So long as Damian agrees to the terms, then we do."

"I agree," he said.

"Very well. The bargain is made." Morrigu stepped back, and a gray mist started billowing from the floor around her. Her gaze went to Damian. "Your mother took the chalice and hid it from me. Good luck finding it." As she started to fade, she turned toward me, offering one final smirk. "See you on the Solstice . . . if you live."

Then she disappeared.

For a long while no one spoke. Then Brigid heaved herself off the couch. She rounded the coffee table and enveloped me in her arms. She hugged me tightly, and then let me go. "I think my mother likes you."

"How can you tell?" I asked.

"You're alive." Brigid turned to Damian. "You're going to Germany, then."

"It seems so. My mother wished for us to be in the temple on Winter Solstice, too. It appears our fates will be determined there."

"What about Patsy? And Broken Heart?"

"One trial at a time, *Frau*," he said.

She inclined her head as both acknowledgment and good-bye. Then the air went electric, gold sparkles lit the air, and she was gone in the blink of an eye.

"Can werewolves do that at all?" I asked. "Because that's a cool superpower."

"The *loup de sang* can," he said, "but only because they are part vampire."

I stepped away, too agitated to either stand still or sit down. I wandered into the kitchen, and opened the fridge. Damian followed me, watching as I pulled out a can of Sprite. "Want one?" I asked.

"No, thank you."

I stared at the can, and realized I didn't really want it, either. So I returned it to the case and shut the door.

"I should've told you," he said.

"You mean about being a god?" I asked.

"Demigod," he said. "Tark was mortal when we were conceived."

"So you're not immortal?"

He looked away, swallowing hard, and then returned his gaze to mine. "My mother's blood will allow me to live forever," he said carefully, "but I can be killed. Not easily, that's true. A pure-blood immortal cannot die."

"Your sudden concern about babies happened *after* our little visit to Dr. Michaels. You didn't really believe Dante, did you? You thought he did something else to me, and I wasn't at risk to have children. Then the doc tells me I'm going lycan, and you realize what that means."

"Kelsey."

"Don't! Your DNA and Jarred's are inside me, without my permission. If either of you were regular paranormals, then the lycan DNA would triumph. I'd be okay. Well, if turning into a werewolf can be considered okay—not to mention whatever the hell Jarred is."

"Nobody knows," he said. "We thought him a friend."

"Yeah? Me, too." I threw my hands up in the air, and started pacing. "The only way I'll survive is if this formula and ritual of Morrigu's works. And that doesn't even include the dream hint that my changeling DNA was donated by someone other than the woman who raised me. If that's true, it means I was paranormal this

whole time. I mean, other than the whole empath thing."
I paused. "Or maybe that's why I'm an empath." I
rubbed my face. My brain felt like a tornado had blown
through it and wrecked all my thoughts.

Damian grasped my arm, but I pulled out of his grip.
"I don't want to be coddled. I'm angry with you. I need
some space."

"All right," he said.

His sorrow and regret whispered to me, so I put up
my shields. Not that it did much good. It seemed Damian's feelings were armor-piercing rounds.

His cell phone rang. I think we were both relieved by
the interruption. He took the cell from his front jeans
pocket and looked at the display. "It's Darrius."

"News about Jarred," I said. "You should take it."

I returned to the living room and picked up the copy
of *Werewolves Are Real!*, which I had already skimmed
through several times. Damian told me that the author
lived in town part-time, and she and her husband had
spent a lifetime researching and studying the paranormal. Then their daughter, Libby, got turned into a half
dragon. She lived in Broken Heart, too, along with her
vampire husband and their family.

This town was beyond weird.

"They have Dante," said Damian as he entered the
living room. "He's in one of our holding cells. He's re-
quested to see you."

"I don't want to see him," I said. "You should go. But
don't hurt him."

He grimaced. "I promised not to leave you, Kelsey."

"Well, if I want you to leave, that's not breaking your
promise," I said. "Just go. I'll stay here and read and try
to get my equilibrium back."

"Can you forgive me?" he asked. He sounded so pitiful, my heart twisted.

I stood up and crossed the distance between us. "It's a lot to think about, Damian. You're not just a lycan, you're almost immortal. What does that mean for me? For us?" I looked into his eyes. "Why didn't you tell me?"

"No one knew," he said. "My parents asked us to keep it secret."

"But I'm not just anyone, am I?" I shook my head, sadness a weight inside my chest. "You were waiting to see if I survived."

His expression confirmed my supposition, as did the regret that arrowed through my pitiful psychic shield. For some reason, a random piece of our last conversation with Dr. Michaels popped into my mind.

"Your blood saved some vampires—the ones who can turn into wolves."

"Not the *loup de sang*," he clarified. "But, yes. A few years ago, a disease called the Taint was killing vampires. It was incurable. When Lorcan got it, my brothers and I offered our blood to do the transfusions."

"Because demigod blood would trump the disease."

"It also gave him, and a couple of others, the ability to shape-shift into our forms. And when Lorcan shared his blood with his wife, Eva, she gained the same ability."

"And they were already immortal, right? So you didn't have to worry they might discover your secret." I sighed. "You've lied to everyone."

He didn't deny it.

"It makes everything else you've done worse," I said. "You understand that, don't you? You gave up on the pack, fired yourself as the leader, and found somewhere to hide. Your mother is the goddess who embraced a cursed people—and you abandoned them."

"They found a new queen." The words dropped like acid, but he couldn't hide from me. He'd carried that guilt, too. Probably the only time in his life he'd failed to honor his duties, which was why he tried so hard now to fulfill them. It was impossible to change the past, but no one could heal from old wounds unless they acknowledged their mistakes, and yes, felt every ounce of that pain. It sounded weird, but bearing responsibility for your actions actually lifted the emotional weight. I owned that I'd messed up with Robert. What I did to him allowed him to take innocent lives. I could never change that. But I could learn from it. I could keep vigilant over my gift and remember that it was not my place to fix people. People had to fix themselves.

Damian was still imprisoned by his past, trapped in the pain of wounds that would never heal. He wouldn't let them. And until he faced that pain, and made peace with his past, he would always be ruled by the emotions he tried so hard to bury.

"They needed a new leader, didn't they?" I asked, keeping my voice gentle. "Did you ever consider your decision to leave Germany and let the pack scatter is why Patsy was made queen? If the lycans had their true leader, she wouldn't have been necessary."

He stared at me, his expression stony. "You weren't there. After we buried our dead, we found out that several lycans had been captured, including Danielle. We got there too late to save her, to save any of them."

"I'm sorry," I said. "What happened to you and to your village was terrible. But you can't let it rule your life—not like this. If you want that tragedy to be motivation for your decisions, then let it be for the good."

"You think I forced the creation of the prophecy."

"Isn't that what Astria hinted at when she was trying to explain the nature of prophecies? Damian, I've met Patsy once and even I can see how overwhelmed she is. She's one person with all these powers and responsibilities, not to mention trying to be a wife and mother. It's too much for her."

"So the Vederes see a new prophecy in which she is no longer queen of lycans or vampires? Only of the *loup de sang*?" He shook his head. "She has the seven powers of the Ancients."

Something niggled at me. "Aren't there eight?" I asked. That was me, mistress of the inconsequential.

"She could not absorb the eighth power," he said distractedly. "My parents will be free of Morrigu's bargain on the Winter Solstice. It is not coincidence that a new prophecy has appeared."

"Because you're ready. Because it's time. And you know it."

"If the prophecy is true, then you are my mate." He put a hand on my stomach, and I sucked in a breath. "Hope renewed."

"Let's just see if I can get through the next week and a half, okay?" I kissed his cheek and then backed away. "Go see Jarred. Maybe if we find out what's in the serum, it'll help."

"Things are still not right between us," murmured Damian.

"No," I said. "But they will be."

"Now who's lying?" he asked. He grasped my wrist and lifted it to brush a kiss across the pulse. "I'll return as soon as I can."

I nodded because the words had stalled in my throat. I walked to the front door and watched him cross the yard to the driveway. The garage door rolled up and he came out with a big, black motorcycle. He straddled it, kicked it on, and then gave me one last look before roaring away into the night.

I locked the door and returned to the living room, feeling empty with a side of awful. I plopped onto the couch and picked up *Werewolves Are Real!* After glancing through the chapter on "The Bigfoot Connection," I put it down.

I didn't want to read about werewolves. I wasn't sure if I even wanted to be one. Not that I had a choice. Still, being a supernatural being was better than being dead. Unless the afterlife was a big party. That'd be nice.

Wondering about where my soul might go after I bit the big one wasn't comforting, so I dropped that line of thought and let my gaze wander over the living room. It was such a man room. Big, dark furniture and chunky brass lamps. Damian didn't own a television or a stereo system. He lived like a monk. Well, except for the sex. What did he do when he wasn't being the security boss? He liked to read, that was obvious. But I wasn't sure what else he did, other than work. Maybe he didn't know what he liked anymore, either.

My gaze fell on my mother's book. It lay on the coffee table like a forgotten nightmare, taunting me with its stark cover. Big red words scrawled across the white background as though someone had written in blood: *A Mother Betrayed.*

I dreaded the very idea of opening that book, but it was time to face what my mother had written. I couldn't resist peeking at the dedication page first. It had become a habit over the years because I'd always hoped that one day I'd see my name there. My brother and sister, even my dead father, and Ames had all been listed in one book or another, usually more than one. But me? Nary a mention.

I glanced at the page, and my heart tripped.

For a moment, I couldn't comprehend that my name was actually there, black on white: *To Kelsey Rose.* The giddiness receded soon enough, though. She owed me dearly for the content, didn't she? Underneath my name was a Benjamin Franklin quote. I smiled. Mother did love quoting him: *As we must account for every idle word, so must we account for every idle silence.*

I skipped the acknowledgments and other nonsense, stopping only when I got to Chapter One:

The day Kelsey Rose Morningstone came into my life was the same day my husband confessed he'd been unfaithful. He punctuated his betrayal of our wedding vows by presenting me with a pink-cheeked girl, barely two months old, and asked me if we could adopt her.

For a moment, I couldn't breathe. I placed the book flat on my lap and stared at nothing. *If it wasn't for me, you wouldn't know about your father's little indiscretion.* That's what Robert had said in my dream, or I should say that's what Morrigu said. How had she known about my real mother? I shouldn't be so shocked at the confession there in black and white. Not really.

But it hurt. It hurt to know that Margaret Morningstone raised me out of loyalty to her husband, not love. Never love.

"Oh, God," I said with a soft, pain-filled laugh. It wouldn't have mattered if I'd won the Nobel Prize or discovered the cure for cancer or won an Olympic medal. She would've never approved of me. I was proof that her life wasn't perfect, that her marriage hadn't been solid. All those years of giving advice in books and on radio and on TV, of telling the world how to create a faithful marriage and a loving family, using her own as an example, of course—and then her cheating husband made it all a lie.

I inhaled deeply, picked up the book, and because I was obviously a sucker for punishment, I read on:

I was blindsided. Here was the man who'd held my heart for almost twenty years admitting he'd had an affair—and that he'd fathered another woman's child. He begged for my forgiveness and pleaded with me to accept his daughter as mine, too. You see, he had no choice but to ask for my mercy.

I rolled my eyes. Egotistical much? God, she was melodramatic. Had it really played out this way? She could say anything she wanted. My father was dead, and I was a disgrace. Any attempt on my part to speak out would only be viewed as the crazy talk of a disgruntled, ungrateful orphan. I hadn't known my father, certainly no charming toddler memories popped out, so I had no idea what he'd really been like. My mother had kept his papers and pictures, other than the family portrait she'd kept on the living room mantel, locked away. My few attempts to ask to read his journals or cull through the photos resulted in lectures so blistering, I stopped asking. She'd claimed my father, and whatever legacy he left behind, for herself—and she had no intention of sharing.

His young lover had died, you see. Though Bert would not tell me more than that, I could see through the pain of his betrayal, his love and devotion for me. Everyone makes mistakes. And everyone deserves a second chance.

I took a moment to absorb that my birth mother was dead. I couldn't harbor the fantasy I might find her, or reunite with a parent who actually wanted me. I supposed it was a good thing, in a way. After all, I might not be around to make any reunions. I swallowed the knot in my throat. I would think about it later. I had to find my own redemption before I could seek that of others.

Even though I risked spontaneous combustion, I continued reading:

As I have advocated often to other couples facing marital hardships, I considered what I wanted, and what I needed, and the answer was easy: Bert. He'd been my rock for so long, I realized that I could forgive him for this indiscretion. I knew I could, and should, soldier on. For me. For Bert. And for Kelsey.

My husband and I recommitted to our marriage, and we raised Kelsey as our own. Even when my darling Bert died two years later, I remained committed in my duty to the child I'd claimed. I believed that with the right guidance and firm affection, she would grow into a lovely young woman and a productive member of society.

And she did.

She graduated from both high school and college with honors. Not long after her twenty-fourth birthday, she "put out her shingle," and in no time at all, she'd found career success as a psychotherapist.

I paused. She actually sounded proud of me, but I knew better. This was a typical Margaret tactic—she would build me up by stating all the things I'd done right . . . so she could tear them all down by pointing out every single thing I'd done wrong. For just this teeny-tiny second, I wanted to bask in the approval. How pathetic was that? I'd been riding Damian about this very issue, and look at me, holding on to the past just as hard. I ached so badly for my mother's acceptance. Would that feeling *ever* go away?

I could close the book. Leave it alone. Pretend Margaret meant those kind things, that I was a daughter she could be proud of.

No. I'd learned my lessons from Robert. Fear wasn't an excuse for inaction. No matter how scared I was, how much I did not want to know the depth of my adopted mother's resentment, I couldn't turn away from her words.

Of course, how could I know that such a gifted child harbored within her a terrible monster? I had no information about her genetic propensities. Bert told me only that his paramour's name was Sylvia, that she was an artist, and that she was healthy in both mind and spirit.

It became my goal to understand why he felt the need to step outside the marriage, to assess his needs, and my own, and meld them together to better our relationship. During this process of reflection, my conclusion was that Robert's midlife crisis had propelled him into a relationship with a flighty woman who fed his fantasies of being youthful and robust. He had to believe that she was "healthy," because to admit, even to himself, she was mentally unstable would mean his daughter might one day suffer from those same destructive behaviors.

He would not tell me how Sylvia died, and it soon become clear she had committed suicide. I had many hints from my husband about this truth, though he did not confirm it—except through psychological clues that only I could discern. I further determined that Sylvia had gone into post-partum depression after the birth of her child. As many case studies have shown, post-partum depression affects women on so deep and terrible a scale, some attempt to kill their children or themselves.

It certainly was not Kelsey's fault she inherited her mother's frail mental health. But her subsequent actions, both as a psychotherapist and a human being, were her own. How the daughter of my heart could put aside all that I had taught her and fall in love with a serial killer, I will never know.

If only I could turn back the clock and help her to be a different person. But we all know you cannot change the past, and you cannot change others. I did all I could as a mother and a mentor to help Kelsey be a good person.

It is no one fault's but hers that she allowed Robert Mallard into her life and into her bed. Her love for him blinded her to the atrocities he committed in her name. Even so, she was not a victim. She was a passive participant in a serial killer's sick games, and she very nearly paid with her life.

I dropped the book. For the longest moment, I couldn't even think straight. All the lies and suppositions and bullshit Margaret had manufactured was for one purpose only: to seek revenge on a man who'd been dead for more than thirty years. She couldn't make him pay for the loss of her pride, for the one imperfection that marred an otherwise proper existence. I would always be the living, breathing reminder that her husband had not wanted her. Was it that I was the only available target for her rage? Did she actually believe this drivel she'd contrived? Had my father's adulterous behavior truly broken her? Or had something else happened between them? Margaret Morningstone was nursing a pain so big, so horrifying that the only way she could lance it was by destroying me.

And she thought I was the one mentally unbalanced? Hah.

I didn't realize how furious I was until I ripped the book in half. I tossed the mutilated pages to the floor and stood up. I wanted to scream.

I was done with this crap. I was tired of being her goddamned scapegoat. She had no right to lie about me, to write those vitriolic things about me and my father and my mother. *Who the fuck did she think she was?*

Somewhere inside me the lycan poked up its snout and howled. I felt off kilter, my mind fogged by my fury, but I had clear intentions. Oh, yes. I knew exactly what to do. I grabbed the BMW keys Damian had left on the coffee table and hurried out of the house. Quarantine, my ass. Quarantine this!

I started the car and plugged in my moth—*her* home address into the GPS. Then I peeled out of the driveway, laying on the gas. *Nomorenomorenomore.* It was my mantra, the only thing I could think as I automatically followed the cheerful electronic voice's directions.

I don't know how long it took to get there. I only knew that I sorta woke up parked in the crescent driveway, just a few feet from the porch steps. *She* lived in a stately manor with perfect winter landscaping. I cataloged random details: Widely spaced marble columns. Big, square windows accented with black shutters. A set of red double doors pinioned with two huge Christmas wreaths. The house of my childhood. A place I'd never really felt welcome, and now I knew why.

Before I realized I'd even moved, I was at the door. But I didn't knock. Courtesy? She didn't deserve courtesy. I yanked on the shiny gold handle and to my surprise, the door opened—well, more like it came off its hinges. I tossed it behind me.

"Frau."

I looked over my shoulder and saw one of Damian's brothers. I shouldn't have been surprised that he made sure I was being watched over. "Which one are you?"

"Drake."

"Why didn't you stop me?"

"You are not a prisoner," he evaded. Then he grimaced. "Damian found the book. He read what your mother wrote. He's on his way, *Frau*. He said to do what you must."

The knot of anger pulsing inside me loosened. Damian had my back. He didn't care that I'd taken his car and left Broken Heart. He knew where I was going. He trusted me. And he wanted me to do whatever I thought best.

"Kelsey?" The horrified voice of Margaret filtered in from the foyer. She was dressed in a pink silk robe, a gin and tonic clutched in her hand. "What happened to the door?"

"If you touch the house alarm," I said, my fury instantly going to inferno levels, "I will kill you. Do you understand?"

"Don't be ridiculous," she snapped.

Drake whipped past me, a blur of silent motion, and in a nanosecond, he was next to her, hand wrapped around her throat. She looked shocked, and then terrified.

And I took a helluva satisfaction in that.

"Answer her question," he said in steely voice.

"Yes," she said. "I understand."

"The living room is to the left," I told him. "Is anyone else here, Margaret?"

She hesitated too long.

"Where's Ames?"

"He doesn't live here anymore." Her expression soured. "We're getting divorced."

Well, that was interesting news. Good for Ames. "Then who's here?"

"Selma, of course, but she's been asleep for hours."

Selma was my mother's longtime housekeeper. She lived in the small guest house on the southern edge of the property.

Drake led her into the living room and pushed her onto one of the sofas. He stood next to her, his expression cold. "Don't worry about the guards," he said. "I took care of them before I joined you, Kelsey. Damian and the others will be here soon." He peered down at Margaret. "She may let you live, you know." He bared his teeth in a terrible smile. "But I doubt my brother will."

She paled, and then she turned her gaze to me. "Kelsey," she said in that dictatorial tone I knew so well. "You cannot be upset with me for writing the truth. I wanted to call you and let you read the manuscript first, but my lawyers cautioned me that maintaining contact could indicate my own culpability."

"You are so full of shit," I said.

She glanced at Drake and offered him a trembling smile. "I don't know what she told you, Mr.—?"

Drake lifted an eyebrow, and didn't answer.

"—ah, that is, she's suffering from delusions. Do you really want to be mixed up in all of this? The police have been searching for her for more than a week. I'm afraid she's in a lot of trouble."

"I think you are confused about who is in trouble," he said. He offered a polite smile. "I'll give you a hint, *Frau*. It is not Kelsey."

"The police?" I asked, alarmed. Then it hit me. "Your book came out, and you made them look like assholes for believing I was a victim."

"You are a person of interest," she said smugly.

"Because you accused me of colluding with Robert!"

"Didn't you?" she asked. Her eyes gleamed triumphantly. "Through my research, it became obvious to me that you were obsessed with Robert. His idea of courtship was serial murders. Why do you think he brought that girl to your house?"

"Wow. That's a lot of hatred, Maggie. Couldn't hurt your precious, imperfect Bert for fucking around on you, so you painted a bull's-eye on me."

Her calm facade fractured, just a little, but she rallied. "You have no idea what you're talking about."

"I was an infant! It wasn't my fault I was born to my father's mistress, or that he asked his wife to raise me." Rage churned in me, and it took all my self-control to push it back. I wanted scream at her and pummel her. She knew it, too. If I broke, I would make her lies into truth.

She shook her head sadly and then offered Drake a conspiratorial "see what I mean" look. "Oh, Kelsey. Your father made a mistake, and I forgave him. I took you in. I raised you."

"Did you love me?"

Her expression froze, and she visibly swallowed. But she was too much of a trained professional, not to mention an experienced television personality, to give anything else away.

"That's what I thought," I said. "How long did you wait for me to mess up so badly, you could finally justify all that festering resentment of yours?"

"I didn't fall in love with a serial killer," she pointed out in a completely reasonable tone. "You did. And you've compensated for that horror by painting me as a villain."

"How could I paint you as a villain? I didn't know I wasn't your daughter until I read it in your book." Well, first I'd been told in a dream, but I wasn't going there. "All I've tried to do my whole life was measure up to your expectations. I sat straighter, I got all A's, I ate all my vegetables—even Brussels sprouts!" I looked at Damian. "She made them with this awful sauce that made them slimy. It was like eating swamp poop."

He shuddered. "That's disgusting."

"You have no idea," I said. Fury was roiling inside me like lava spilling over a volcano's edge, and with it, came a torrent of tears and a suffocating sense of grief. "You always had another criticism, another lofty goal I fell short of, another payment due for what my father did. Do you get that part? I didn't hurt you. He did."

She faced me calmly, her expression giving nothing away. God, she was cool customer. And why did I even bother? What had I hoped for here? Closure? Margaret would never admit she was flawed. She'd never find redemption or healing because she couldn't admit she wasn't perfect. She'd convinced herself that she was right. About everything.

"You told the world I was in love with a serial killer. You said that I'd slept with him!"

"You did, Kelsey. Don't deny it. I have evidence—"

"The hell you do," I said.

"You're not well, darling," she said in a soothing tone. "Now that Robert's dead, you can admit how sick—"

Drake's growl interrupted her. She gaped up at him and put a quaking hand against her chest. She sucked in a breath, and then opened her mouth again.

"If I were you," he said in a low, scary voice, "I would not speak."

Her lips mashed together, and she looked down at her lap. She must've only then realized that she still held the vodka and tonic. She downed the whole thing in one, long gulp, and put the empty glass on the side table.

Drake reached up and squeezed my shoulder.

I felt the buzz of electricity and then there were three pops of gold sparks. Six people appeared in the foyer: Patrick and Jess, Lorcan and a dark-haired woman, Ruadan and Damian.

"Kelsey!" He strode across the room and yanked me into his embrace. "Are you all right?"

"No," I said.

He looked at my face, which was probably red and puffy from crying and from the anger clogging my pores. His kissed me, and then tucked me into his side. Suddenly, I felt better. Oh, I was still pissed off, but not the crazy, dark kind of way that had carried me to Margaret's door.

Damian and Drake held a rapid-fire discussion in German, which ended with them both glaring at my ex-mother.

She seemed to shrink inside herself. Maybe she finally understood she was trapped in a situation she could neither control nor escape. "I'm giving all of you one chance to leave my home," she said coldly. "I suggest you take it."

Or not.

Chapter 12

"Aw. She's cute," said Jess. "You know, in an evil bitch kind of way."

Margaret gasped in outrage. She shot up from the couch and waved her arms. "Get out! All of you!"

"Sit. *Down.*" Damian's voice held absolute command, and she deflated onto the sofa like a popped balloon.

She pinned me with a hard stare. "I see your taste in friends has not improved."

"Ow. Stop. That hurt," I said in a flat, bored voice.

"Mind your manners," said Damian, "or I'll rip out your tongue."

I glanced up at him, and I could see he meant it. Gross. I was angry with Margaret, but that didn't mean I wanted to harm her. Well, not much. Certainly not in a way that would leave her tongue-less. Though the idea she would never be able to talk again held merit.

"Wow," said Jess. "Nice house. So this is what you get when you trade in on the pain and suffering of loved ones." She rounded the couch, her gaze assessing Margaret as though she were a particularly nasty roach.

"And yet we could buy this piece of crap . . . hmm." She glanced at her husband. "What do you think? Six times over?"

"More like twenty," he said. "Probably more."

Jessica grinned. "Sweet. We're way richer than I thought." She put out her hands and twin beams of light flared. When they dissipated, two gold half swords with bejeweled handles appeared in her fists. She swung them in a small, tight arc, Zena-style.

"What is the meaning of this?" asked Margaret. Her composure was flaking away, but she had too much iron control to completely freak.

"We're serial killers," answered Jess cheerfully. "We had a meeting and decided our new victims would be mean, old bitties with shriveled-up hearts. Guess what? You were at the top of the list."

I snorted back a laugh. Jess glanced at me and winked.

"We could make her disappear," said Drake. He studied Margaret as if trying to determine the size of her coffin. "Ruadan? When's the last time you visited the Adriatic Sea?"

"'Bout six hundred years ago," he said. "I could do for another visit."

I thought Margaret might faint. She sorta listed to the side for a few seconds before she managed to catch herself. She inhaled and then exhaled slowly. She gripped the edge of her robe and stared at us defiantly.

Everyone ignored her.

Jessica seemed to be having a great time practicing sword moves, though after she nearly gouged Patrick's rib cage, she moved to the left side of the marble hearth, where there was more room. She made sure she stayed within sight of Margaret, who, despite her take-no-prisoners stance, was starting to look a little green.

Patrick moved to study the paintings on the far side

of the room, and Ruadan was busy touching all the knickknacks—which were plentiful thanks to Margaret's need to show off what money could buy.

Crash!

We all looked at Ruadan and then at the pile of blue glass. He shrugged. "Sorry there, love. Clumsy fingers, you know."

Margaret flinched.

"Eva," said Drake. "Three guards tied up in back. They need new memories."

The dark-haired woman nodded and said, "No problem." She waved at me, smiling widely, and then she and Lorcan left, presumably to go do something vampire-rific to the guards.

Margaret was sullen. She had no idea that she was dealing with paranormal beings who could outrun her, outthink her, and outmaneuver her.

And they were on *my* side. That's the part that flipped me out the most. They didn't even know me all that well, but they had come to help me. I was Damian's, and therefore I belonged to them, too. It was a heady feeling. I couldn't remember a time that I'd had this level of acceptance and support.

"What do you want from me?" asked Margaret icily. "No, wait. Let me guess. You want me to tell my publisher to stop selling the book, which won't matter because it's already sold a million copies. And if you think I will publicly admit that anything I've written is not true, I won't do it. Go on and kill me, Kelsey. Then the world will know you really are a monster."

"You think that will make you a martyr?" I asked. "You really do have a bloated opinion of yourself. You know what I want, *Margaret*? I want my father's papers, journals, photos, everything."

"No," she bit out.

I had expected her response. After all, she'd been saying it to me my whole life. "You wouldn't even let me have a memory of my father. And you couldn't keep from tainting my mother's name, either, could you?"

Margaret stared at me, unable to keep the hatred from her gaze. I didn't dare open my shields to that blistering antipathy.

"What a bitter, bitter soul you are," I said, and for the first time, a new emotion cut through my anger. Pity. Margaret had helped thousands of people through their tragedies, their problems, their failures, but she'd been unable to deal with her own. How could she spout all that rhetoric to those who were genuinely suffering without giving away the emptiness of her own heart? She was so pathetic. And with that thought, the rest of my anger dissipated. She deserved my rancor, but it would make no difference. Being pissed off at Margaret Morningstone would do nothing except poison me—filling me up with acrimony until I couldn't breathe. If she cared about me at all, she would've been sorry, just a little about what she did. Obviously, she'd been prepared for me to seek her out—that's why she had guards outside her place. Maybe she hoped to capture me. Wouldn't that have been a feather in her cap?

But she hadn't expected that I would have backup.

And she had no idea how dangerous my new friends were.

It made a girl perk right up.

"All you want are your father's things, *Schätzchen*?" asked Damian. I recognized the question that echoed within the one he'd spoken. *Do you want payback, too?*

"I don't want to be angry anymore. And I don't want revenge," I clarified. "It's time to let this all go."

"I don't need your forgiveness," sneered Margaret.

"Give it rest, Ego-zilla," I said. "You've lost your

whipping girl. I don't need to forgive you. Not even a little. I don't care anymore. Not about you and not about your book." I leaned down and got nose to nose with her. "And you know what? You'll miss me when I'm gone."

"Who thinks too much of herself now?" she said quietly. If she was trying for dignity, she was failing. Her tone was too hostile. "I won't give you anything."

"No kidding. Why start now?" I looked at Damian. "She'll never tell us where she keeps his stuff. She wouldn't even let me peek at old photos or read anything he'd written while I was growing up."

"Oh, she'll tell you," said Eva. She and Lorcan had returned from outside. "I gave the guards instructions to reawaken in an hour."

"Plenty of time for us to finish up," said Drake.

Crash!

We all turned to look at Ruadan, who stood next a shelf filled with items Margaret had purchased on her travels. He looked down the ceramic shards that had once been a very expensive vase from India. "Oops."

"Stop destroying my treasures!" demanded Margaret.

Ruadan laughed. "Me? You're the one who spent nearly thirty years trying to destroy the treasure standin' before you. You know nothing about gaugin' worth." He punctuated the statement by knocking off another trinket. I think it was the gold-etched dish she'd brought back from one of her trips to Russia. It shattered instantly, and turned into a pile of shiny nothing.

Damian guided me away from the couch, and Eva took our place. She sat carefully on the edge of the coffee table. "Look at me, Margaret," she said in soft, lyrical voice.

I could tell my mother didn't want to look at Eva, but

she couldn't resist the command woven into the woman's musical voice.

As soon as she met the vampire's gaze, Margaret's eyes glazed over and she started breathing deeply.

"Where are your husband's things?"

"In his study."

Eva glanced at me, and I shook my head. "He doesn't have a study."

"She can't lie to me," said Eva.

"Eva's Family power is glamour," Damian whispered to me. "She's very good at it."

"Family power?" I asked.

"Remember when I explained about the eight Families? Each has their own special talent."

"Oh. Right." We'd talked about the vampires and other paranormal beings, at least those who occupied Broken Heart, during Werewolf 101. That had been a postcoital conversation, as I recall. Then again, most of them were. Heh.

Eva had turned back to Margaret. "Where is his study?"

"Across the foyer."

"That's a wall," pointed out Jessica. She raised an eyebrow. "I think Cuckoo for Cocoa Puffs over there has already left on the train to Nutsville."

"Push the panel with the cardinal," directed Margaret. "Bert did so love bird-watching. Cardinals were his favorite."

"That's nice," said Eva soothingly. "And everything's in there?"

"Everything," she confirmed. "It's mine. *He* was *mine*."

Damian took my hand and led me across the wide foyer to the wall. It was a pale blue and featured a white chair rail. A variety of birds had been hand-painted above the white trim. There was only one cardinal. I put my palm on it and pressed.

It was like being in a spy movie and discovering the secret entrance to the villain's lair. The panel pushed in about an inch, there was a click, then *whoosh* . . . the wall slid open.

"Why do I feel like the Green Hornet?" asked Jess as she peered into the dark space.

"Kato was the ass kicker," said Patrick, joining his wife. "He never gets the proper credit." He made an "after you" gesture to Damian and me.

Damian gripped my hand tightly as we stepped into the office. He found the switch, and when the lights flickered on, we all let out a collective gasp.

"Creepy," said Jess.

Creepy was right, though it wasn't the look of the place, but the feeling of it. Like we'd found the sacrificial chamber of an ancient cult. It seemed as though my father had just stepped out for a moment. Everything was shiny and clean, the hearth filled with cedar logs, and Christmas decorations layered the mantel. It was a typical enough study—with floor-to-ceiling bookshelves, an oversized antique desk with a leather wingback, Persian rugs accenting a dark wood floor, a sitting area near the fireplace, and a fake window.

Jess studied this feature. "Soooo . . . she walled over the real window, and then added a fake window with a picture of a thunderstorm."

"She said it was raining the day he collapsed. He was rushed to the hospital, but he died on the way there. Heart attack."

"Way to commemorate it." She shuddered and turned away. Her gaze fell on the desk. "Dude. I bet it looked that exact way when he died."

It was a mess, but it looked carefully constructed. My

mother, that is Margaret, had kept everything clean to the point of mania, but had apparently returned items and papers to their exact spots.

"All right," said Jess, rubbing her hands. "What do you want to take?"

I looked around. "If I disrupt her fantasy, it might send her into a nervous breakdown."

Everyone was quiet, their gazes on me. I felt the whisper of guilt. Did I really want to send Margaret into a mental tailspin?

"Hoo-kay. I'm waiting for the bad part," said Jess.

I huffed out a laugh. "All the papers. Journals. Photographs. Anything that looks important. I'll look through the books, too."

"I have boxes," said Ruadan, joining us. He tossed down several flattened cartons. "Seems she was packin' up your stepfather's things."

"Probably so she could burn them in a nice neat boxy pyre," I said.

"Your da will get his things, darlin'. Eva's plantin' new memories, too, and puttin' that blight of humanity into a deep sleep."

"Thank you," I said. "Thanks to all of you." I felt a lump in my throat as I offered my gratitude to these people, these paranormals, who showed me more respect and acceptance than anyone ever had.

It was crazy. Crazy and perfect.

"Let's get to work," said Damian. He leaned down and a brushed a kiss across my lips. "You okay?"

"I will be," I said. I cupped his face. "And we're okay. Totally, completely okay."

He smiled.

"Holy shit," said Jess, grabbing her chest as though having a heart attack. "I can't get used to him turning his frowns upside down."

I chuckled, and Damian smiled wider. Jess made gagging sounds until her husband swept her into his arms and shut her up with a kiss.

Then everyone grabbed boxes and started filling them up.

Drake was the first to leave—on the motorcycle he'd driven when he'd followed me to Oklahoma City. The boxes filled the trunk and part of the backseat of Damian's BMW. To my surprise, Lorcan slid behind the wheel. Eva gave me a quick hug, and took the front passenger seat.

"I knew I shoulda yelled shotgun," muttered Jess. She punched me lightly on the shoulder. "Good luck. After everything's all official, we'll have a party. You ever have a chocolatini?"

I shook my head.

"You poor thing," she said, clucking. "I'll remedy that travesty."

Patrick walked around the car and tucked her into the backseat.

"If they're taking the car, then how are we getting back?" I asked Damian.

"We're not going to Broken Heart," he said. "Patrick and Ruadan are taking us to Germany. More specifically, to my family's castle."

"Oh."

Ruadan's back was to us as he studied the row of thornbushes on the right side of the porch. He squatted down and poked his head close to the underside.

"What is he doing?" I asked.

"Sometimes it's better not to know," said Patrick as he joined us.

Lorcan gave a quick honk, everyone in the car waved, and then they took off, leaving the three of us alone on the snow-crusted driveway.

"Da," called Patrick, "it's time to go."

"Don't go gettin' your knickers in a twist," muttered Ruadan. He shoved an arm into the brambles, and when he pulled it out, he held a small, squirming gray creature. He carried it to us. "Poor thing. Must've been stuck in there for a while. He's a mess."

"It's a pug," I said, delighted. "May I?"

Ruadan handed me the puppy, and I cooed to it. He was so small and thin. He had a squished-in black face and bulgy eyes. The ugliest cutie I'd ever seen. It was a wonder he'd survived any amount of time out in the cold, and it was obvious he was starving.

"What will you do with him?" I asked.

Ruadan and Patrick shared a look that was the equivalent of yelling "not it!"

"I can't believe you're not dog people," I said.

Damian laughed, and embarrassment flushed my cheeks. How could I forget I was dating a werewolf? Or that I was becoming one?

"Can we keep him?" I asked.

"Do you see the irony in us having a dog as a pet?"

"I can live with irony," I said. "He looks like a Jeff. What do you think?"

"If you want him," said Damian, looking askance at the pug, "then he's yours." He turned his gaze to Ruadan. "Can you add a second passenger?"

"Sure enough."

Since there was a seven-hour time difference between Oklahoma and Germany, we arrived very close to dawn. That meant our transpo-vampires had to do what Patrick called "turn or burn," which Damian described later as a pilot joke. (And no, I didn't get it, and I forgot to Google it.)

One thing you can say about insta-beam travel was

that there wasn't any jet lag. All the same, the roller coaster argument with Damian, the emotional confrontation with Margaret, and the culling of items from my father's study had worn me out.

We stood in a hallway roughly the size of a football field. Massive gray stones made up the floor and walls. Big tapestries covered most of the right side wall and there was a *Titanic*-sized stone stairway to the left.

"I expected it to be darker and dustier," I said. "Maybe a few cobwebs and some creepy organ music wafting through the hallways."

He laughed. "My brothers and I do not live here anymore, but we make sure it is well taken care of. Every few years, Drake or Darrius returns to check on everything."

"But not you."

"Not until today," he admitted softly.

Jeff whined and snuffled closer to me.

"Aw. He's hungry."

"Come. We will feed him and then we will rest."

"It's less than a week until the Solstice," I said.

"Plenty of time to find the chalice," he said as he guided me past room after sumptuous room. After a few twists and turns, we found ourselves in a modernized kitchen updated with stainless-steel appliances and granite countertops. It still had an old-world feel, though, with the huge hearth and the cauldron hitched inside it by a big, iron bar. Copper pots and pans hung from a dangling rack while another held drying herbs and flowers. It smelled divine. It also felt charming and cozy, despite its size.

"Is anyone else here?" I asked.

"Yes. Tomorrow you will meet Hilda and Arnold. They are the caretakers, and are in charge of the staff."

"And how many employees are there?"

He shrugged.

"Soooo . . . a lot."

"Ja."

After Jeff lapped some water and chomped down minced steak and carrots, Damian led me up a back staircase, through another wide, twisty hallway, until we arrived in a room that was bigger than my entire apartment at the Dante Clinic.

Of course, there was a hearth—oversized stone in an arched pattern. A stack of fresh logs sat within the cavernous opening. Two big, wingback leather chairs were angled to face the fireplace, and a small antique table sat between them.

There was a separate sitting room, a bathroom with a hot tub, steam shower, and sauna. "You need a map for this place," I said as I wandered through what amounted to a personal spa.

Damian followed, studying the features. "This was done in my absence. I suppose the hope has always been that I would one day return home." He paused, and touched my shoulder. "Does this please you?"

"Are you kidding? I could live in this bathroom paradise."

"Really? Perhaps after you see the bedroom, you might rescind that statement."

He was right. It was the biggest four-poster bed I'd ever seen. It was dark wood, an antique, and so tall that when I stood next to it, my hip didn't even hit the top mattress. There was a little wood staircase nearby, and Damian pushed it to the bed, and I used it to climb up.

Jeff was eager to explore. He sprung out of my arms and loped around the thick, patchwork comforter, yipping happily.

I fell into the mountain of pillows and sighed contentedly. Damian joined me, rolling me so that we lay facing each other.

"What do you think, *Schätzchen*?" he asked.

"I think this is where I want to live," I said. "But only if there's room service."

"You will have a dedicated servant to see to your every need," he promised, his tone going smoky.

"Oh, really? Breakfast in bed? Foot massages? Neck rubs?"

He nodded.

"Hmm. And just who is this wonderful new servant of mine?"

"Me," he whispered, swooping down to conquer my mouth. "Only me."

My whole body went molten. I slid my leg along his, wrapping myself closer. One hand coasted over my hip to cup my buttock, and he gave a little growl. My stomach twisted with excitement. I let my shields down, and opened myself up to his. And let myself feel everything: his need, mine, the lust that broke over us like a waterfall.

God, we could drown.

He stopped tormenting my lips, but only so he could torture my neck with soft kisses and little hot flicks of his tongue. He pushed on my shoulder and I took the hint, lying fully on my back.

While his hands snuck under my shirt and cupped my breasts, I dragged his T-shirt up and touched the warm, solid muscle of his stomach. Through the bra, his fingers tweaked my nipples and I sucked in a startled breath.

"Wow. Whoa," I said. He did it again, and I moaned, my hands digging at the waistband of his jeans.

"Now, that's what a man likes to hear. And feel," he said thickly as I managed to unhook the button and jerk on the zipper.

"I hate underwear," I muttered as his boxers blocked my immediate target.

He laughed, and sat up, shucking his boots and socks, and then wiggling out of his pants and boxers.

"Shirt, too," I demanded.

He took it off, and it joined the rest of the clothing on the floor.

"Better?" he asked.

"I think you should walk around naked all the time," I said. "It would make it easier for you to serve me."

"I don't think Hilda would forgive me if I showed up to dinner wearing nothing but a smile."

"Spoilsport."

"Hmm." He settled next to me, him leaning on his side and me still on my back, feasting on his beautiful body. Then with two fingers he grabbed the top of the very nice blouse and *riiiiip* . . . he turned it into scraps.

"I kinda liked this one."

"I'll buy you a replacement." He unbuttoned my pants and then stripped them off efficiently along with my socks and shoes.

He gazed down at me, one blunt fingertip tracing an erratic line over my stomach. I was wearing a black bra and panties fringed in delicate lace and ribbon, another set from the insanely expensive collection of lingerie he'd bought for me.

His eyes went dark as he traced the top of the panties, and my heart stuttered as a wave of hot need flowed over me. That belonged to him, but it echoed my own. I was wild for him. No matter how many times or how many ways we made love, it was thrilling.

I gripped his cock and started stroking. He was already hard, but he seemed to swell even more under my touch. He groaned, his eyes closing briefly as he enjoyed my attention. Feminine satisfaction curled through me.

Then we heard a happy bark, and tiny gray blur leapt onto my stomach.

"Oof!" I let go of Damian as our new doggie planted himself between my breasts and leaned forward to lick my chin.

"That's my woman, runt," said Damian. He picked Jeff up by the scruff. The little dog twirled around. Damian misjudged the distance between him and the puppy. Jeff was in tongue range, and he slobbered all over Damian's cheek with enthusiasm.

"This isn't a threesome," he told Jeff. He eyed me. "You find this funny?"

My lips quivered and I mashed them together. Jeff yipped, his tongue lolling as he split his bug-eyed gaze between the two of us. *"Ohmygod,"* I wailed. "He's soooo cute. And he lurves you." Then I laughed so hard my body shook and tears leaked from my eyes.

"Ah, romance," said Damian dolefully.

He scooted off the bed, obviously too much a man to use the staircase. He turned and scooped up my torn blouse, and then he stalked toward the bathroom. He returned a few minutes later.

"He's in that gargantuan tub, nesting in your shirt."

"Glad to know it went for a good cause. Do you think he'll be okay in there?"

"We had a talk. He said he would sleep while I made you very, very happy."

"Oh?"

"And then I promised to retrieve him for long-term snuggling."

"You are the best servant ever."

He bent over me and kissed the humor right out of me. It didn't hurt that his lust was easily renewed, and he sent wave after wave of red-*beauty*-passion to me, *through* me, until I was ruled by it. By him.

I ached for him to take me, to fill me.

But he wasn't in a rush.

One of his hands clamped my hip, to pin me securely while he nuzzled my breasts. I clawed at the bedcovers, my toes curling as he sucked one nipple into sweet agony. He was definitely taking the lead on this, and I was okay with that (more than okay, really), but I had limited access to his body.

One of my hands was around his neck, my fingers threaded into his hair, convulsively tugging as he continued to bedevil my breasts with that tongue of his. The other was pressed against his rib cage, just underneath his fiercely pounding heart. I was undone by his attention, and I wasn't doing a good job at returning the favor.

It's like he heard my thoughts, or maybe he just read my emotions.

"Let me love you, Kelsey," he murmured.

I relaxed, and stopping trying to figure out the who-was-touching-who-and-how-much ratio. I enjoyed. I tingled. I ached.

Breathing? Not so much. Who could breathe? Pant. Gasp. Huff. Yep. I had those down, but drawing a full breath was impossible. This intoxicating man was like my new drug. I was addicted to Damian. And it seemed he was addicted to me as well.

"We'll burn each other up," I whispered.

"Every time." Then he lightly nipped one turgid peak, and I nearly launched off the bed.

So he did it again. Electricity jolted straight into my womb. My panties were soaked, and my thighs trembled.

He reached behind me and unsnapped the bra, then oh-so-slowly pulled the straps down my shoulders. He revealed each breast like it was a newly discovered treasure, and then, because he obviously wanted me to spontaneously combust, he renewed his torments.

Erotic heat poured through me. My skin was so sensitized that the lace fabric of my panties brushing against my agitated clit—which Damian had not even touched—offered tiny trills of pleasure.

Damian kissed the center of my cleavage and then wove of spell of want, of need, as he dragged lips over my skin, tasting me as his hands worked off my panties. Then he knelt between my thighs and lowered his mouth toward my sweet spot.

His lips grazed the quivering flesh of my inner thigh.

"You bastard," I gasped.

He repeated the mouth torture on the other thigh.

"If you want to live," I gritted out, "you will get busy."

He chuckled; then he pressed one light, unsatisfying kiss against my clit. He gazed up at me. "What do you want?"

"You. Inside me. *Now.*"

He kissed my flesh from the hollow at the base of my throat to the undersides of my ankles. He took his time, but the quivering of his hands, and the need that threaded into his desire, betrayed his slipping control. His hands coasted over my stomach, drifted across my ribs, then paused to once again torment my breasts. Fingers rolled my nipples into tight buds.

Then fingers dipped through my curls to tease my clit.

I shuddered, and gasped, and moaned.

He covered me fully, and dragged his lips over my neck, and I felt the rasp of his tongue tasting a sensitive spot under my ear. Then he was kissing me, his need filling me. He let his emotions go, all of them, and I felt his passion for me, his worry that he would lose me, the regret he harbored for not trusting his parents, for disappointing his people, and tying it all together, beat the warm, sweet pulse of his love for me.

Oh, my God.

Damian loved me.

I tried to squeeze back the tears, but he noticed.

"Schätzchen," he murmured.

"I need you," I said. "I need you."

I stroked the strong contours of his back. His tight buttocks flexed under my palms. *Sweet mamma jamma.* He was big and muscled, his hair so long it tickled my arms.

His cock nestled against my wet heat, nudging my entrance.

"Damian," I begged. "Please."

His cock inched inside. The velvety-smooth penetration of his cock offered a new kind of torment. When he was sheathed fully, I wrapped my legs around his waist and we stared at each other, the connection of our bodies and the connections of our emotions seemed to arrest us, just for a moment in pure splendor.

I loved him, too.

And I sent it into him. Fully. Without doubt. We might not have many tomorrows, but we had now, we had this moment. And it would be enough.

His eyes widened, and he sucked in a breath. "Kelsey."

"Love me," I said.

"I do," he said helplessly. "I do."

I clung to him and met his slow, measured thrusts.

Delicious, sensual fire rolled over both of us. I wasn't sure who was feeling what now, but did it matter? It was the same. It was scary and beautiful and overwhelming.

I tightened my legs, urging him deeper. His hands curled under my shoulders as he thrust harder, faster. Sweat slicked our bodies as we strained toward mutual satisfaction.

His teeth scraped my neck. His groan was a low rumble that became a growl. I surprised myself by answering with one of my own.

He thrust deeply, stilling, panting harshly and, as he spilled his seed inside me, I flew over the edge with him.

For a wondrous moment, the world sparkled, and all I knew, all I found, was absolute pleasure, and within it, the shining grandeur of love.

Chapter 13

The next morning ... er, afternoon, I awoke to puppy kisses and muttered curses. I looked sleepily up at Damian, who was wiping drool off his cheek.

I laughed.

Then we heard a faint ringing.

"My cell," said Damian. He scrambled out of the covers and hopped off the bed. Jeff thought that was a fine idea, and because he didn't realize the bed was forty-seven million feet off the ground my death-wish doggie made a flying leap.

By the time I'd opened my mouth to yell, Damian whirled around, caught him with one hand, and then leaned down to scoop his BlackBerry from his jeans pocket. He was back on the bed with phone and puppy in hand before I uttered a strangled squeak.

Damian answered his phone, dumped Jeff into my lap, gave my breasts a lascivious stare, and then leaned against the pillows as he listened to the caller. I petted my poor, half-brained pooch and slowly, my heart rate returned to normal.

A minute later, Damian ended the call. He did not

look happy. "Dante escaped—minutes after I joined you at Margaret's house. My brothers and Adulfo have been searching for him, but they've found no trace."

It didn't sound like the opening salvo to a conversation either of us wanted to have, so I threw myself on top of him and made him forget about Jarred, and everything else. We even managed to ignore Jeff, who got bored and went to nap on a nearby pile of pillows.

Afterward, Damian took a quick shower and went off to check in with Hilda and Arnold. Then Jeff and I took advantage of the steam shower, and got dressed (me, not the dog. Oh, but wouldn't he look cute in a teeny shirt that said STUD MUFFIN?). Damian had managed to ship all my clothes and lingerie (of course) from Broken Heart. It was amazing what he could accomplish with willpower and wealth.

When Damian returned, he walked me down the hall to another huge room.

It was mostly empty except for a couple of chairs, a table, and all the boxes we'd packed from my father's study.

"I can't believe you managed to get it all here." I paused. "Wait. Yes, I can. Because you're you, and nothing's impossible for you."

"Almost nothing," he said, the whisper of sadness cut me like a thin blade. Then he smiled at me, and I melted into a puddle of love goo. "I'll go get us something to eat while you get started." He kissed me. I grabbed his shirt and kissed him back. He staggered out of my grip and shook his head. *"Nein,"* he said with a laugh. "We will never get any work done."

"That's true," I said crankily. "So maybe you should start looking around for the chalice, and I'll look for clues about my mother."

"And get to know your father."

"Yes," I said, my heart tripping over in my chest. In those boxes were there remnants of a man I hadn't known—and would never know except through what he'd left behind. I was saddened by this thought, but not devastated. It was difficult to miss what I'd never really had.

Damian offered me another smile, and then he scooped up the pug. "Come, runt. I will introduce you to the gardens, so you can water them."

"Shouldn't we get him a leash?" I asked worriedly.

Damian looked at me, arrogance etching his features. "I am the crown prince of all lycans, *Schätzchen*. I can command one tiny puppy."

"Does Jeff know that?"

He sent me a haughty glance, which he softened with a half grin. Then he and Jeff left, and I turned to the boxes.

And to the unmasking of my true past.

Three days later, I knew my father had been a sucker for foreign films, deep-dish pizza, and nature walks. At the beginning of his marriage to Margaret, he was a producer for a local radio station; after she hit it big, he turned to managing her career.

To my great disappointment, my father's journals held all kinds of information about plants and birds, as well as some observations about nature, all random notations with the occasional crude drawing of a cardinal or flower. But there were no mentions about me, or his mistress, or his actual life. After a while, I began to realize how much was missing, all carefully removed by his enraged wife.

I went through every letter, every ledger, every book, every goddamned piece of paper. I found an elementary-school drawing done by my brother, one of my sister's high school report cards, and a postcard from Ireland that Margaret had mailed to him twenty years ago.

By the end of day three, I reached the conclusion that I would never know Bert, or my mother, or their story together.

None of the photographs included me. They were all pictures of Bert and Margaret together, Bert alone, usually in some nature setting, or with them with their two children. Throughout the years, I'd been part of the Morningstone photographic history. But she'd erased me. She didn't want me to exist, and so she did everything possible to make sure I disappeared.

That level of hatred was difficult for me to comprehend. She'd been tough on me, but even my older siblings had admitted she'd always been a stern disciplinarian. She never hit me, and while her criticisms wounded, she didn't call me names, and she never made me do any Mommy Dearest–type things. Of course, she was under the public microscope. If she stepped one toe out of line, she risked losing everything. Who would believe her "firm but fair" child-raising tactics if it was found out she'd been secretly abusing her own daughter? Or rather, the orphaned child of her late husband's paramour?

Why had she snapped? Could she have truly bided her time, twenty-eight long years, while she waited for the opportunity to finally exorcise me from her world? It didn't make sense. But insanity rarely did.

Come to think it, neither did love. Emotions didn't operate with rules. And sometimes, there was no logic to them at all. How many times had I heard patients admit, "I know I shouldn't feel this way, but . . ."

Exactly.

I sat among my father's effects feeling tired, and truth be told, weepy, too. But it wasn't grief for him. It was grief for her, for Margaret. She'd been the only mother I'd ever known, and it hurt that she didn't want me. There was relief, too. Sure. Because I no longer had to worry about what she thought about me, or what I could do to earn her approval. Maybe one day I'd feel better about everything. I'd be able to let go. Maybe.

"Did you find anything about your birth mother?" asked Damian.

Jeff stirred from the pile of papers he'd flopped down on a half hour ago, then jumped to his feet, tail wagging. Then he trotted over to the werewolf and yipped. Damian scooped him up, and bent down to kiss me.

"I got nada. Any luck tracking down the chalice?"

"Nein," he said. "Only three days until the Solstice."

"I know." My heart gave a tug. Three days for a new life to begin, or for the old life to be over. Permanently. "You think we can get these boxes to my sister?"

"If you like. What if she returns them to Margaret?"

"Her choice," I said philosophically. "But I think she and my brother should know about this stuff. And it'll mean more to them."

"All right, *Liebling,*" he said. "I'll help you."

Damian was an efficient packer, and we worked in a comfortable silence. At least until Jeff grabbed one of my father's leather journals and dragged it off. By the time I'd convinced the dog we were not playing a rousing game of tug-of-war—or should I say, he got bored, let go, and ran over to see why Damian was laughing so hard—the journal had been chewed thoroughly.

"Shit." I wiped the drool off on my jeans, and then opened it to the back to inspect the damage. The decorative paper had been ripped and poking out from it was the corner of something. I tore it all the way, and a narrow strip of photos fell out.

I picked it up, and gasped. Five squares of black-and-white photos revealed Bert, a pretty girl with dark hair and darker eyes, and between them an infant. In the first photo, they kissed each other while holding the baby. Then they kissed the baby. The next two photos were silly faces, me in the center of the fun, and in the last one I was crying, my mouth caught forever in a wide-open wail.

"Kelsey."

"He loved her. Us." I showed him the photos. "I wonder where they took these."

"Carnival, maybe," he said. "Hard to say." He studied the photographs. "It looks as though they were happy."

"But he was married," I said. "He had no right to go off and seek happiness with someone else—not unless he had the balls to tell Margaret good-bye."

"Do not judge him, Kelsey," he said softly. "We don't know his reasons, or his motives. And your mo— Margaret has proven unreliable."

"He didn't beg her for mercy," I said, suddenly sure. "He wanted a divorce. They'd raised their children, hadn't they? He was miserable. And she was . . . well, *her*. Maybe my real mother isn't dead."

He handed me back the strip. "Kelsey, if she were alive, your father would not have stayed with Margaret."

He was right. It was only five tiny photos commemorating the days or weeks before everything changed. No doubt my mother had died, and Bert had done the only thing he could for me, asked his wife to help him raise me. I wanted to believe that he thought he'd be around to protect me, and to one day tell me about my mother. I supposed if he'd gone off and tried to raise me alone, I would've ended up an orphan. Would foster care have brought me any better of a life?

I searched through the journal once more, but there were no other hidden photos or messages. I tossed the book into the final box, and Damian taped it up.

I would never know the story of my parents. And they wouldn't know mine. It wasn't the kind of information or closure I wanted, but life didn't always tie up nicely. I had to live with the unanswerable questions, and it sucked.

But at least I had a consolation prize.

I smiled at the photos, and decided to believe my mother and father had been reaching for happiness.

That's all we can do—reach for the stars and hope.

"Your castle is too big. It would take an army and a year to search this whole place thoroughly," I griped as Damian and I headed downstairs. Jeff was too little to tackle the wide stone steps, so Damian, who was a big ol' sucker, carried him tucked under one muscled arm. We'd spent the last few hours combing through rooms that seemed to hold everything except a silver engraved cup.

"Mother would not have left the chalice where Morrigu could find it easily."

"You think Morrigu snuck in here and searched for it?"

"I wouldn't doubt it. My mother's clever. I believe she either made the chalice part of the bargain, or acquired it as an insurance measure."

"That makes sense." We reached the end of the staircase, and I waited for Damian to take the lead. I knew the general direction of the dining room, but I had yet to figure out the labyrinth of hallways and staircases. I needed a personal GPS (which was currently Damian). "I know we have only two days left," I said. "But I would love to do something fun. Something that's awesome and frivolous."

"Ah. I believe I have just the thing," he said. "But first, dinner."

Damian took my hand and tugged me along. As she had every meal, Hilda waited by the massive table, food plated and wine poured. She was a big woman with apple cheeks, sparkling blue eyes, and a penchant for fussing. She wore dresses that featured colorful flowers, which she covered with a crisp, white apron. Her graying blond hair was always neatly braided, a yellow ribbon tied at the end. I loved that ribbon. It was whimsical.

"Jeff! *Mein kleiner Frechdachs*," she said in a thick accent as she plucked the pug from Damian. "I take him to kitchen." She flapped her free hand at me. "Ach! Too skinny, *Frau*. Eat, eat!"

Damian and I settled down to dine and to converse, and I thought about how nice it was to be here, with him, doing something so normal. These moments offered an easy comfort, like donning a favorite coat, or tucking under a cashmere blanket.

Several times, he reached across the table to squeeze my hand, or just to hold it for a few moments. I'd noticed that the closer it got to the Solstice, the more we sought to solidify the connection between us. We were both afraid about what might happen. Even if I survived the transition, would Damian still want me for his mate? I knew he loved me, though we had not verbalized it other than that one intense moment.

I supposed that was an issue we'd explore after the Solstice.

Damian went to reclaim Jeff, and I stacked the plates and put the soiled napkins on top. The last time I'd tried to help Hilda with the dishes, she'd acted so affronted that I never asked again. Still, I did what I could at the dinner table—and she pretended not to notice.

"Ach!" protested a soft voice. A waif of a girl, wearing a blue dress with a starched apron, scurried across the dining room. She looked over her shoulder, and then turned her cornflower eyes on me. I realized she was the only one of the staff, other than Hilda and her husband, whom I'd ever seen.

"My name's Kelsey," I said.

"Eleonore," she said. She gave a tiny curtsy. "You go, *Frau.* I clean."

"Okay," I said. Looked like Hilda was making sure I stopped helping altogether. I offered the girl a smile, which she returned shyly. Then Damian returned, and he took my hand, leading me out in the hallway.

I have no idea how we got there, but we entered a room that appeared to be filled with every game imaginable—from pinball to pool. Farther back, in the corner, was a sixty-inch television. Positioned in front of it was a Rock Band kit—at least I thought so. It looked a lot different than the ones I'd seen displayed in the stores.

"Rock Band Three," said Damian.

I shook my head. "I've never seen this version." The drum kit, guitars, and keyboard were wrapped in metal.

"Jessica and Patrick were the first ones to try out this game," he said. "Jess's enthusiasm broke several drums. So Patrick started a small company that upgrades gaming materials for parakind. Those two have parties all the time." He picked up a guitar and put the strap over his shoulder. "Have you ever played?"

"No," I said, eyeing the drums. I sat on the stool and picked up the sticks. "You'll have to help me figure it out."

"I've never played, either," he said.

"But you said Jessica and Patrick had parties." I glanced up at him and saw his expression. "You never went to one?"

"It seemed trivial to spend my time playing a video game when so much needed doing." He used the guitar's frets to maneuver through Xbox 360 menu.

"But you still wanted to."

"It looked fun," he admitted. He gestured around. "My brothers outfitted this place. They are much better at letting out their inner children."

"Well, everyone needs to let loose. Even you."

He grinned.

We spent almost ten minutes arguing about what we should name our virtual band. Jeff interjected his opinion with a series of barks and yips, and then he flopped on to his back and went to sleep.

I suggested Jefferson Pugship followed by Belly Scratchers, which earned eye rolls from Damian. He countered with Butt Sniffers and spent a good minute being amused by his own guy humor. Then, because he obviously never wanted to have sex with me again, he offered up Sixty-Nine and the Tongue Lashers.

"How about The Werewolf Sleeps Alone?" I asked archly.

"Suggestion rescinded."

Eventually we settled on Lycan Therapy.

We rocked into the wee hours of the night, choosing songs, switching instruments, and teasing each other mercilessly. Damian got the hang of the drums much faster than I did, but I totally whooped him on the keyboard. Neither one of us had much voice talent, but man, we had enthusiasm. (Huey Lewis and the News, eat your heart out.)

All in all, Lycan Therapy kicked serious ass.

"I know where it is."

"Whaaat?" I rolled onto my side and blinked sleepily up at Damian. He stood next to the bed, dressed and looking incredibly chipper. "Your morning perfection burns me." I made hissing noises and covered my eyes.

"Tomorrow's the Solstice," he said.

"Noted." I collapsed back onto the covers. My tired mind flipped back to his first sentence. I jolted up. "You know where the chalice is?"

"In the temple."

"There's a temple in your castle?"

"No, there's a temple *near* my castle." He leaned over the bed and kissed me. "It's the perfect place. Morrigu cannot enter religious ground not dedicated to her unless she's invited. That's why she needs us to get it."

"How is she going to perform the magical ick potion if she can't go inside the temple?"

"After my parents return, Mother will grant her access."

"You seem sure."

"We are following our destiny," he said. He kissed me again. "We are meant to be together, *Schätzchen*."

With that lovely thought as motivation, I got out of bed and got ready.

Within an hour, we were on our way to the temple. I figured we would be bundled into a car and drive to another castlelike structure. But the castle and the temple were actually connected by tunnels through the mountainside.

So, once again, I found myself following Damian through another mystifying set of twisty hallways, stairways, and finally, we entered a wide tunnel lit by torches.

"I feel like I've fallen into the medieval era," I said.

"We have rarely used this passage," said Damian, glancing around at the soot-stained rock. "Perhaps we should consider updating with electricity."

"Put it on the to-do list," I said.

From the crook of Damian's arm, Jeff barked his agreement.

It was a good fifteen-minute walk to the temple. The tunnel dumped us into a cellar, which was filled with crates and barrels. It smelled musty, and it was dark. Luckily, Junior Explorer Lycan brought a big flashlight, and with it, he was able to guide us up a set of ancient wooden steps.

We reached a solid, heavy door, which swung open easily.

"This is the only temple left that honors Aufanie," said Damian. Since the empty kitchen we'd entered was well lit, he clicked off the flashlight. The place wasn't as updated as the castle's, though it was just as clean and tidy—and it had the same kind of huge hearth (but without the cauldron). "There used to be many all throughout Germany. She was worshiped by many peoples, not just the lycans."

"People stopped believing in the gods and goddesses."

"Mostly," said Damian. "A mere thousand years ago, many humans still used magic and married into paranormal clans. But as advances were made in science and technology, the humans stopped following the old ways. They hunted us, ignored us, hated us . . . Finally all the creatures who'd once lived in harmony with mankind went into hiding."

"That's sad."

"It is survival."

"Prince Damian?" The woman gliding toward us wore in a long red dress trimmed in gold, her feet shod in matching gold slippers. The pendant swinging from her neck was a large teardrop ruby. She wore her dark hair as long as Damian's, her darks eyes glinting with wariness. She stopped before us and curtsied deeply to Damian.

"Maria," he said. "It's nice to see you."

"And you as well." She rose gracefully, and cast me a curious look.

"This is Kelsey Morningstone," he said. He smiled at me. "Maria is an old friend."

I shook her hand briefly, and introductions done, she turned back to Damian. I had my psychic shields up, but I had the distinct impression she was displeased with my presence. Was it that I was obviously not a lycan? Or that I had claimed a man she wanted?

"We were surprised to learn you had returned. As I recall, you swore to never step foot in this place again."

"Things change," he said, gripping my hand tightly. "People change."

"They must," she agreed. "When you called asking about the chalice, we were hopeful that you were embracing the new prophecies."

"I'm working on it," he said. "The chalice?"

"The high priestess is its guardian," she said. "I'll take you to her." She gave me another veiled look—somewhat hostile, if you asked me—then turned with a swish of skirts and led the way.

We climbed staircases—three different sets—before reaching a narrow arched doorway set inside a curved wall. Obviously it was the entrance to a tower

"Through here," she said. "She's waiting for you." She placed a hand on his forearm, her gaze searching his for a long, uneasy moment, and then she left.

Jeff barked and wiggled out of Damian's grip, so I took him, letting him lick my cheek before securing him.

"She likes you," I said as Damian opened the door.

"Who?"

"Oh, please. Maria. Did you guys date or something?" He flushed.

"You *did*?" I asked, jaw dropping.

"I was much younger."

"How much younger?"

"Two or three hundred years ago," he said.

"Oh."

Conversation over, we peered up into the tower, and I looked forlornly at the winding stairs.

"Crap," I muttered.

Damian chuckled, and then he led the way.

When we reached the top, we found the door open. Inside was a richly appointed chamber lit by flickering candles. A single square window sat too high to offer much natural light. On one side of the room was an altar. In its middle was the gleaming silver statue of a tall woman, her hand resting on the nape of a wolf. Aufanie and Tark. The statue was surrounded by lit white votives, and on either side were cones of incense, thin trails of fragrant smoke rising into the air.

"Damian, Crown Prince of Lycans," said a raspy voice.

We turned to the other side of the room. Sitting in an oversized red velvet wingback was a woman—at least in form. She wore a more elaborate version of Maria's dress, except hers was black and gold, and she wore a black veil that completely covered her face.

Damian studied her with a frown. "You are the high priestess?"

"I am." She rose and executed a graceful curtsy. "Your Highness."

Damian had been unable to stop staring at her, his expression confused. "Alaya?" he choked out.

She inclined her head.

He grabbed her into a fierce hug. "We though you lost! Why did you never contact us?"

"We all have our destinies," she said, her odd voice rife with emotion. "And our sacrifices."

He pulled back from her. "Darrius searched for you. For weeks we all combed every inch of the village and the mountains looking for you and other survivors. We found none."

"I'm sorry he suffered, that you all suffered," she said quietly. "We were separated after the first explosion, and he followed you to protect Anna. The second explosion was practically under my feet. Maria and another priestess found me. Somehow they got me to the temple and cared for me. It took a long time for me to heal, and even when I regained my full strength, I was left scarred. Too scarred, Damian."

"You do a disservice to my brother," said Damian harshly, "if you believe that matters. He sees you with his heart."

"I freed him."

"You freed yourself."

She pulled out of his embrace. "It does not matter, Damian."

"It will," he said softly. "We are coming home to rebuild the pack."

"I know. You must promise not to tell him about me."

"I cannot."

"Would you hurt him with the truth? He has the chance for a new life now. Let him have it." She paused, and placed a slim, gloved hand on his cheek. "Swear it, Damian. Please."

His shoulders sagged, defeat in his gaze. "Very well, Alaya. I will honor your wish. For now."

"Always the caveat with you." She laughed softly; then she turned to me. "You are Kelsey—Damian's mate."

"Yes," I said simply.

"We never know what lies ahead, so all we can do is live each day fully, with hope." She looked down at Jeff snuggled in my arms. "He's adorable." She scratched behind his ears, and Jeff rewarded her with a tongue-lolling.

"I need to find Morrigu's chalice," said Damian. "My mother hid it somewhere."

"And Morrigu promised to save your mate if you returned it to her." Alaya sighed. "It's an ancient magic, an extension of the goddess who crafted it. It's the cup from which Ruadan drank Morrigu's dark blood, and became the first undead," she said. "Now her blood will save the lycans, too."

"You know about the ritual?" asked Damian.

"I received a vision," she said.

"Then you know where the chalice is?"

"I know where it will be," she said. Sadness threaded her voice. "And that your mate must be worthy, or your sacrifice will be for naught."

"What does that mean?" I said as foreboding crimped my stomach.

"We will see soon enough."

Was it a rule that paranormal beings had to be cryptic? Talking to Alaya was like trying to get a straight answer out of the Caterpillar. He'd asked Alice the same question in a way: Who are you?

I knew who I was. And who I wanted to be—Damian's mate. *So, go ahead, Fate, bring it.*

"We are preparing the main chapel," she continued. "Tomorrow eve, our goddess and god will come home, and we will celebrate the marriage of our new alpha and his mate."

"Your vision confirms this?" he asked.

"No, Damian." She placed her gloved hands on our shoulders. "My hope does."

We made our way to the cellar and headed into the tunnel. Jeff insisted he be let down, but he made it only three feet under his own power. He decided that making his own way wasn't as much fun as Mommy carrying him.

He pawed at my calf and yipped, but Damian looked at him and said, "Scoot, runt."

Jeff plopped onto his butt and cocked his head at us.

Damian tugged me into his arms. He kissed me, and I felt a whisper of good-bye in that hopeful meeting of lips. It made the nerves plucking my stomach tighten. Fear crept up my spine like icy spiders. *What if I don't make it?*

Damian pulled back, looked me in the eyes, and said, "I love you, Kelsey. And I will never love another. You are my mate."

His words destroyed my already wobbling psychic shield, and I leaned forward to take another kiss. "I love you, too," I said, tears crowding my eyes. "And you are my one and only."

We stood there staring at each other. My heart was so full that I didn't discern the wisps of hostility right away.

I grabbed onto the emotion and tried to follow it to the source. I didn't get too far, but whoever was leaking the emotion was close. "Damian."

"Go back," he said, immediately concerned. "I'll check—"

We heard screams and crashes echoing into the tunnel. There were sounds of fighting, too, and then gunfire.

"Run, Kelsey!"

"Not without you." I scooped up Jeff, my heart pounding, as a barrage of emotions ravaged me. *Pain. Fear. Shock. Anger. Determination.*

"The priestesses are being attacked," I whispered.

"Go, damn it!" Damian spun me around and pushed me toward the direction of the castle. "Warn Hilda. She'll know what to do."

Jeff whined in my arms, but I couldn't leave Damian. I was sick with terror. I stumbled back, heading toward the temple.

Damian was running toward the melee, and I followed clumsily, weeping, hugging the puppy tightly to my chest.

When I caught sight of Damian, he'd just reached the point where the tunnel became the temple's cellar. Military-garbed figures swarmed toward him, and then bright, loud pops of sound and color burst through the darkness.

The force of the bullets jerked Damian off his feet.

I screamed, and ran faster, Jeff clutched in my arms.

One of the men stepped between Damian's legs. Damian's chest was shuddering, blood soaked his shirt and spattered his face, and through his rippling, awful pain, I felt a sudden, red-*beauty*-passion-love flow from him. It wrapped around me, and I clung to it fiercely. He wanted me to know that he loved me, before he—

"No!" I cried. I stumbled to a stop, my horror so great I couldn't breathe.

A man dressed in black combat gear stepped forward, aimed a sleek, black pistol at Damian's heart, and pulled the trigger.

His body jerked, and then he went limp.

Damian's last emotion, his love for me, faded into nothing.

One must die, so the other can live. Morrigu's chalice appeared right in front of me. It spun slowly, as though dangling from an invisible wire, pulsing with gold light and old magic.

I grabbed it and clutched it to my chest, pressing it next to Jeff, who was whimpering and shaking.

It was too late. Too goddamned late. No, no, no!

Rage and grief pounded through me, and I couldn't keep the feelings inside. I screamed and screamed. Tears poured from my eyes, my throat clogged.

"Take the girl and get that damned cup," he ordered flatly. "Christ! Shut her the fuck up." He pointed the pistol at Damian's head.

The whole world snapped into cold, clear focus.

I know what you are, Kelsey. You must shed your old skin. You must walk in the darkness with me.

Two men came forward and laid hands on my shoulders. But they could not move me. I wouldn't let them.

You will be who you were always meant to be. I understand my purpose. I understand your purpose.

Jeff growled and snapped at them. *Good boy.*

Blood will tell.

I opened my senses wide and let myself feel everything. Pain. Grief. Loss. Love.

They took from me.

And so I would take from them.

Everything.

Take what's yours, Wolf of Silver.

"Don't move," I said, and I pushed out the command to them all, filling it with authority, coating it with fear. "You're scared of me, you bastards. You're fucking terrified."

Every soldier froze. Like statues. Like *toy* soldiers.

Within me, their emotions pulsed, like a thousand heartbeats, but I controlled them. I could cull through them like hanging ribbons, choosing what I wanted, shredding, cutting, destroying.

Stupid humans.

I looked at the man who'd killed my mate.

It was so easy. How simple it was to make him pay. *Make them all pay.*

I reached inside him, deep where his fears lay, and pulled out the nastiest one. Claustrophobia. Then I draped it over him like a freshly spun web: *You are being buried alive.*

He choked, dropping the gun, and fell to his knees. He was pushing at air, at nothing, tears clogging his eyes. "No," he yelled. "Stop shoveling dirt on me!"

"They stole from you," I whispered to my jailers. I

weaved in fury and betrayal, pushing those fetid emotions in so deeply, they would taint everything inside
them. "Your money. Your women. Your homes. They
took them."

Their gazes went glassy, their expressions turned
murderous.

They let go of me, drawing their guns as they marched
toward the other soldiers.

"You assholes!" one shouted. He started shooting.

His friend joined in.

I pushed wave after wave of fear, of greed, of fury out
into the cellar. I planted emotion after emotion until
they were drowning in their own hatred. As I watched
them destroy each other, I released their emotions, and
the ribbons went liquid, bleeding away, like a painting
caught in the rain, its colors running until the canvas was
blank once more.

Then I felt nothing. Nothing at all.

Jeff whimpered and wiggled, until I crouched down
and let him go. He ran barking toward the castle. "Good-
bye," I whispered.

I sat down next to Damian. I held the useless chalice
in one hand, and with the other, I grasped his cold, still
hand.

And waited.

Chapter 14

"*Frau.*"

I looked into the cornflower eyes of Eleonor. She was leaning over me, carefully keeping her gaze from Damian's prone form. It was quiet now. Everyone was dead or gone. I idly wondered if any of the priestesses were still alive. Whatever had been in those bullets had been meant to kill lycans. Otherwise Damian wouldn't have succumbed.

I noticed then that Eleonor held Jeff, who gazed at me and whined. I reached out and patted the top of his head.

"I'm fine," I said. "I'm just waiting."

"For what?" she asked.

"For it to be over. It's almost the Solstice. If I don't drink Morrigu's potion, I won't survive the change. There's no point now, you see?"

"You should not give up," she said.

"I'm making a choice."

She looked at me, her blue eyes mercurial. Huh. They looked gray now, and somehow oddly familiar. "Then, I, too, must make a choice." She withdrew something long and silver and stabbed it into my shoulder.

"Ow." I stared up at her, dumbfounded. Her face wavered and I swore I saw the strong, masculine features of Jarred Dante superimposed on her waiflike features. Then my body went boneless, and I slid mercifully into unconsciousness.

When I awoke, I was tucked underneath a thick comforter in a small, windowless room. Jeff lay curled up between my neck and shoulder, snuffling in his sleep. It was a wonderful two seconds.

Until I realized Damian was dead.

"Kelsey." I looked up and saw Jarred sitting in a nearby chair, his gaze wary. "I couldn't let you die."

"Didn't you kill me?" I asked without rancor. "That serum of yours is what fucked everything up."

"I know. I should've realized the consequences before I authorized Dr. Ruthers to inject you. My judgment was . . . clouded."

"Thinking with your dick," I said.

"Wrong organ," he said with a sad smile, and put his hand over his heart.

That was kinda sweet, and the gesture made me feel bitchy, but I guess I had a right to feel however the hell I wanted. "What now?"

"We fix you."

"I'd rather you didn't," I said.

"Do you think Damian would want you to give up?"

My heart clutched, and I tried to push down the grief. It came anyway. "Don't play armchair psychologist," I said. "It doesn't suit you."

"And playing the victim doesn't suit you."

I sighed, too weary to feel the jab of his very sharp

point. "You're going to do what you want no matter how I feel about it."

"I won't do a damned thing if you plan on wasting your chance to live." He stood up and straightened the sleeves of his jacket, once again looking untouchable and imperious. "Decide quickly. It's already the Solstice. We're two hours away from midnight."

I blinked up at him. "Already?" I'd been unconscious for a really long time. "You'll get me to the temple?"

He shook his head. "Your redemption should not be left in the hands of Morrigu."

I sat up. "Where's the chalice?"

"On the nightstand," he said. I looked to my left. On the nightstand sat the goblet. The one Damian had died for. Why the hell would Aufanie sacrifice her son to make the chalice appear? It didn't make sense. A blood sacrifice was needed to unlock the hiding place—which had been where? The cellar? The tunnel? The freaking ether?

It didn't matter. Not anymore.

Jarred's gaze searched my face. "Don't get me wrong. Morrigu keeps her bargains. But she's also very good at finding loopholes."

"You know her."

"Quite well," he said.

I studied him. "What are you?"

"Maybe I'll tell you one day. If you decide life is worth living."

My breath hitched. *Damian.* "Where is . . . Did someone . . . ?"

"The priestesses will prepare him for funeral rites. I'm sorry, Kelsey," he said, and I could actually feel wisps of genuine sympathy. "I truly am." He tucked his hands into his front pockets and rocked back on his heels.

"ETAC found him again. It's a government organization that handles paraterrorism. They know about us, and they're either killing us, or experimenting on us, or finding ways to extract our abilities."

"I know. That's why they took Damian." God. It felt like a lifetime ago that I'd been watching him pace in that induction room. He'd been so strong, so beautiful. How could that kind of vibrant life be snuffed out so cruelly?

"I destroyed the lab after his extraction. Whatever intel they'd gathered is cyber dust, I promise you." He sighed. "But ETAC's new weapons were already in production. I managed to snag a couple of their weapons and their bullets in the tunnel. We'll figure out their tech and create countermeasures."

"Who's we?"

"Mostly me," he said.

"So you're a good guy?"

"Sometimes."

Silence unfolded between us, and waves of grief crashed through me. My heart ached so much. "He's not coming back, is he?"

"It's too late for him," he said. "But not for you." Jarred gave me one last pitying glance, then turned and left the room.

I had no idea where I was, only that I knew it wasn't Damian's castle. What did it matter? I could be in France or South Dakota or hell. Who cared?

I wanted to be with Damian, if not in this life, then the next. How did one go on after love was ripped away like that? I couldn't fathom it. I couldn't draw a full breath without feeling like razors were scraping my lungs. I understood now how Aufanie must've felt when she bargained for Tark's life. Damian was a demigod. He shouldn't have been felled by humans. By bullets. I couldn't escape from the ache that stole through me. I felt like I had swallowed rocks and shards of glass and acid.

Jarred was right. Damian wouldn't want me to give up.

I took the chalice and studied it, hoping for inspiration or wisdom or something. But it was just a freaking cup. Old, magical, and worthless.

Except to Morrigu.

Rules, my ass. She would help me, or I'd make sure her goblet was melted down into nothing.

Fucking immortals.

I didn't want to eat, but Jarred insisted. I took a few sips of soup and then gave the rest to Jeff. I sat on the edge of the bed, feeling tired and chilled. I was wearing a set of pajamas that weren't mine, and I couldn't bring myself to care about the fact that Jarred had bathed and dressed me while I was still unconscious.

"Morrigu isn't going to be happy that I'm breaking the bargain."

"So long as she gets the chalice, she'll consider the terms met."

"Will she?"

"That's up to you."

"So everyone tells me." I scratched around Jeff's ears while he finished off the soup. "If we're doing this the science-y way then why are we waiting for midnight?"

"Only thirty minutes more," he said, ignoring my question.

I put the empty bowl on the nightstand, then snuggled with Jeff and tried not to think about Damian. Or Damian's lifeless body riddled with bullet holes, soaked in blood.

All kinds of scenarios had entered my mind. The vampires could Turn him. His mother could breathe life back into him. Morrigu could let him drink from the chalice.

Hope was a tiny flame inside me, even though my own heart told me the truth: Damian was gone, and I was lost without him.

"Do you feel that?" I said. The air felt electrified. Jeff lifted his snout, cocked his head, and then he barked. The hair on the back of my neck rose. Wary, I scooted off the bed, hugging Jeff, as I looked around the room.

"Shit," said Jarred. He stood up, too, and shoved the injector into my hand. "Skip Morrigu's blood spells and use this."

"What?" Stunned, I looked at metal tube the size and shape of a cigar and then at Jarred.

"The problem with the first serum was that I donated DNA in my weakest form. Still, my demigod blood was enough to disrupt the theria genotype's natural process. It was trying to encode Damian's DNA, but mine was just potent enough to, as you so kindly put it, fuck everything up." He grimaced. "He's getting through the protections faster than I thought possible."

"Who?"

"Your friend," he said with an almost smile. "The new serum includes lycan DNA coding."

"Dr. Michaels said that adding more lycan DNA could overload my system."

"It's your choice," he said. "Morrigu's dark blood or my lycan DNA."

"But you're not a lycan!"

"I can be," he said. "That's my curse. I can be anyone. Anything."

"What does that mean?" Panic was started to claw through me. My heart pounded fiercely, and I felt an intense heat gather in my belly. "Why are you helping me?"

"I'm the one who hurt you. I need to make this right."

"I appreciate that," I said warily. "What, exactly, are you?"

"I'm a therianthrope," he said. "The only one left on this earth. And you are the daughter of the last known changeling. My last hope to find a mate." His gaze filled with anguish. "I wished you could've loved me the way you love him."

"Oh, Jarred." My heart broke for him, even though I was feeling wretched. My bones hurt, my muscles felt rubbery, and inside me, something foreign scrabbled, wanting out. The inner me, the werewolf who wanted to live.

"Good-bye, Kelsey." He disappeared. Literally. No sparkles, or electric air, or anything. Just gone.

The moment he left, gold sparks burst inside the room, and when they dissipated, I saw Ruadan. He cocked an eyebrow at me. "There you are, love. C'mon, then. You've work to do yet."

I walked into his arms, holding my dog, the chalice, and the injector.

Then we went all sparkly—and did our own disappearing act.

We arrived in a huge room with a vaulted ceiling, stained glass windows, and large stone dais at the front. Pain radiated through me, and I was having a tough time drawing breath.

"The change is upon her," snapped Morrigu, who stood. "Hurry!"

I briefly wondered how Morrigu could be in Aufanie's chapel without the Goddess's invitation, but I was tired of trying to figure out the policies of supernatural jerkfaces. Screw 'em.

I put Jeff down, and he trotted off—probably to go pee in a corner. Ruadan helped me to his grandmother, who stood a few feet down the aisle in front of the dais. Her gaze was on the chalice in my hand. She couldn't have it unless I gave it to her, not until the bargain was met.

On the left of the platform stood Alaya, who was dressed in even more formal robes. Her black lace veil was so dark, it was a wonder she could see through it. Damian's brothers stood on the other side. They were looking at me, but I could see Darrius stealing looks at Alaya and frowning.

Someone else was there, too.

Damian.

Even though it felt like I was being turned inside out, I climbed up the steps and grabbed the edge of the smooth, worn rock. He lay on the flat stone, looking too much like a sacrifice. He'd been stripped and cleaned, and wore a black and gold robe.

"Damian," I whispered.

"You must mourn later, child," said Morrigu, "lest you want to join him in the next world."

"I want to join him in *this* world," I said raggedly. I turned, and stumbled. "If he drinks your potion, will it save him?"

Morrigu narrowed her gaze. "That was not the bargain."

"Do you want the chalice?" I asked bitterly. "I'm changing the terms. Answer the question." I fell to my knees, sucking in harsh breaths. I heard an odd cracking sound and agony shot through my limbs. I kept a death grip on the chalice.

"Foolish girl," she said softly. "Yes, the potion will save him. He will live again as he was—but the magic is meant for you. Do you love him so much that you would give up your only chance to live?"

"Yes," I said, and it was true. But I wasn't giving up my life. At least I hoped I wasn't. The injector was still in my hand, hidden by the sleeve of my pajama top.

"Very well," said Morrigu. "I will trade Damian's life for my chalice."

Well, at least she hadn't told me something cryptic and stupid. I gave her the chalice. She held the edge of it by her fingertips. She raised her other arm and a small, silver dagger appeared. She drew the blade under her wrist; black blood dribbled into the cup.

As the Morrigu whispered words I didn't understand, the dagger disappeared. In its place, she held a grape-sized lustrous gray rock, which she put inside the chalice. I heard a metallic plop, and then silver sparkles emitted from the concoction.

"Silver, blood, antimony, chalice," said Morrigu. "Life reborn." She walked to the dais, leaned over, and lifted Damian slightly. She whispered into his ear, and his mouth opened wide.

She poured all the contents down his throat.

I burned.

My muscles were pulling away from breaking bones.

I screamed.

"She's trying to shift," said Drake, kneeling next to me. "I've never seen anything like this."

"Kelsey."

I looked up and saw Damian peering at me over the edge of the altar. He looked alive and healthy, as though he'd never spent a second as a corpse. My love. My mate.

Morrigu had kept her promise.

I lifted the injector and slammed it into my thigh.

"No!" He leapt off the dais and cradled me. He picked up the silver tube and looked down at me with a horrified gaze. "What have you done, *Schätzchen*?"

"It's okay," I said. I pressed my palm against his cheek. "I thought I'd lost you."

"Never, my love. Never."

"Aufanie and Tark are coming through the portal," said Alaya.

I saw a bright light somewhere to the left of Damian, but I couldn't look away from him.

"Family reunion time," I said. My body started to shake, and my vision grayed around the edges. I tried to fight off the creature growing inside me, but I was helpless. And scared. Damian held me, never looking away, pouring his strength and love into me, wave after wave of it. It sustained me. Panic receded.

"Damian." The sweet face of Aufanie and the stern visage of Tark leaned over me.

"S-say hello to your mother," I told Damian. "Don't be rude."

He barked a laugh, and then he broke eye contact to look at his mother. "I understand," he said in a broken voice. "I would do for Kelsey in a heartbeat what you did for my father. I'm sorry, Mother."

"You forgive me," she whispered. Crystalline tears fell from her eyes.

"As do we all, Mother," said Drake and Darrius together as they joined the circle of faces above me. This was my family. The family of my heart. The ones who loved me. I felt that truth, that unalterable joy pulsing all around, filling me, healing me, buoying me.

"The circle is closed," said Morrigu. I couldn't see the Goddess, but her voice was close. "The bargain is met, Aufanie. Blessed be."

"Blessed be, Morrigu." Aufanie looked at me, her smile beatific. "Peace, child," she said soothingly, and placed her palm against my forehead.

Tark covered her hand with his and said, "Welcome, daughter."

Inside me, beyond the shadows of my soul, something wonderful stirred.

The beast nestled inside me, the one that felt like hope, like belonging, bloomed to the surface. A voluminous whiteness burst around me, and the terrible agony faded.

Everything shifted back together, but in a completely different way.

I was reborn.

I felt the power, the strength in my muscles, the wonderment that beat within me with the same ferocity of my pounding heart.

I lifted my snout, and howled.

"Wolf of Silver," said Aufanie. "Life-mate of the lycanthrope king."

I stood next to Damian, and he put his hand on my scruff. Jeff meandered over and looked up at me, his bug eyes assessing my new form. I leaned down and licked his face. He snuffled, then lay down, putting his head on his paws.

I watched as Aufanie lifted off her crown and placed it on her son's head. And then Tark removed his collar and clasped it around my neck. Happiness rippled through me, and I barked.

Aufanie and Tark bowed to us.

"All hail the new king and queen of lycanthropes," said Alaya in her scratchy voice. Everyone offered us their obeisance.

Even Morrigu.

Epilogue

Three months later . . .

"Any word from Alaya?" I asked as Damian drove down Sanderson Street to Jessica and Patrick's home. It was the first time we'd been back to Broken Heart since the night Damian had us whisked away to his castle.

"*Nein.* Maria promised to keep us informed."

Maria had been named the new high priestess, and she'd been a lot nicer to me now that I was her queen an' all. Heh.

Slowly but surely the lycans—full-bloods and Roma alike—were returning to Schwarzwald. A new community was being built—in a location far away from the original one. The remnants of the first village had been razed, and a small memorial erected. Damian wanted everyone to remember what had been sacrificed sixty years ago, but he didn't want them to, as Jessica so often said, wallow around in the past.

I knew Alaya had left because of Darrius. Damian had kept his promise to her about not revealing her identity, but Darrius had been nosing (hah) around, asking questions. Her disappearance had only whetted Darrius's appetite to know who she was . . . and you know, *I* hadn't promised Alaya not to say anything.

But I also knew Damian had kept his mouth shut to protect his brother.

I'm not sure, however, that Darrius would think of it as a favor.

Aufanie, Tark, and Damian's brothers all resided with us at the castle. We had a lot of guests these days, mostly the lycans who were helping to build the new town. The castle was big enough to hold a thousand or so people, so we had plenty of space. I was still getting lost, too, but that was the perk of having a goddess for a mother-in-law. She always knew where to find me.

I hadn't heard from Jarred except once. Not long after Damian and I were official married (in the chapel where we'd saved each other), I received a bouquet of lilies. The card only said, "Be happy. J."

I wanted Jarred to find what he was looking for, but I hoped he found a better way to go about his search.

Damian parked the BMW. Then he took my hand and pressed his lips against my wrist. I melted instantly. "Are you ready?"

"As long as I have you, I can do anything."

The weapons of war were being carefully arranged by the leaders of the combatants. Two big-screen televisions, two Xbox 360s, and two sets of Rock Band 3 paranormal-ized (as Jess called it) were being set up, while the captains of the opposing sides—Patrick, the vampire, and Damian, the lycanthrope—eyed each other suspiciously.

I stood between Jessica and Patsy, behind the safety of the couch, eating a cupcake. I'd been craving them more than usual, but I figured that just meant that the child growing within my womb totally got the delights of sugar and fat. And also, she was a girl. I just knew it—even though Damian and I had decided to be surprised. (He thought we were having a boy. Hah.)

"I never got a crown," said Patsy, as she gazed longingly at the one perched on my husband's head. "Seriously. I ruled vampires and lycans for eight freaking years, and I never got any cool accessories."

"Does Gabriel count?" asked Jessica.

We snickered. She plucked another truffle from the gold box she held. I peered inside, sniffing, and she looked at me, baring her fangs.

"You are so selfish," I said. I pointed to my belly. "Do you want my child to suffer?"

"I'm protecting your ass," she said. "Literally. You're getting some junk in the trunk, girl."

I gave her my best puppy-dog look.

"Christ. All right, already." She jabbed the box toward me and pointed to the corner piece. "That one's like lemon pie."

"Thanks." I grabbed it and popped it in my mouth. "Mmm. Good."

Jessica stared at me, horrified. "You have no idea how to properly eat a Godiva truffle. It's impossible that we're friends."

"I think I'm more a sapphire kind of girl," mused Patsy. "Maybe some platinum gold. Hey, Damian, how do you feel about loaning out your headgear?"

"No can do, *Liebling*," he said, flashing a smile. He looked at me and winked. "It's part of a set."

"It still freaks me out to see him all smiley," muttered Jessica. "It's like the sun turned purple or something. You know. Unnatural."

"Says the vampire," said Patsy. She looked at me, her

belly more rounded than mine. "You hear that Margaret Morningstone was committed to the loony bin?"

I nodded. "By her own children." I glanced at Eva, who was reading an instruction manual and telling Lorcan how to set up the drum kit. "She had a nervous breakdown. And then some journalist discovered her latest bestseller was a bunch of lies."

"Interesting," said Jessica, who didn't sound interested at all. "Don't fuck with karma."

Or with vampires or their friends, I thought, inwardly smiling. "Have you heard anything else from the Vederes?" I asked.

"Nothing that makes any sense," said Patsy. "'Bout the only thing we know for sure is that I'm not gonna be queen of the vampires for much longer. And you know what? Just watching over the *loup de sang* will be fine by me. I might even resign from the Broken Heart council and go on an actual vacation."

"We're done," declared Patrick.

"Woot!" Jessica put her chocolates on a nearby table and literally flew over the couch to jump into her husband's arms. "Nice job, honey!"

I joined my husband on our side. He leaned down to kiss me, flattening his palm against my slightly rounded belly. "Are you ready to rock, *Schätzchen*?"

"And roll," I said.

Damian kissed me again. "I love you," he whispered against my lips.

"Love you back," I said, my heart full of love—and a serious need to wallop some vamps on Rock Band. "Now let's kick their asses."

"As my queen commands." He lifted my hand and turned it up, pressing his lips against the pulse point. I shivered. I don't think I'd ever get tired of him doing that.

"This ain't a game for sissies," said Jessica. "Grab a guitar, Romeo, and quit pawing your drummer. Sicko."

Damian laughed.

Jessica sat down by her drum kit and did a neck roll. "It's time for the Broken Heart Bloodsuckers to school Lycan Therapy."

"Try not to cry when we spank you," I offered sweetly.

"Oh," said Jessica, grinning broadly, "it's on, sistah. It's on like Donkey Kong."

And it was.

THE BROKEN HEART TURN-BLOODS

*Jessica Matthews: Widow (first husband, Richard). Mother to Bryan and Jenny, and to adopted son, Rich Jr. Stay-at-home mom. Vampire of Family Ruadan. Mated to Patrick O'Halloran.

Charlene Mason: *Deceased.* Mistress of Richard Matthews. Mother to Rich Jr. Receptionist for insurance company. Vampire of Family Ruadan.

Linda Beauchamp: Divorced (first husband, Earl). Mother to MaryBeth. Nail technician. Vampire of Family Koschei. Mated to Dr. Stan Michaels.

MaryBeth Beauchamp: Nanny to Marchand triplets. Vampire of Family Ruadan. Mated to Rand.

*Evangeline LeRoy: Mother to Tamara. Teacher at night school and colibrarian of Broken Heart and Consortium archives. Vampire of Family Koschei. Mated to Lorcan O'Halloran.

Patricia "Patsy" Donovan: Divorced (first husband, Sean). Mother to Wilson, and to *loup de sang* triplets. Former beautician. Queen of vampires and *loup de* *sang*. Vampire of Family Amahté. Mated to Gabriel Marchand.

Ralph Genessa: Widowed (first wife, Teresa). Father to twins Michael and Stephen, and to daughter Cassandra. Dragon handler. Vampire of Family Hua Mu Lan. Mated to half dragon Libby Monroe.

Simone Sweet: Widowed (first husband, Jacob). Mother to Glory. Mechanic. Vampire of Family Velthur. Mated to Braddock Hayes.

*****Phoebe Allen:** Divorced (first husband, Jackson Tate). Mother to Daniel. Comanages The Knight's Inn in Tulsa. Vampire of Family Durga. Mated to Connor Ballard.

Darlene Clark: *Deceased.* Divorced (first husband, Jason Clark*). Mother to Marissa. Operated Internet scrapbooking business. Vampire of Family Durga.

*****Elizabeth Bretton née Silverstone:** Widowed (first husband, Henry). Stepmother to Venice. Socialite and jewelry maker. Vampire of Family Zela. Mated to werejaguar Tez Jones.

---

*Direct descendents of the five families who founded Broken Heart: the McCrees, the LeRoys, the Silverstones, the Allens, and the Clarks.

GLOSSARY 1

GERMAN WORDS/TERMS

Deutsches Reich: German Reich also known as the Third Reich

Liebling: Darling

Mein kleiner Frechdachs: My little cheeky monkey (rascal, scoundrel)

Nein und abermals nein: A thousand times, no

Schätzchen: Little treasure

Schwarzwald: Black Forest

Was zum Teufel: What the fuck?

Wehrmacht: Unified armed forces of Germany from 1935–1945

GAELIC IRISH WORDS/TERMS

a ghrá mo chroi: Love of my heart

a stóirín: My little darling

a thaisce: My dear/darling/treasure

aiteacht: Inexplicable sense of thing or place that is not right

bard: Poet-druid (see: *Filí*). Storyteller and singer of Celtic tribes

céardsearc: First love/beloved one

damnú air: Damn it

deamhan fola: Blood devil

draíocht: Magic

droch fola: Bad or evil blood

druid: The philosopher, teacher, and judge of Celtic tribes

Filí: (Old Irish) Poet-druid (see: *Bard*)

Go dtachta an diabhal thú: May the devil choke you (Irish curse)

Is minic a bhris béal duine a shrón: Many a time a man's mouth broke his nose

Leamhán sléibhe: A Wych Elm (the only species of Elm native to Ireland)

mo chroí: My heart

Ná glac pioc comhairle gan comhairle ban: Never take advice without a woman's guidance

Níl neart air: (lit. There is no power in it) There is no helping it

Ovate: Healer-druid; healer and seer of Celtic tribes

Solas: Light

Sonuachar: Soul mate

Súmaire Fola: Bloodsucker

Tír na Marbh: Land of the Dead

Titim gan éirí ort: May you fall without rising (Irish curse)

OTHER WORDS/TERMS

Centurion/Centurio: Professional officer in the Roman army in charge of a century, or *centuria*, of men

Century/Centuria: Group of 60 to 160 men in the Roman infantry led by a centurion

Durriken: Romany boy's name that means "he who forecasts"

Fac fortia et patere: Latin for "Do brave deeds and endure"

Gadjikane: Romany for "non-Gypsy"

Muló: Romany for "living dead"

Roma: Member of nomadic people originating in Northern India; gypsies considered as a group (Also the term used for cousins of full-blood lycanthropes who can only shift during a full moon and who hunt rogue vampires)

Romany/Romani: The language of the Roma

Strigoi mort: Term for Romanian vampire

GLOSSARY 2

Ancient: Refers to one of the original eight vampires. The very first vampire was Ruadan, who is the biological father of Patrick and Lorcan. Several centuries ago, Ruadan and his sons took on the last name of O'Halloran, which means "stranger from overseas."

banning: (see: *World Between Worlds*) Any one can be sent into limbo, but the spell must be cast by an Ancient or a being with powerful magick. No one can be released from banning until they feel true remorse for their evil acts. This happens rarely, which means banning is not done lightly.

binding: When vampires have consummation sex (with any person or creature), they're bound together for a hundred years. This was the Ancients' solution to keep vamps from sexual intercourse while blood-taking. There are only two known instances of breaking a binding.

Consortium: More than five hundred years ago, Patrick and Lorcan O'Halloran created the Consortium to figure out ways that parakind could make the world a better place for all beings. Many sudden leaps in human medicine and technology are because of the Consortium's work.

Convocation: Five neutral, immortal beings given the responsibility of keeping the balance between Light and Dark.

donors: Mortals who serve as sustenance for vampires. The Consortium screens and hires humans to be food sources. Donors are paid well and given living quarters. Not all vampires follow the guidelines created by the Consortium for feeding. A mortal may have been a donor without ever realizing it.

Drone: Mortals who do the bidding of their vampire Masters. The most famous was Renfield—drone to Dracula. The Consortium's code of ethics forbids the use of drones, but plenty of vampires still use them.

ETAC: The Ethics and Technology Assessment Commission is the public face of this covert government agency. In its program, soldier volunteers have undergone surgical procedures to implant nanobyte technology, which enhances strength, intelligence, sensory perception, and healing. Volunteers are trained in use of technological weapons and defense mechanisms so advanced, it's rumored they come from a certain section of Area 51. Their mission is to remove, by any means necessary, paranormal targets named as domestic threats.

Family: Every vampire can be traced to the one of the eight Ancients. The Ancients are divided into the Eight Sacred Sects, also known as the Families. The Families are: Ruadan, Koschei (aka Romanov), Hua Mu Lan, Durga, Zela, Amahté, Shamhat, and Velthur. Please note: At this time only one known vampire of the Family Shamhat exists.

gone to ground: When vampires secure places where they can lie undisturbed for centuries, they "go to ground." Usually they let someone know where they are located, but the resting locations of many vampires are unknown. Both the Ancients Amahté and Shamhat have gone to ground for more than three thousand years. Their locations have yet to be discovered.

Invisi-shield: Using technology stolen from ETAC and ancient magic, the Consortium created a shield that not only makes the town invisible to outsiders, but also creates a force field. No one can get into the town's borders unless their DNA signature is recognized by both the technology and magical elements.

loup de sang: Translated as "blood wolf." The first of these vampire-werewolves were triplets born after their lycanthrope mother was drained and killed by a vampire. For nearly two centuries, Gabriel Marchand was the only known *loup de sang* and also known as "the outcast." (See: *Vedere Prophecy*) Now the *loup de sang* include his brother, Ren, his sister, Anise, his wife, Patsy, and his children.

lycanthropes: Also called lycans and/or werewolves. Full-bloods can shift from human into wolf at will. Lycans have been around a long time and originate in Germany. Their numbers are small because they don't have many females, and most children born have a fifty percent chance of living to the age of one.

Master: Most Master vampires are hundreds of years old and have had many successful Turnings. Masters show Turn-bloods how to survive as a vampire. A Turn-blood has the protection of the Family (see: *Family* or *Sacred Sects*) to which their Master belongs.

PRIS: Paranormal Research and Investigation Services. Cofounded by Theodora and her husband, Elmore Monroe. Its primary mission is to document supernatural phenomena and conduct cryptozoological studies.

Roma: The Roma are cousins to full-blooded lycanthropes. They can change only on the night of a full moon. Just as full-blooded lycanthropes are raised to protect vampires, the Roma are raised to hunt vampires.

soul shifter: A supernatural being with the ability to absorb the souls of any mortal or immortal. The shifter has the ability to assume any of the forms she's absorbed. Only one is known to exist, the woman known as Ash, who works as a "balance keeper" for the Convocation.

Taint: The Black Plague for vampires, which makes vampires insane as their body deteriorates. The origins of the Taint were traced to demon poison. After many attempts to find a cure, which included transfusions of royal lycanthrope blood, a permanent cure has been found.

Turn-blood: A human who's been recently Turned into a vampire. If you're less than a century old, you're a Turn-blood.

Turning: Vampires perpetuate the species by Turning humans. Unfortunately, only one in about ten humans actually makes the transition.

Vedere prophecy: Astria Vedere predicted that in the twenty-first century a vampire queen would rule both vampires and lycans, and would also end the ruling power of the Ancients. This prophecy was circumvented by a newer proclamation that the lycan crown prince would take a mate and rebuild his pack. Please note:

Patsy was granted only seven powers out of the eight. No one is sure why.

World Between Worlds: The place between this plane and the next, where there is a void. Some beings can slip back and forth between this "veil."

Wraiths: Rogue vampires who banded together to dominate both vampires and humans. Since the defeat of the Ancients Koschei and Durga, they are believed to be defunct.

Read on for a sneak peek at the
next book in Michele Bardsley's
Wizards of Nevermore series,

NOW OR NEVER

Coming from Signet Eclipse
in March 2012

"She's filthy."

Norie Whyte stared dully at the man in the black robe, his tall, bulky form hidden by the layers of shining cloth. The hood covered his face, but even through the mush that was currently her mind, she recognized her kidnapper's voice. The two guys holding her up were leaning away as much as possible. She'd gotten used to the stench.

"You said to make sure she couldn't escape again. You didn't say nothing about keeping her clean." This protest rang out from the bald guy on the left, the one who liked to stare at her breasts and touch himself. He knew better than to try to get his jollies with her. She used to have three guards, but one had made the mistake of trying to rape her.

The man in the black robe had punched a hole in the guard's chest with his fist and magic, and then coldly watched the horny bastard bleed out on the floor. Then he'd used his magic to turn the guard's body into ash. Just . . . *poof*. No more rapist. Then he'd looked at the other two, who'd both pissed themselves, and said calmly, "Do you also require an explanation of what 'virgin sacrifice' means?"

They didn't.

She didn't know Black Robe's name, his title, his House, or his face. But she knew one thing quite well: He was an asshole.

"I won't do it." She wasn't sure whether the words actually made it past her throat. Then Black Robe swung toward her, and she knew he'd heard the hoarse protest.

"It's your destiny, Norie."

"Bullshit." Her voice was stronger this time, but still sounded like a rusted hinge.

He slapped her hard across the face. She felt the shock of that blow all the way to her toes, and she would've fallen had it not been for her captors holding her so tightly. Her cheek bloomed with wicked pain, but she still managed to turn her head and stare at Black Robe with as much defiance as she could muster.

Gods be damned! She wanted to punch him. She wanted to knee his balls and claw his face and pull out his hair. But she hadn't the energy, and her anger was sliding away into the fog of apathy, into the resignation that was nearly as familiar as all the other wretched things about her life. She knew then that the newest dose of magic-laced drugs was kicking in. Her tongue felt thick and her head felt as if it were stuffed with cotton.

"Are you feeding her?" Black Robe asked.

The guards shuffled their feet. "We try to, but she won't eat."

"She can't die before the ceremony, damn it." Black Robe sighed. "Very well. It's obvious that she requires care other than yours now."

"Aw right. You want us to clean up here?" asked the bald guy. He made the sound of an explosion. "Y'know, like we did the other places?"

"I can take it from here." Black Robe grabbed Norie, sweeping her against his chest and raising one hand toward the startled men. Through her graying vision, she saw the fireball emerge, split in two, and hit each of her guards square in the chest. She wasn't exactly sorry to see the bastards burn.

They screamed and flailed, falling onto the floor and trying to roll around. But the fire was born of magic, so it wasn't like a mundane-created fire—it couldn't be doused or suffocated.

Black Robe threw her over his shoulder and walked away. She realized vaguely that she'd been holed up in a warehouse. She could smell the sea air, which wasn't exactly refreshing, what with all the dead-fish and garbage stink. Nausea roiled through her. She almost wished she would throw up so she could ruin His Highness's robe.

The building started to go up in flames, and in moments, it was completely on fire. Norie stared dazedly at the flames licking the wood, snaking toward the wharf. The whole dock would be on fire soon. Someone from Magic Protection Services would have to be called in to combat the spell. And the bastard holding her like a moldy old sack of potatoes probably didn't give a shit if he burned down the whole city.

Black Robe tossed her into the back of a limousine. By the time she hit the seat, Norie was nearly unconscious.

"Everyone has a destiny," said her tormentor again. "And you will fulfill yours."

Those were the last words she heard before darkness claimed her.

Sheriff Taylor Mooreland slammed shut the door to his crotchety old SUV, grimacing at the creaking sounds of rusted springs and tired metal. He should have put in for a new vehicle, but doing so would have meant yet another change. And there'd already been a lot of changes around Nevermore, Texas.

Made life unnerving, damn it.

He liked routine. Order. Knowing that what happened today would probably happen tomorrow. He took comfort in consistency.

He pulled his thick wool coat tighter, zipping it up to the neck. Then he leaned against the side of the SUV and stared up at the twinkling stars.

It wasn't even dawn, for fuck's sake.

He scrubbed his face, trying to wipe off the tiredness, but he still felt like a zombie. He needed more coffee, and that meant hauling his ass up to his office and wrestling with that newfangled machine. His assistant, Arlene, had requisitioned a new coffeemaker, and Gray Calhoun, Dragon wizard and current town Guardian, had one imported from Italy. Italy! The thing was huge and shiny and covered with a thousand dials and spouts. It looked like something out of a Dr. Seuss book.

The wind whipped at his coat and brought with it the ashy-sweet scent of incense—from the temple, no doubt.

He shifted, then paused. The wind carried another scent, too—a wonderful smell that brought back memories of his mother in the kitchen baking. A pang of longing sliced through him. She'd been gone almost six years now. And not a day went by that he didn't miss her.

He sniffed the air. *Well, I'll be.* It damned sure did smell like cookies.

Sugar cookies.

His favorite.

He looked around, but Main Street was dark and quiet. The brick buildings looked the same as ever, and so did the sidewalks and the street and there, where Main Street ended in a large cul-de-sac, gleamed the shining brass dragon, and behind it the Temple of Light. People showed up every week to pay homage to the Goddess and to the Dragon ancestor Jaed. The big wooden doors were always unlocked to allow supplicants into the inner chamber, with its polished oak pews and shining stained-glass windows. Magic kept the torches on the walls burning red and orange, the colors of Jaed. The colors of dragons. The temple was open to anyone, night or day.

He felt a sudden urge to walk down there, to slide into one of the pews, and to ask the Goddess for guidance. He'd always had a goal, a purpose. But lately, he'd felt unbalanced. Like the ground beneath his feet was about to shift and swallow him whole.

Damned nightmares. He hadn't had a single good night's rest in the past six days. He didn't want to admit that the nightmares were costing him physically and emotionally. All the same, he figured it wouldn't hurt to talk to Ember. She was a good friend who ran the local tea shop, and she had an herbal remedy for everything; surely she could whip up something tasty and magical to help him sleep.

Taylor stared at the temple, a beacon of solace in the darkness; then he turned toward the steps that led up to the sheriff's office. It wasn't that he had anything against the Goddess, or religion, for that matter. He deeply respected not only the faith of believers, but the right of everyone to worship whatever deities they liked. But he wasn't a church kind of guy.

Pain throbbed in the center of his forehead and he rubbed at the aching spot. Looked like aspirin was in order, too. After a final sweeping glance down the empty street, he headed up the stairs and unlocked the door.

The smell of sugar cookies followed him inside.

"Please describe the . . . er, creature," said Sheriff Mooreland. His pen was poised above the form his assistant, Arlene, had created specifically for this particular situation. He glanced up at the man sitting in one of the leather wingbacks facing Taylor's oversized antique desk.

"Red," said Henry Archer. "Definitely red." His cowboy hat was perched on his knee, his fingers tapping the crown. His gaze was steady, the same as his manner, but the man's expression kept wavering between disbelief and shock. "Scaly, too."

Taylor nodded, then looked down at the form, with its neat rows of boxes. His pen scratched over the crisp paper. "What else?"

"Wings," admitted Henry. "It was a big son of a bitch. Blotted out the moon, Sheriff. Startled me so badly last night, I tripped over my own two feet and went ass over teakettle into Maureen's begonias."

Taylor's lips quirked. "And how'd she take that?"

"'Bout as well as you might think," said Henry, also smiling. "Don't suppose Ant might be willing to come over and see if they can be coaxed back to life?"

"I'm sure my brother could be talked into it," said Taylor. "Especially if it means he can get within snatching distance of one of Maureen's apple pies."

"Three were cooling in the kitchen when I left," said Henry. "The more agitated my wife gets, the more pies she makes." He chuckled. "Sometimes I rile her up just so I can get some of her blackberry cobbler."

Taylor's smile widened as he looked over the report. "All right, then, Henry. Anything else?"

Henry hesitated, and then he sighed. "I saw a dragon, Sheriff. It's almost like the statue in our town square came to life. You don't think one of the magicals did a spell on it or something . . . ?"

Henry was looking for an explanation other than, yeah, he'd seen a dragon flying around Nevermore's skies. In a world where some people could talk to the dead, control the elements, or, like Taylor's little brother, grow a garden from barren soil, the idea of an honest-to-goddess dragon still freaked people out.

"The statue's protected. No one could pull a prank like that even if they were fool enough to try," said Taylor. He studied his friend. His instincts were humming, and he knew Henry was holding something back. "What else?"

Henry grimaced. "I swear I wasn't drinking," he said. "We got into the habit of not keeping alcohol in the house because Lennie . . . well, you know. We never was much for the hard stuff, anyway." He paused, his gaze dropping.

Taylor let the man have a moment. Eight months ago, Henry and Maureen's youngest son, Lennie, had been killed. The young man's demise was one of three deaths that had been facilitated by Taylor's former deputy and half brother, Ren Banton. Ren had been killed, too, and that was just as well. Hell's bells. By the time it was all said and done, six people had gone to early graves. The whole debacle still weighed heavily on Taylor's mind, but at least life had gotten back to normal—if life in Nevermore could ever really be called "normal."

"Anyway," said Henry, "I saw someone on its back."

Taylor blinked. "You saw a person *riding* the dragon?"

Henry nodded. "A woman. I think she was wearing . . . uh, you know. A nightie."

Oh, for the love of— Taylor stifled a groan. He dutifully added the description under "More Details," and then put the pen down. "That all?"

"Yessir." Henry stood up and plopped the cowboy hat onto his head. "Thanks for taking the time to hear me out."

"I appreciate you coming in," said Taylor. He stood up, too, and rounded the desk to shake Henry's hand. Then he walked the man out of his office and into the main foyer. "You headed back to the store?"

"Yep."

"Tell Maureen I said hello."

"Will do."

Taylor watched the man leave, and then glanced at

Arlene's desk, just as big and old as his own. It gave him a sense of satisfaction to see everything in its place. The office had been changed here and there over the years but, like most things in Nevermore, it had stayed mostly the same. He liked the continuity of it all, the way this building and all that it housed had been used by those who'd stood vigil over the town before him.

Arlene kept everything spotless and orderly, just the way he liked it. The black and white checkered linoleum floor gleamed despite its age. He suspected Arlene bought magic-enhanced cleaners, which was fine by him. He didn't want to dip into the coffers to replace anything, for one thing, and for another, he wasn't a big fan of new and different.

New and different meant trouble.

He thought about Lucinda Rackmore—well, Lucinda Calhoun now. She was all kinds of new and different. She'd turned Gray's world upside down, not to mention that of the whole town, and it seemed like—though he didn't much fancy admitting it—everything was somehow better.

Taylor clasped his hands behind his back and looked around. Off to the left of Arlene's desk was a locked door that led to the archives. Only Arlene ventured inside there, and not even he risked invading that domain. To the right of the foyer was the entrance to his office, which faced Main Street. The picture window allowed him a proper view of downtown, not that there was much to watch.

He did a quick check around, a habit motivated by Ren's betrayal. The deputy had used his access to the office to rifle through files, break into Taylor's safe, and paw through Arlene's precious archives.

A narrow hallway led to the former deputy's office, a supply closet, the bathrooms, the break room, and the back door that opened onto the alley. Beyond the break room was the secured door that led down to the basement, and to the rarely used jail cells. One had been built especially to dampen the powers of magicals, but he'd never had cause to use it.

Satisfied with his inspection, Taylor returned to the foyer and breathed deeply. Yep. Life was all right so long as it had order.

He checked his watch and frowned. Arlene had been gone for more than half an hour. A couple of times a day she'd go across the street and check on Atwood Stephens; the man, who looked like an exhausted rhinoceros, owned both the town garbage service and the weekly paper, *Nevermore News*. His health had been deteriorating rapidly, and not even Lucinda's gift of healing had been able to do much more than slow the decline. Atwood's nephew Trent Whytefeather had been taking over more and more of his uncle's responsibilities. He was a senior in high school, and despite the burdens of his home life, was still a straight-A student.

Taylor turned to go into his office, but he heard the rattle of the front door, so he turned back. He expected to see Arlene chug inside, already complaining about Atwood's stubborn hide, but to his surprise, he saw Gray Calhoun. The wizard still wore his hair long, but these days he kept it neatly trimmed. His nose crooked in the middle, and the angles of his face were as sharp as blades, as sharp as the look in his blue eyes. A faded scar on the left side of his face twirled from his temple down his neck, hiding beneath the collar of his T-shirt.

"Gray," he said, offering a congenial nod.

"Hey, Taylor," said Gray, smiling.

He did that a lot these days. He was the happiest son of a bitch in town, and Taylor felt, well, jealous of his friend's connubial bliss. It made him feel petty, so he shook Gray's hand heartily and said, "C'mon. Arlene finessed that damned machine into a fresh batch of coffee."

"You might want something stronger," said Gray as he followed Taylor down the hall and into the break room. "I just got word that my mother will be here in time for our Samhain celebration. With all twelve of her *lictors*."

"A dozen bodyguards?" Taylor gestured for his friend to sit at the table, and Gray grabbed a chair and slid into it. "I thought she traveled with only three."

"Every Consul has been encouraged to keep all their *lictors* close. Things are tense in political circles," said Gray. "There are rumors that the House of Ravens might secede from the Grand Court."

Shock stilled his movements. He didn't much pay attention to things outside Nevermore, but damn, that was bad news all the way around. "Can they do that?"

"There's no precedent," said Gray. "Not in two thousand years since the Houses and the first Grand Court was formed. If the Ravens withdraw from the current governing structure, it may well start a war."

"That would mean a whole lot of scrambling for the mundanes, too. Nonmagicals won't like the idea of rogue witches and wizards."

"Let's hope the current Consuls can make the Ravens see reason."

"Yeah," said Taylor. "Let's hope." He paused. "So, you got enough room in that house for your visitors?"

"Not for twelve giants and certainly not for my mother's angst. When I told her about marrying Lucinda, I think her head exploded."

"Well, you did marry the sister of your ex-wife, who sold your soul to a demon lord."

"I'm aware," said Gray dryly.

Taylor handed the Guardian a mug and then took the

spot across from him. "I'm surprised Leticia didn't come down long before now."

"No doubt she stayed away so she could plot in private." He shook his head. "That's not fair. I know she's upset, but once she meets Lucy, she'll be fine with it."

Taylor wasn't so sure. Leticia was a spectacular woman, but she was also as stubborn as the day was long. "How long is your mother staying?"

Gray blinked. "Ah. Well, through the Winter Solstice Festival."

"So she'll be here for . . ." Taylor narrowed his gaze. "Oh crap. You haven't told her?"

"No. Other than you, Ember, and Rilton, we haven't told anyone."

"Well, you don't have to," said Taylor, rolling his eyes. "Not with all the reports I've been getting."

"Sorry. We try to be discreet, but it's not easy."

"Shifting into a dragon is no small feat." He gave Gray a level gaze. "And neither is flying around with Lucy on your back."

"Oops."

"Yeah, *oops*."

"After the Winter Solstice, everyone will know."

"Not sure that's a good thing," said Taylor. "All those stories about the magical ancestors being shifters . . . Well, people think they're myths. And you're gonna go prove 'em wrong. Everyone will know you're Jaed's champion."

"You're worried people will figure out that Nevermore is a goddess fountain."

"Bound to come out eventually."

"We have to trust the Goddess, Taylor."

Taylor nodded, but he looked away. He wasn't a magical. He lived with them, was related to them, and worked for them, but he was a mundane. And he didn't like the idea of a magical war. It would be bad for everyone, but especially for those without magic.

Gray drained his coffee mug. "I gotta get back to Lucy. The Halloween party is more than two weeks away, but she's already futzing over the decorations. You'll be there, right?"

"Wouldn't miss it," said Taylor. "I'm gonna win that pumpkin-carving contest."

Gray laughed, smacked Taylor on the shoulder, and then he left, giving Taylor one last wave before he headed out.

Taylor took their mugs to the sink and rinsed them.

Pain shot from his temples to the center of his forehead, throbbing in a circle of agony. He dropped the mug, barely hearing its protesting clatter. He staggered forward, pressing his palm against his head. Gods be damned! Bright light danced behind his eyes and he groaned. Then he heard a swooshing sound, like wings.

Accept what belongs to you, Taylor.

Then the pain disappeared.

He slowly straightened, wiping the sweat beading on his brow, and tried to get back his equilibrium.

What the hell?

He took a few deep breaths, clenching and unclenching his fists. With some effort, he pushed away the dread squeezing him as tightly as a constricting python.

"Taylor!"

The panicked voice of Arlene had him shaking off the fear, the ghosts of pain, and rushing out of the break room, down the hall, and into the main office. He found her in the lobby, chest heaving, a quivering hand pressed against her throat. Her eyes were as wide as saucers.

"It's Atwood!" she cried. "The dumb son of a bitch went and killed himself!"